FATAL DESIGNS
A Patrick MacKenna Mystery

Peter H. Green

www.peterhgreen.com

To Dave, Enjoy Patrick's adventures! Peter

FATAL DESIGNS

A PATRICK MACKENNA MYSTERY

Peter H Green 4/2/2012

PETER H. GREEN

GREENSKILLS PRESS
ST. LOUIS, MISSOURI

Fatal Designs, A Patrick MacKenna Mystery
By Peter H. Green

Publisher: Greenskills Press, May 25, 2015

Copyright ©2015 by Peter H. Green

Cover Design by Jennifer Stolzer
Cover Photo: Peter H. Green
Interior Book Design: Greenskills Press

Address comments and inquiries to:
Greenskills Press, Publisher
An imprint of Greenskills Associates, LLC
P. O. Box 11292
St. Louis, MO 63105

First Edition

All rights reserved. No part of this publication may be reproduced, stored in retrieval system or transmitted in any form by any means, electronic, mechanical, photocopying, recording or otherwise, without written permission of the copyright holder, except for brief quotations used in a review.

This is a work of fiction and is produced from the author's imagination. Any resemblance to specific individuals is purely coincidental. People, places and things mentioned in this novel are used in a fictional manner.
ISBN: 978-1-941402-07-8-Amazon Edition
ISBN-978-1-941402-09-2 Trade Paperback
eISBN: 978-1-941402-08-5 -Kindle Edtion
eISBN: 978-1-941402-10-8 -e-book
Library of Congress Control Number: Applied for
Visit us on the web at www.peterhgreen.com

For Connie

PART I: RUMBLINGS
ONE

When the thugs removed the blindfold, Trooper found himself in a basement room, staring at a disfigured face, a knife leveled at his eyes. On the floor above, a wailing saxophone protested, an electric bass boomed and the muffled beat of a drum shook his body. He cringed, sweat dripping from his forehead into his eyes.

"Pay up," the enforcer said.

"I did, last week. Delivered it to the man myself."

"Your mistake. I'm not responsible for that creep. It was my money."

"I paid my debt to him. There's no more where that came from." Why hadn't he turned away from booze, girls and gambling when he still could? Now it was too late.

The man leered with a cruel grin. "I thought so. What a pity. Here's what you can do for me instead."

A bald bruiser closed on him from the shadows, wrapped a thick arm around his throat and held his left wrist in a hammerlock.

"Give him the gun."

The thug placed an automatic rifle in his free hand and turned him toward a man gagged and bound to a chair in a dim corner. He released his other arm and held him steady, pointed at the prisoner. When the captive recognized the shooter, his eyes widened and darted around the room, searching in vain for a way out. With muffled cries of protest, the victim struggled against the ropes, rocking the chair from side to side.

"I can't kill him! He's—"

To ensure steadiness of the target, the suit turned the chair to face the wall and hit the side of his captive's head with the fist gripping the butt of his knife. The restrained body slumped forward.

Ugly man closed in behind Trooper, the point of his dagger jabbing the skin over his right kidney. A moist sensation warmed his back and then another spread down his legs as he wet himself. A long forgotten voice returned. *Soldier, your job is to kill...* Trooper's mind drifted back to those terrible, memorable days in Vietnam

One night on patrol his company had split up—one squad to round up and guard the natives at the center of the village, his squad to search the hootches for weapons, tunnels and evidence of Viet Cong propaganda. The haunting image returned.

A terrified old man remained behind to protect his family, his daughter and a granddaughter no older than six, and defend their home. Inside, a soldier faced them, weapon raised. Someone made a sudden noise. A semiautomatic weapon roared in response. When the smoke cleared, the old man lay on the floor, his daughter sprawled, dead, and the little girl lay prostrate on her back, her blood oozing through her beautiful coal black hair.

He had lived for his buddies. He couldn't let them down, even if it meant "collateral damage." He'd repaid his debt. He couldn't understand what had gone wrong. Why this? Why now?

The knife dug deeper. He struggled to wrest the gun free and turn it on his captors, but the bruiser held one arm in an iron grip and the knife-wielder held the other rigid. Trooper's muscles tightened in reflex; his right hand clenched. The knife dug deeper. His muscles tightened in reflex; his right hand clenched. *You've got to get them before they get you...squeeze, don't pull, the trigger.*

Cymbals crashed overhead. A deluge of sound descended from above and the band launched into "The Stripper's" razzmatazz finale.

"Now!" The enforcer pressed his knife deeper into his flesh.

It's him or me. His hand contracted. The weapon unleashed a thunderous volley, inaudible above the drums' finale and the cheering, clapping crowd. Lead rained on the hapless victim and tipped the chair forward.

Released by the brute, Trooper fell flat. The automatic clattered to the bare concrete.

He craned his neck toward the wreckage he had wrought. The man's knees and head made three-point contact with the floor, the chair still roped to his back.

Trooper writhed in pain, more from the sight than his wound. "NO! My buddy—I'll rot in hell."

The song had ended and the applause had died. The weapon and the thugs were gone,

Had it only been a horrible nightmare?

Hardly. The stench of cordite and a sweet, coppery smell confirmed the evidence before his eyes. All that remained in the room were Trooper, the victim perched atop a pool of his own blood and the deathly silence.

Two

Erin MacKenna stood trembling at the door from the kitchen to the garage. The whine of machinery assaulted her ears through the thin panel, and her heart pounded in her chest. She didn't want to start a fight, but she had to do this. She entered.

Patrick MacKenna, an architect who was always making something, was absorbed in his work. He stood over his lathe, his tall frame bent over his task. The worry lines that typically made his boyish face seem older were relaxed. Erin admired him most at times like this, with his confident, imaginative approach to creative work. Except when it came to his single-parent supervision of her activities. It caused her to dread this moment all the more.

"Dad—"

"E-e-e-yaiou," The knife bit into a stout spindle of hickory.

"Dad, I have to talk to you!" she shouted

"Huh, what do you want?" He looked up and lurched. The piece splintered in half.

"Will you please turn off that machine so I can say something?"

Patrick flicked off the switch. Silence. "Dammit, Erin!"

"I wanted to remind you about the outing I planned next weekend with the seniors and sophomores for our float on the Current River."

"What outing?" Patrick stared at her in disbelief. "*Just* a float trip. On a river."

"What, Dad? Geez! Our school float trip. You said it was okay. If you ever listened to me you'd recall a long conversation we had about this."

"Oh, I suppose we discussed it," Patrick said. "At the time I assumed you'd have me along, like last time. But I can't make it next weekend. I've made plans with Meg. Besides, I don't want anything to do with a river."

"Discussed it? You signed the permission slip."

"What if I canceled my plans with Meg this weekend and came along? Just like last time, remember?"

She remembered. When he and the twins' mother, Liza Sharpe, were gathering firewood, they met in a clearing and were no role models for youth.

"I can't allow it. Rivers are dangerous. That's how we lost your mother."

"But—, but, when I fell off that pony, you put me right back on it. You said, otherwise, I'd be afraid of horses for life." She flipped back a lock of orange hair and flashed an arch grin. "Anyway, that's the usual place to paddle a canoe."

"This is serious."

"You always looked forward to outings on the Current. You've taken me out there since I was five years old. You loved the chance to get out into nature. You're making a mountain out of this."

"The Ozark Mountains, to be exact. Infested with bootleggers, druggies and killers for the past hundred years. That wilderness is no place for young girls to be alone."

"Oh right." Erin made a sarcastic snort. "The area's history hasn't changed since the last time we went. Even the headmistress at St. Agnes approved it. And we'll have chaperons. But this time, Sister Jeanne-Marie said you can't be one of them. She knows. Instead of gathering wood, you were carrying on with Mrs. Sharp."

He flinched as if he'd been punched.

Touché. "So there."

Her father avoided her eyes and stared at the ruined spindle. "You cost me an hour's work."

"Is that the chair arm you broke in the sabotage case?" A murderer had snuck into their house, handcuffed him to it and tried to kill him

"As a matter of fact, it is. I was planning to restore it anyway. The killer merely moved it up on the priority list."

"How come I have all the rules, while you're the one who's always in trouble?"

"Look, Erin. I have a lot of responsibility, for your upbringing, your education and your safety."

"And I don't? I'd be thrilled if you'd own up to *your* responsibility. I didn't break your stupid spindle—you did."

Patrick stared at her, silenced.

"You don't care about me. You weren't even at the field hockey championship when Kelly shot a rocket across the field and I knocked in the winning goal."

"I'm sure I had a very important business reason to miss it."

"Oh, right. When I got home you and Meg were enjoying dessert after a cozy candlelight dinner. You'd been apple-picking in Illinois!"

"You'll have to admit she made a very good pie."

"I don't know. I wouldn't eat it. Look, you've got to let me go."

"Erin, it's too risky—you girls out there in the wilderness, alone."

"We'll have two moms with us. Don't you think I know the ropes by now? Heck, I organized the trip, planned where we would go, and even called to make arrangements for canoe rental." When they began sponsoring girls from the city, their annual Big-and Little-Sister Weekend had become an Outward Bound adventure, adding a new feature to the school tradition.

"That's got nothing to do with it. You may not go, period."

"Hey, that's not fair!"

"Seems fair to me, and to you—to keep you alive."

"I can't tell my friends the trip is off. They'll be crushed, especially the city kids. They're all counting on me." She was shouting again, this time through tears

"Aw, honey, I just want the best for you." He reached out to hug her.

Erin dodged his embrace "I hate you!" She ran back into the house, her face red, her heart drumming a war chant.

It was too late to change their plans. She would defy him and find a way to go anyway. She would not be demeaned—again.

Three

On Saturday morning fourteen girls and two mothers gathered at dawn in the school parking lot, piled into two cars and a van—with backpacks, duffel totes, sunglasses, coolers tied shut with rope and sacks of provisions stowed by Kelly's mother in waterproof trash bags—and set off for the launch point, deep in the forest about three hours' ride southwest of St. Louis.

Erin had spent the night at Kelly's house. She hadn't told either of them that her father believed she was spending the weekend at Kelly's house, and she figured she'd be just as well off if they never knew. .

On the road at last, Erin settled into the back seat with her "little sister" Aliesha and the backpacks. Kelly chatted in the front with her mother, who was driving. When they got past the outer belt highway, the urban streets gave way to wooded areas between developed sites and views of distant hillsides filled with homes, roadside shopping centers and churches on hilltops. When they crossed the Meramec River, she wondered why her father had become so fixated on the river's danger. While she had the same reasons to fear the risks, she preferred to embrace its many other roles—discovery, adventure and host to human settlement and natural creatures.

"Look at all those cows in that field," Aliesha said from her back seat next to Erin. "They're not locked up. Couldn't somebody come along and take them?"

Kelly grinned back toward Erin. Her mother, at the wheel, shot a glance back at Aliesha. "Honey, those would be cattle rustlers. If the ranchers caught them before the sheriff, they'd be likely to hang them—and the law might not interfere!"

Erin marveled how different her experience was from that of the city kids and was doubly glad she'd planned the trip.

The interstate plunged into the heart of the Ozark Mountains, so old in geologic time they'd been worn down to hills, gently rounded like buffaloes' backs and flocked with the new green of sprouting leaves

Erin checked her text messages.

Jimmy S: Where are u?
She began typing.
RedErin: Headed 2 canoe float.
What? U promised.
Promised what?
2day is my commissioning.
2day? Honest , Jimmy, I didn't kno.
I told U at Xmas.
Huh???
It's starting now.
She groaned.

"What's with the sound effects?" Kelly asked.

"Oh, I'm toast. Jimmy's commissioning ceremony with the U. S. Army is right now, After we broke up. I didn't think he'd want me there. And I'm a hundred miles away.."

"Well, fifty, anyway," Kelly's mom said.

"Dang and double dang."

"Sounds like a triple to me," Kelly said. "This is serious."

"He's being made a Cadet Colonel. It makes him eligible for a top rank in college ROTC and the best four-year scholarship they offer."

"I'll bet you're proud of him," Mary Epley, said.

"Yeah. Like I really show it." Erin typed a reply.

U never called. I didn't think U wanted me there.

Not even her best friend could help. She owed Kelly a detailed explanation later. All her careful preparations for this trip, one by one, were blowing up in her face.

Just outside Rolla at the sign, "Missouri 68, Ozark National Scenic Riverway," Mrs. Epley turned off the interstate.

They wound through the forest on two-lane roads for another hour and arrived at a clearing on a bank of the Current River. A shack by the dock bore a weathered sign hand-carved with the letters, AKERS FERRY. The campers climbed out of the cars, stretched their legs and warily sniffed the crisp country air.

Erin stood beside the pristine woodland stream of her youth, which flowed calmly now beside the dock. When the banks narrowed, with little warning nor mercy the river could turn into a raging torrent. She could barely wait to break out on her own, but now her father's dire premonitions upset her. She had already sacrificed too much on another river. Nonetheless, she resolved to put that out of her mind. She'd get back on that horse and try again!

Erin fingered the locket at her neck bearing her grandmother's initials, with her mother Kitty's picture as a teen inside, a family heirloom her mom had given her on her thirteenth birthday. She patted it for luck. *Let's go, Mom!*

"Check him out," Kelly said, jolting her back into the present.

The lanky canoe rental guy, in Levi's, a partially buttoned plaid shirt with rolled up sleeves and a battered Stetson, hefted aluminum canoes singlehanded and plopped them into the water. He reminded her of a starving cowboy.

"He's too skinny," Erin said. "But his smile is kinda cute."

"Listen up, girls." He displayed an irresistible grin. "You're gonna have lots of fun out here. But we got a few basic safety rules. You might wanna pay attention. If you're not a strong swimmer, you need to wear your life vest. And stick together so nobody gets lost. If anybody gets hurt, you call me on your cell phone at this here base, and we'll pick you up. Otherwise we'll see you at Round Spring tomorrow afternoon. When you get there, walk over to the bubbling pool, check out that icy cold water and its deep blue color—just don't fall in! Now, whenever you're ready, you in the first four canoes can shove off, so I'll have room to set the last four in the water."

Erin stepped into hers, arranged the floating seat cushions, hauled in a backpack and tote bag and set a cooler full of provisions next to the center thwart. Her senior classmates and the little sisters, who put on their life jackets, piled into the other three canoes at the dock. Aliesha Robinson, the girl from the inner city Erin was sponsoring, lowered her backpack into Erin's boat and stepped gingerly into her position at the bow.

"Have you ever floated before?" Erin asked her.

"No, but we had lessons at the Y. They put a boat in the pool."

"Great. I'll show you more once we get going."

Aliesha cast off, Erin pushed out into the stream and feathered her paddle while the current took hold. Guided by Mary Epley and the other chaperons, the rest of the party climbed aboard and next four shoved off, completing the launch of eight canoes in the party.

After waving a final farewell, Cowboy stood beside the shack, hands on his hips, surveying the scene. The animals seemed agitated. His horse pulled at the rope, kicked at the shack's side wall and sent a hail of pebbles in all directions. A cat scrambled from inside to the back porch, scratched a single spot on the boards and rolled on it, either with pleasure or to scratch off fleas, and leapt alarmingly high in the air, squealing a lament. The hounds bayed as if to a full moon, although it was still midday. Erin wondered at the sight. Shouldn't they be used to tourists by now? Or was it something else?

They were under way, with squeals of delight from Aliesha, who caught on fast and dug her blade deep into the water, eager to do her share.

Kelly caught up with Erin and pulled her canoe alongside. "How'd you finally convince your dad to let you come?"

"I didn't. He thinks I'm staying at your house for the whole weekend."

"Oh, boy! My mom doesn't even know?"

"I'm through with his stupid rules."

"Mom thought you had it all agreed. You realize, kiddo, if anything happens, we're in deep do-doo."

Erin fell silent and pulled into the lead.

They paddled for a while down the narrow stream and glided speechless in the spell cast by the dark, deep woods. "Wow," Aliesha said, "they've got no roads, or signs or motels out here."

"In the early days this must be how this land looked to the Indians."

"Oh, look!" Aliesha pointed to a still pool by the bank. A turtle sunned itself on a log. A fish leapt in a graceful arc, leaving no trace but circular ripples on the surface.

These creatures on the stream recalled Erin's earliest river trips.

She'd worn her straw hat and sunglasses. Her mother, so young then, tied a tiny life jacket over her one-piece swimsuit and placed her in the center of the canoe. They glided the streams as hawks circled far above and insects hummed in the sweet-scented forest. That same sun, still filtering through the trees, set her mother's long, coppery locks on fire, brought out her freckles, and put a glow in her emerald eyes. In her strong Irish brogue she recited the names of the trees, the plants, the insects, the fish and the other natural creatures they encountered. Those names—wild blueberry, thistle, dogwood, chokecherry, onion grass—flooded back, along with memories of happier times.

Before the next bend the current slowed between wider banks. She showed Aliesha how to steer around rocks in their path by extending her paddle across the bow. Approaching a sandy island ahead they had to veer sharp left of its gravel bar to avoid a snag-clogged chute and stay in the main channel. Aliesha tried out her new skill while Erin helped from the stern by stroking wide on the opposite of the boat.

A stiff breeze turned the calm surface to gooseflesh, and the water shimmered in the hazy light with its own pellucid glow.

"You won't believe what's ahead." Erin pointed to a tall, forested hill on the left bank. As they rounded the bend it exposed a sheer limestone cliff, which rose two hundred feet into the air. On its face, indented with tan and grey stone ledges, scrub trees grasped for a roothold in the sparse soil on the shelves. At the waterline, branches of the stream disappeared into dark caves.

"It's like the Grand Canyon!" Aliesha exclaimed.

"This is the neatest part." Erin steered their craft into the cave's dark interior. Cool air rushed from deep inside, and their voices echoed from the walls.

An unexpected sound, a deep rumble, rose from the depths beyond. Erin almost dropped her paddle. Dust and pebbles from the cave roof rained on them, and larger stones plopped in surrounding water and into the canoe.

"Hey! What's this?" Aliesha cast a bewildered look in Erin's direction.

"Aliesha, backwater, now! We have to get out before we're trapped." With her heart hammering, Erin wheeled their canoe about. They raced back through the cave mouth for safety under the open sky.

But there was no respite here. Huge boulders tumbled down the sheer face, bounced off the slope and landed in the river, roiling the surface and spewing geysers aloft. The air reeked of sulfur and the stream sloshed from side to side between the banks, forming spume along the shore. As suddenly as it began, the rumble stopped, replaced by a roar, which competed with the pounding in her ears.

"Wow," Aliesha said. "Those rocks just missed us."

The other lead boats had escaped further downstream. But it wasn't over. By the time they could accelerate from a dead float, the fallen boulders had turned the lazy river into a torrent.

"Look, the rocks made new rapids!" Aliesha struggled at the bow to steer.

"Paddle hard! Now." Erin exclaimed. It was all both girls could do to keep their craft upright and pointed forward. At last they reached slack water below, still afloat. Barb and Cassie also made it, but Kelly and Sarah had shot the rapids so fast they were broadsided by the flow against a fallen tree. Erin watched helpless as the undertow beneath the trunk capsized their canoe. Thoroughly doused, but none the worse for it, the two girls stood waist-deep in the water, laughing.

Downstream, her friend Barb, and Aliesha's classmate Cassie raced to recover floating backpacks and plastic bags of food from the swamped craft before they sank. Erin and Aliesha paddled hard upstream to reach the tree. They jumped into the water to help the others empty the canoe, set it upright and helped Kelly and Sarah climb back in.

"What caused that?" Cassie asked.

"An earthquake," Erin said, "it's just like my father described."

"We were almost crushed," Aliesha said.

"Thank goodness we were outside and not in a building," Erin said. "Dad said that's even more dangerous."

"Bad enough," Kelly said. "We were under a cliff."

"Yeah. Besides, it's four o'clock already," Erin checked her watch. Although thoroughly immersed, it still worked. "We'd better pull out over there and make camp." She pointed to a flat clearing on the left bank.

The six girls paddled to the spot and beached their canoes.

Erin reached for her cell phone to hook up with Mary Epley and the other campers. She got no response; "Oh, no! I got it wet. Kelly, try yours." She had their only other phone.

"Guess what? I had it in my pocket when we jumped in. I can't get a peep out of it."

"Now what're we gonna do? I'm cold and wet," Cassie said.

"We're screwed." Aliesha's tone was matter-of-fact.

"No kidding," Erin said. "We can't even call anyone to say we're okay."

"Two of us could hike back upstream," Kelly suggested.

"We've only got a few hours of daylight. I'm not sure we can find the others and return safely."

"They must have stopped so they wouldn't have to shoot the rapids." Kelly pointed upstream at the roaring torrent. "Let's wait for them to float by tomorrow."

They began their preparations to ward off the dangers of the night—further earth tremors, the chilly air, an unruly river, wild animals—and other forces threatening six defenseless girls alone in the wilderness.

Four

After Erin's Friday departure to Kelly's for the weekend, Patrick had planned dinner out and invited his fiancé over to stay.

"I hope the girls have fun together this weekend." Patrick refilled their Delft coffee cups. "We crossed swords over that float trip she wanted to conduct."

"You wouldn't let her go?"

"She's all the family I have left. I just couldn't bear the thought of losing her."

"Seems unlikely. You trained her in canoeing and camping on the river."

"It's gotten too dangerous these days. I can't let her take the risk without me."

Meg didn't respond. Loud ticking from the Bavarian cuckoo clock filled the room. The mechanical bird opened the doors and announced the hour: two o'clock, ending the awkward silence.

As if on this cue, a rumble sounded from far away. Parnell, his aging cockapoo, joined in. He yapped in their faces with an awful racket.

"Can't you shut that dog up?"

"That dog, as you call him, saved me from a murderer. He's trying to tell us something." He planted his feet, stood upright and winced as his right knee cramped.

The thundering sound came closer . A cacophony of car alarms added to the din.

"What on earth is it?" Meg's eyes reflected fear.

The floor shuddered beneath them, Patrick's coffee jiggled and sloshed out of its cup. He steadied himself on the back of the chair. As if to retaliate for the attempt, the earth trembled again, this time knocking him off balance.

Like a barrage of rifle fire, loud cracks echoed up and down the suburban street and through the half open patio door.

"Drop, cover, and hold on!" Patrick dove for shelter beneath the maple top.

Meg followed, clambering to a spot next to him. "Why are we doing this?"

"Earthquake!" The teapot rattled on the stove and cabinet doors swung open. Glasses and cups crashed to the floor.

He grasped Meg around the waist, grabbed a hefty table leg with his other hand and sustained this contorted, white-knuckled posture until the shaking subsided.

"Looks like it's stopped for the moment. Let's go outside to be safe."

Patrick guided Meg through the patio door into the rock garden. The sun, filtered through new growth in the woods, shone with cold indifference.

"You have no time when an earthquake hits. The whole building can collapse on top of you. We should be okay, but Erin—? I've gotta call her." He grabbed his cell phone off his belt and punched in her speed-dial code.

He got her recording and left a message. "Hey, Erin, it's Dad. We just had an earthquake. I wanted to make sure you girls are okay over there. The house is fine here. Love you."

"Are the girls in danger?" Meg asked.

"That's what I'm afraid of. Buildings are the most dangerous places. He called the Epleys' home number—no answer."

"At the mall, I'll bet. Let them enjoy their weekend."

Patrick walked the perimeter of his house, examining the walls. The crisp spring air promised a lovely day, but the cloudless cobalt sky felt as claustrophobic as an inverted steel bowl. His fingers followed widened cracks at a few joints next to window frames. "I was lucky. There's not much damage here a caulking gun won't fix."

"Look, the chimney across the street is about to fall down."

"Yeah, leaning masonry extremely unstable. Fortunately, Mrs. Jameson is away for the weekend. I'll warn her Monday. When I built this house I reinforced the brick with steel and designed flexible foundations, like Frank Lloyd Wright's Imperial Hotel in Tokyo. That building survived a huge quake."

"Is it over?"

"Maybe, but this could be a mild warning of bigger things to come. The house looks okay and we have our escape route. We can go back inside."

He clicked on the television set. After a lengthy interview with a large, matronly woman about daycare, the anchorman appeared.

"Here are the breaking news headlines: Two earthquake tremors of an estimated 4.5 and 5.1 magnitude were recorded at 2:03 and 2:07 PM today. The epicenter was near Potosi, Missouri… the Mayor of Brooklyn, Illinois, is still missing since he failed to return home last Thursday night… A five-year-old girl in North St. Louis was killed by random gunfire from a passing car while she was playing on her front porch. Is severe weather in our forecast? Tune in to the News at Five for details."

"If it's so important, why don't you just tell me now?" Patrick yelled at the screen. He switched it off.

"He can't hear you." Meg grinned.

"Magnitude 5.1—that's stronger than we've had in a long time."

At 3:15 the phone rang and Patrick grabbed it. "Erin?"

"Patrick, we've had a tremor—two, in fact. I'm at the office."

"Oh, hi, Ed. Look, make it short. I'm waiting for my daughter to call. How bad is the damage?"

"So far it looks minor." Ed Mossbach was the structural engineer Patrick worked most closely with at the firm, and an expert in earthquake resistant design.

"We felt it out here and I just saw it on the news. How's our building?"

"A few cracked windows. It's not The Big One, for sure. But Gary Archer called me at home to say some walls cracked in the Deerpath City Hall."

"We warned him about that. Ed, I've got to get off this phone—"

"He's still angry about our budget overruns on the expansion project."

"At least he called us to report damages. He doesn't sound like he'll go away mad, at least not yet. Why don't you go over there Monday and see what happened?"

"It's going to take both of us to calm him down."

"Right, right, Ed," he said absently.

"Was that a yes?"

"Do you think this quake could have had an effect out in West County?

"I'd have to check the new data. Why?"

"Erin's at a friend's house out there."

"Most homes have only minor damage. She should be fine."

"How do you really know?"

"No reports of serious effects so far."

"But if you look at the earthquake risk maps, the risk zone that takes in St. Louis wraps in a wide band around the city. The impact can be felt and for miles to the west."

"It might be worse out there—"

"Exactly. Goodbye." He hung up. "I thought I'd never get him off the phone."

"Erin probably won't call you. They're too busy having fun."

"She will. If not, I can only assume the worst."

"If you must know, why don't you call Mary Epley's cell phone?"

"Good idea." He placed the call.

"Patrick, thank God you called. Our party got separated by the quake. Erin and two other friends' canoes got ahead of us. Then the earthquake hit. A landslide tumbled into the river. And now we've got rapids between us and them. With ten people it's too dangerous to proceed further at this late hour."

"Canoes? But…I thought she was staying at your house."

"I can't get through to their cell phones." In her agitation, Mary wasn't hearing him. "Kelly and Erin are strong swimmers and experienced campers. I'll call for help, but we can't shoot the rapids, leave the other eight campers alone here and hope to make it back upstream to them by nightfall. If the canoe rental man can't find them, they should be okay until we catch up with them in the morning."

"This is incredible! I specifically forbade her to go. They're in trouble besides?"

"You wouldn't let her go? She didn't tell *me*. Oh God, Patrick. How could this hap—?"

"That willful girl went on the trip anyway. I'll have her hide!"

"Oh Patrick, I'm so sorry. They had permission from the school. It never occurred to me to ask you. I didn't see any harm in letting my daughter go on the trip."

"Of course you didn't. You're there to chaperone. I offered, but apparently I'm persona non grata over there."

"Oh—that. But still, she shouldn't have lied to both of us."

"Call me the minute you contact them." Patrick said and slammed down the phone.

"Don't take it out on Mary. It was Erin who lied to you."

"That child— why has she become impossible to help?"

"For one thing, she's no longer a child. Trust their skills. They're probably happy for the challenge, coping just fine."

"I knew something like this would happen. She's totally out of my reach. Dammit!"

Meg didn't realize the gravity of the girls' predicament. He hadn't been fooling about the legacy of bootlegging, marijuana culture and and, more recently, illegal methamphetamine production that flourished, hidden in those hills. She didn't understand the Ozarks' history—an ancient Appalachian culture, whose people are bent on avenging blood feuds and gaining advantage over all comers, regardless of the consequences.

"You'll have to let go of her someday, Patrick. She can't depend on you forever."

He threw up his hands. "She can't even depend on me now. We can't have a normal conversation. I can't even take her shopping for clothes. I look for nice dress and she chooses skin-tight jeans and boots. Have you seen what they want for that stuff?"

"She should have them, too. You're not poor. A good chunk of my salary goes for those little luxuries."

"She feels cheated, losing her mother that way. We can't even talk in a civilized tone."

"Maybe I can referee. The next chance we get, let's sit her down and talk about real things. Maybe we can make some progress."

"If we even get another chance."

Five

"When can we eat?" Cassie said.

"I can't dry out." Her classmate Sarah stood shivering beside the fire.

"Calm down," Erin said. "We said we wanted to go out in the wilderness and see how strong and brave and clever we are. Let's show it. Stand here by the fire and dry your front side and then your back. Barb, Kelly and I will see what kind of food we have with us and make us some supper."

"I'll help with the firewood," Aliesha said.

"Me too." Cassie joined her in combing the nearby woods for pieces they could carry.

Barb took inventory of the food the plastic bags had kept dry. Kelly helped them pitch tents and set up camp. To avoid fouling the stream, Erin followed a trail leading deeper into the forest and used her entrenching tool to dig a latrine, marking the spot with a roll of toilet paper on a dead branch. By the time they pitched their three Army surplus pup tents in a casual arrangement around the fire, the sun had sunk below the tree line, and the river lay shrouded in shadow. They stood around the campfire, trying to dry out and ward off the evening chill. Barb improvised a meal with the hot dogs, cheese and bacon in their portion of the group's provisions.

By nine, Sarah and Aliesha, who shared one pup tent, and Barb and Cassie, who shared another, said they were exhausted and turned in. Kelly and Erin lingered by the dying fire, listening to the rushing stream and savoring the oak and hickory smoke. Cold and too tired to change, they slid fully dressed into their sleeping bags and lay with their heads poking out of the tent, looking up at the stars.

"This trip is turning into a disaster," Erin said. "I was looking forward to getting away, so my problems might look easier."

"What really happened between you and Jimmy?" Kelly, her closest friend. asked.

"Jimmy and I have been close since Mom died. He helped me deal with grief."

"I know you haven't seen much of him lately, but—why? "

"We broke up after our fight. Over what he did with Moira Sharpe."

"Oh, he claims she was hitting on him. I think that's true."

"That's what I want to believe. She won't leave him alone. Now that the news of our fight is all over school, I'm afraid she'll move in and I won't have a chance. I was so upset with him. Those Sharpe twins are so sneaky."

"I know." Kelly propped herself up on one elbow. "They take after their mother. Barb told me how they got Kevin away from Julie. First, Moira tempted him and set up a date. They're identical twins—everybody gets the two of them confused—so Myrna was actually the one who went out with him. She took him to bed. I only know because he bragged about it."

"Wasn't Moira angry with her sister?"

"No, that's their routine, pretending to be each other to fool the guys. Moira was more interested in Julie. I think she's gay."

"I hate them!"

"Don't worry, I'll fix Moira and Myrna. Compared to their scummy reputation, you're the Virgin Mary."

"Not anymore."

"What, exactly, are you talking about?"

"It goes a long way back. You remember when Mom was alive, Dad and I used to be pretty tight? Now he thinks I'm having sex every night."

"You do spend a lot of time with Jimmy. No wonder. His looks are to die for, and he's sweet in his nerdy way."

"It's more than that, Kelly. He understands me. We talk for hours. When Mom died, he came over and helped me study. I can't talk to Dad about personal stuff. He's so wrapped up with his job and with

Meg. Jimmy's there when I need him.

"Darn, he really loves you. We'll have to get you two back together."

"He never talks about himself, but he will with me. He's still hurting from losing his brother in the Iraq war. He blocked a roadside bomb to save his buddies. He hurts as badly as I do."

"Wow, that's tough."

"We were so close."

"It shows. When you two are together, everyone can see how much you love each other."

"I thought Jimmy loved me, too, but then he went and kissed Moira Sharpe at our dance. He says it's her fault, but the rumors won't die. Everything's gotten so hard since Mom died. Dad loves Meg more than me. I try to open up but he doesn't listen. Jimmy's the only one I can confide in—at least he was.

"Then, when Dad went to the architect's convention last month, Jimmy came over. I'd promised to help him catch up with his freehand drawing. He had to fill a sketchbook to get his semester grade. I posed for him."

"Oh?"

"It was innocent enough. First I wore a skirt and blouse, so he could work on draperies.

"His instructor gave him some Conté crayon, in a rich burnt umber. Jimmy said it was perfect for my red hair, with the manila sketch paper just right for my skin. When I saw his first sketch, my clothes were ruining the smooth flow of the lines, so—"

"I think I see where we're going with this."

"Oh, Kelly, it seemed so natural. It's as if he already knew me, and I had nothing more to hide. He's the only person who sees me as I am."

"So was the drawing good?"

"It was beautiful. I was so excited, I kissed him. He kissed me, and then... I can't describe it."

"Come on, you've told me this much."

"I can't—you'll talk. My rep is already in the toilet."

"I swear to God, I won't, Erin. I need to know."

"Well, pretty soon his clothes were gone, too. We wanted each other so much, and he was so perfect."

"Shut up! Did you two *do* it?"

"I was trembling. I wanted to let go but my hands wouldn't obey. I had to know how he felt—like that. I talked myself into believing there was no harm in trying, just once."

"O-o-oh. Did it hurt?"

"Yeah, a whole lot, at first. But then—Jimmy made me feel so good."

"You're so lucky, to have it go like that your first time."

"Now look at us. He hasn't talked to me since our fight. I gave myself to him, Kelly!"

"Oh. My. God, Erin! Didn't you use protection?"

"No. It was just supposed to be a study date. All he brought was his sketch pad. Oh, Kelly, What am I gonna do?" She broke down in gut-wrenching sobs.

"Don't panic. Maybe there'll be no problem at all."

"I miss him…I miss Mom…. Nothing's right anymore." Her sobbing resumed.

Kelly stroked her hair and pillowed her head on her breast.

"Look, people make love every day—sometimes two or three times, I hear." Kelly giggled and tightened her hug. "They don't die from it. I'm happy for you. No matter what happens, we'll stick together, okay?"

Erin cried herself to sleep in Kelly's arms.

Six

When Erin awoke, a half moon was shining in her eyes. It was full over a month ago, she recalled wistfully, when it shone in the window that night with Jimmy. She needed to relieve herself but was too warm and cozy to budge.

Aliesha crept to her tent. "Erin, I need to go to the latrine and I'm too scared."

"So do I. We'll go together."

She grabbed her flashlight, slipped on her mocs and led Aliesha up the trail to the latrine. As she stood up she heard a noise deeper in the forest, a crunch repeated every few seconds, and low voices. She turned off the flashlight and motioned to Aliesha. She crept silently toward the sound, stole closer and crouched behind a bush, scarcely daring to breathe. Aliesha followed. In a clearing a man in shirtsleeves stood over a big, muscle man in a tee shirt, who was digging by the light of an electric lantern.

The man in the suit muttered, "Hurry up, we ain't got all night." The larger man glanced at him sideways. "Gimme a break, Jake. I'm goin' as fast as I can." He continued to shovel earth on the ground.

"Okay, okay, good enough," said the boss. The big man straightened up and leaned on his shovel. "C'mon," Jake said. "Grab an end."

Erin glanced at Aliesha and put a warning finger to her lips.

The big man climbed out of the trench. The two leaned down and lifted a huge form. The lantern illuminated a man's obliterated face, glistening with congealed blood, so grotesque as to be inhuman. Erin gasped.

At the noise the leader looked up. "What the hell?" He glanced in her direction. "Get 'im, Momo."

Oh, dang.

Erin screamed and stood. She turned to escape down the path, but Momo sprang and caught her by one arm. She squirmed free, but he landed on top of her and knocked her breathless. Jake snagged Aliesha's leg and tackled her. Erin caught her breath and struggled against Momo's immense weight. He held her arms so tightly it hurt and turned her to face him in the moonlight.

Momo towered over her. Her heart hammered and her lips quivered as they tried to form words of protest, but none came out. Even in the moon's pale glow, she could tell he had blue eyes. They widened as the realization dawned on him. She almost saw a glint of recognition. At last he spoke.

"Holy crap—a broad!"

"I got another one here," Jake said. "She's black. Nice tits."

Jake looked them up and down. His lips curled into a cruel smirk. "My, oh my. They're not half bad lookin'."

Just what we need, two creeps for admirers.

"No-o-o!" Aliesha screamed. "Let me go!" She writhed against Jake's firm grip and fought back hard, squirming, struggling and kicking. She landed a knee in his groin.

"Dammit bitch, you'll pay for that!"

"Damn *you*, motha!"

"Wait till I tell Solly about this!" Jake pushed her toward the trail.

Blood pounded in Erin's head, her chest constricted and her vision blurred. What were they going to do to them? Erin was pale and silent. But Aliesha's reaction was more vocal. She stopped dead in her tracks.

"You ain't takin' us to see no Solly! I'll scratch yo' eyes out before you bastards touch me—no way!"

"Why you—" Jake threatened Aliesha with a raised arm.

Even in the dim moonlight Erin could see Jake's face redden and veins stand out on his balding head.

"Hold it, Jake." Momo said. "Don't hurt them. You tol' me if you mess up babes' looks Vince can't use 'em."

Use us? What for? Then it dawned on her all the things Jimmy said bad men did to young girls. "Where are you taking us?" Erin demanded. She already suspected what lay in store—dark thoughts of deprivation, rape and even murder. Certainly they were capable of it.

"Tough luck, kid. You saw way too much. C'mon, Momo, let's get them outta here—and don't get any ideas. This cargo is too precious for the likes of you."

Jake reached down for one of the ropes from the corpse and tied Aliesha's wrists in front of her. "Now march!" He set off, leading Aliesha, with the rope over his shoulder toward a trail on the opposite side of the clearing. Following suit, Momo tied Erin's hands behind her back and brought up the rear of their little procession

Erin's legs turned to rubber. Momo pushed her in front of him, with an occasional humiliating tug on her leash-rope when she stumbled, and forced her to follow Jake as he and Aliesha filed up the trail and away from the clearing, the camp, her friends

Jake led them along the winding path until they reached a dark sedan by a rutted gravel road. The moon peeking over the surrounding oaks and hickories was the last thing Erin saw. Momo came up behind her, knotted a bandanna taut over her eyes and wrestled her into the backseat. They squabbled over who should drive. Momo, who insisted he was the designated driver, won out. This didn't prevent him from sharing Jake's flask of bourbon, its smell wafting back toward the blindfolded girls. She was sitting uncomfortably on her tied hands. Bumps pitched her toward the car's roof as they roared out of the woods. Their bound bodies were squashed together as he swerved to avoid near misses with oncoming cars on the two-lane.

Her discomfort and terrified silence seemed to last for hours. Without a seat belt, she was at the mercy of every lurch and bump on the car's aging springs. They sped up and swept past other cars on the interstate. Traffic slowed, and they reached a more congested area. The car climbed, and she sensed by the silence they had entered a wider space. Cool air poured in the driver's window. When she sniffed the musky breeze, she realized they were crossing a wide span Through the window came the familiar musky smell of the Mississippi's waters.

"We're on the bridge—to Illinois!" she whispered to Aliesha.

"Shee-it!" Aliesha muttered. "This is *not* good." Her voice faltered and she fell silent.

Erin's heart hammered. She'd heard about East St. Louis, its poverty, crime and corruption. Sometimes the guys she knew would drive over to Sauget or Brooklyn to drink at the strip clubs. People in St. Louis suburbs, who seldom went east of Lindbergh Boulevard anyway, insisted that *nice people* didn't go there. As they said around here, it's a wide river.

At least a half-hour after they crossed the Mississippi, the car slowed and crunched down a bumpy gravel lane. She bounced as they jolted along. Stones pinged against the underside of the car. When they came to a halt, Jake barked the order. Momo opened the rear car door, grabbed her by the arm and lifted off the bandanna. Unable to use her hands to rub her bleary eyes, she had had trouble focusing on the cabin looming in front of her, the surrounding forest and the forms of Aliesha and their captors.

"Where am I?"

"This'll be your new home for a while. Momo will take good care of you."

"You…shitheads!" Aliesha spat out.

"They're combing the countryside right now looking for you bastards." Erin figured tough talk was the only language these brutes could understand.

"You wish." Jake shoved her toward the cabin. "Get inside."

Momo pushed the girls into a room with a few pieces of shabby furniture and a dingy oval braided rug. He thrust them down on a moth-eaten overstuffed sofa with sprouting springs that did little to relieve her discomfort. Momo pulled the chain on a bare ceiling bulb and closed the door to the moonbeams. Erin made out an armchair that once matched the couch and a table with three assorted straight chairs around it. An old television receiver with rabbit ears sat in a corner on an aluminum stand. Facing the couch on a low chest of drawers a flat-screen model with an antenna and dish looked out of place. Above it open-riser stairs disappeared through a rectangular hole in the ceiling. To the left a closed door led to another room. On the right, beyond an ancient wood stove, was a kitchen ell with painted wooden cabinets.

Jake grabbed a hammer and some nails from a kitchen drawer and climbed the steps. Erin heard pounding and had no trouble imagining what he was doing. Momo pitched his empty bottle in an overflowing trash bucket in the corner and headed for the kitchen, returning with two beers. After a few minutes of regular hammering, Jake descended.

"Where are we?" Erin demanded.

"Safe in the woods, and you're damned lucky to be here." Jake led the way up the stair, Aliesha and Erin next, with Momo bringing up the rear, still hanging on to her tether. Beneath steep roof rafters, a single bulb dangling from the ridge beam and the moon's rays peeking through an end window illuminated the loft's only furnishings: an iron bed with a thin, sagging mattress and a chamber pot. An old-fashioned orange crate served as a nightstand.

"Yuck," Erin said. "And there's only one bed."

"It's a hole all right." Aliesha jutted her chin at Momo. "Just give us some blankets."

"Hey, what's wrong with my pad?" Momo opened the closet and pulled out its only contents, two blankets and a pillow. "Now I gotta move in with Jake. He snores."

"Untie me and get outta here, assholes," Aliesha said, "I gotta pee."

Momo looked at Jake for assent and struggled with the knot until it yielded and the rope fell away. Then he untied Erin. At first she could barely move her arms, frozen for so long in that unnatural position. She rubbed her hands together to restore circulation and movement.

"Well?" Aliesha said, glaring at Jake.

Jake turned away and descended the stairs. Momo hesitated. "You need anything?"

"I'm hungry and thirsty," Aliesha said.

"Could I at least have some water?" Erin asked, afraid to ask for more.

He went below and returned a few minutes later. He set a water jug, two cups and a couple of cheese sandwiches on the crate..

"Hey, thanks, Momo," Erin said.

"This caper wasn't my idea. This crib ain't so bad, really. Maybe we'll get along okay.'"

With his flat nose, wide forehead and receding chin, his small head sitting on a barrel chest and legs that seemed inadequate for his body, he looked pathetic. And yet his blue eyes stared worshipfully; he couldn't take them off Erin. This seemed to her more than a physical attraction. As he backed toward the stair, Jake called up to him. "Close it." He lifted a trap door from the floor on its hinges, still watching her in the dim light, and let it down as he dropped from sight. A dead bolt secured the hatch with a sickening clank,

Erin scurried first to one window in a dormer and the length of the attic room to the gable window. Each double-hung sash glinted with Jake's new nails. Some crib—more like a cage.

"I think Momo likes me, and not just for—you know." Erin said. "Maybe they won't be so bad."

"You don' wanna know how bad. I'd kill these mothas before I'd trust 'em."

Erin sighed, as her companion banished even that faint hope. "What are we gonna do about sleeping? You can have the bed."

"No way, swee'pea. I'm used to the floor. You wouldn't sleep a wink."

"Hey, that's sweet of you. How come you're so used to the floor?"

"When we first moved into the house my parents bought in the city, Daddy got laid off just when he was about to buy furniture. My sister and I had to sleep on the floor for six months until he got hired back and we could buy beds."

"Ouch."

"Are you scared?" Aliesha asked.

"Terrified. Remember how brave I wanted us to be when we all got wet and discouraged? Now I'm having trouble believing I could ever talk like that. This time we're really screwed."

"This is a little more serious than lost in the woods with wet clothes. We don't know who these dudes are, 'cept for sure they killed that poor sucker out there. That ain't good."

"And they're hooked up with those strip clubs Jimmy warned me about. To them, we're just more cattle ready for slaughter."

"Since you put it that way, more like cows ready to be milked, bred and then killed for meat, or horses pullin' wagons—we'll just be shot when we're no any good to them anymore."

"You hear about kids who've been kidnapped and held prisoner getting free," Erin said, "like that kid Shaun, what's his name?" Erin said, "They were hiding him in plain sight. One day, somebody spotted him coming out of a suburban apartment building, and it was all over."

"Yeah, I heard about it. But don't forget, that didn't happen until he'd been stuck with them for four years. Think about all the other disappeared kids they never found."

"We have to think more positively than that. We've got to make a plan."

"You do that, honeybun. Meanwhile, I'll get some shuteye, so I can keep my strength. I'll prob'ly have to fight my way outta here with my bare hands."

Aliesha grabbed one of the blankets off the bed, made a bedroll and plunked down in the least drafty corner she could find. She soon was dead to the world.

Erin's body trembled. She had encountered death three times today. First in the landslide. Next, their discovery by the dead man's likely killers. Then in their harrowing ride to a woodland prison with their captors. The trembling increased, as if the earthquake had penetrated her bones. She curled up on the cot and wrapped herself in the thin blanket, determined to regain control. Eventually the shaking stopped and exhaustion took over, transporting her into a welcome state of oblivion.

SEVEN

Sunday morning Patrick agonized over the lack of news from the canoeing party.

"Why did she defy me? I was right not to let her go in the first place."

"Maybe you weren't paying attention to her needs."

"But I can't stand it when she's away from me for that long."

"No matter what *your* emotional needs are, she's a teen, and she deserves a chance to break out and try her wings in the real world."

"The real world, especially the Ozark wilderness, is full of thieves, drug addicts and desperate men." Moreover, her open rebellion against him and the authority figures in her life could backfire. If she ran up against any real criminals, in her present state of mind, she'd have all the wrong instincts for self-preservation.

"It's hard to imagine a more innocent outing than a Big Sister-Little Sister canoe float on the beautiful Current River."

"Ha. Innocent as an opium den. She's the only family I've got left."

"How do you think I feel? I've become so attached to her, I'd be devastated if anything bad happened. Besides, I hoped you'd consider *me* family by now."

Uh-oh. "I didn't mean to hurt your feelings, Meg." He'd have to be careful how he talked about this. He proposed to her last fall. But he couldn't marry her until he got Erin's blessing. And she and Erin didn't get along.

He called Mary Epley's cell phone again. "Mary, Where are you?"

"We've finally spotted the girls' campsite, below the rapids. It was quite a ride. Two of the canoes capsized on our way here. I'm so glad we didn't endanger the girls with that so late int he day yesterday."

"What did the canoe renter say?"

"He found the girls, about seven p. m., safely landed, with their tents properly set up in camp. They had enough food, so he reported back to me. He was busy, checking on his other canoeists after the quake, so he left them alone and went on to help others who were stranded.

"Great news. How are the girls?"

"We're about to land at their camp. Look, I've got to go. I'll let you know more later." She ended the connection.

"That is a relief," Meg said. "We can relax for a while. Let's chill and have some music."

She got out her guitar, the one her father had given her and taught her to play—a Spanish acoustic instrument with six nylon strings, a dark rosewood fretboard, the traditional Tacote wood sounding board and an inlaid mother-of-pearl six-pointed star around its circular opening. She played him a Scottish folk song, about a fiancée who offers shelter, out of charity, to a lonely, lost soldier and discovers to her joy that he is her man, returned from the wars.

Meg was trying too hard to divert him. The gentle music from her handsome instrument was actually making him feel worse. His problems mounted hourly. Frankly, he'd rather brood.

"This waiting makes the Deerpath project, with my difficult client and all its obstacles, seem like a minor nuisance. And the new client that showed up unannounced at the office two weeks ago..."

"Who's that?"

"Some guy with an improbable scheme to put a gambling boat along the river, at the very northern tip of the City of St. Louis. He arrived in late afternoon. I told him to come back the next day. But he said he was just in from Chicago, and he had a plane to catch. Besides Doug had suggested he talk to us."

"I guess you couldn't ignore the favor." Doug Marsh, Meg's employer at his land development company, was creator of many of Patrick's best projects, and a very good client. "Who is he?"

"Name's Manny Marancik. He wanted a full-blown design concept for his casino boat. And to top it off he laid a fat check on the table."

"I'll bet that got your attention."

"In fact, I was a bit embarrassed I tried to put him off. I've got the whole architectural team on it."

"Where does he come from?"

"Chicago, with a company called Gold Coast Gaming. He showed up with his development manager, Phil Swanson. He does the same kind of things you do on a project, coordinates it all, clears a path with regulating agencies and makes the day-to-day decisions. Like you, he's a cool head, to temper his boss's wild schemes. You should have seen the two go at it."

"Marancik must be quite a personality" Meg said, her efforts to keep Patrick's mind off Erin now obvious. Mary's update was way overdue.

"Oh, he's a real character—high strung and vain. His talks *at* you, not *to* you, keeps changing the subject and laughs at his own jokes. If Swanson hadn't been there to keep him on the subject, we'd never have gotten out of there."

They sat at the maple kitchen table over their coffee. A cold sun glaring through the glass failed to warm him. The dazzling spring day, rather than cheering him, aggravated his uneasy mood. Conversation dwindled to trivial chit-chat, ignoring the elephant in the room.

At four-thirty the phone rang. Patrick grabbed the receiver from the wall. It was Kelly mother again.

"Mary, where are you?"

"Patrick, something terrible has happened. Erin and Aliesha Robinson, one of the city girls, have disappeared. We just spent two hours at the County building in Eminence, talking with the sheriff. He's—"

"The sheriff...What the hell?" He stiffened and gripped the phone, repeating Mary's words, as if to convince himself he'd heard them. "Three canoes ahead ... separated from the main party... Erin and Aliesha... disappeared."

"We didn't find out until we reached their camp this morning. Their cell phones got wet when a canoe overturned. We had to call the sheriff."

"My God."

"There's a body involved."

"Tell me it's not one of the girls!"

"No, no. It's a man they can't identify."

"Where can I meet you?"

"Stay put. We're on our way. We should be at your house in two hours." There was much more, but she would explain when she arrived.

"Hurry, Mary. I can't stand this." Patrick hung up the phone. "I told you something like this would happen."

"We didn't know that until just now. This is awful." Meg grabbed his shoulders and tried to comfort him.

"I never should have let her go without me along. She's already sacrificed too much, on another river."

The grim image returned—a chill December night in an ice storm, the Explorer sailing off a bridge approach in Illinois, tumbling down an embankment and coming to rest in the icy flow.

Patrick rose and stalked toward the den, oblivious of his surroundings, and collapsed on the sofa. Meg pushed back her chair and followed him. He stared blankly at the shelves—the Belleek vase holding Kitty's last Christmas arrangement, photos of the family's happiest times. He fixated on the first publicity photo he'd taken of Kitty for her act in his father's night club.

He couldn't erase his last sight of her from his mind. Her eyes closing… blood trickling from her ear, black in the clouds' dull glow… his numb fingers plunging into the icy flow, clawing for her seatbelt… his clumsy pokes at the clasp, his head under ice water… released at last … Floating her out of the car to the huge bear of a medic, who clambered up the slope and lifted her litter above his head to pass up the human chain to the road…… the medic's frantic efforts to resuscitate her. Her eyes, closed—forever. The huge medic's tears… his final bear hug… Headlights lined up for miles behind them on the highway, reminding him of their own ruined Christmas plans. Before Kitty's last words: "I'm okay, get Erin."

"Your eyes look crazy. Your face—it's gray…" Meg stroked it. "And clammy".

His vision dimmed. Then he lifted his lids wide and burst into a grin. "You're here, you're safe!" He reached for her and locked her to his chest.

"Patrick, I can't breathe!" She wrenched herself from his death grip.

"Oh, Kitty—it's okay, it's okay…"

Meg screamed. "Patrick, wake up. It's me, Meg!" She shook him. He groaned and rolled over.

Patrick slept where he lay on the sofa in the den.

◊

Meg retreated to the kitchen, where they had first felt the disturbance, and fished in the fridge for a snack. Despite her vigilance to preserve her girlish shape, she nibbled whenever she was unhappy, and now was no time to stop. She found the box containing last night's left-over gourmet lasagna from Charlie Gitto's on the Hill and picked with her fork at the cold, formless remains—sort of like her life. She'd been looking forward to spending the rest of it with Patrick. He had proposed to her after the conclusion of his case last fall. Since her first few relationships had ended in disaster, this was a dream come true, the chance to partner with a stable, serious architect, on the high road at last. But maybe this time was no different—for her, something always seemed to come up to obstruct the path of true love.

When they first started to work together, she thought he was too old for her. His halting gait, due to the knee injury from his accident, his weathered, rugged face and his graying sideburns belied the fact that he was not yet forty. At thirty-three, she'd held out for the right man and at last found him, or so she thought. She could even imagine her hero wielding Excalibur, charging to defend her on his steed toward hordes of evil barbarians.

She chuckled at her fantasy. But he did seem to have a nose for trouble. Last year's mysterious death on his job site, constant friction with his daughter Erin and now this. Just when Meg was hoping to serve as mentor, guide and even girlfriend to this beautiful and rootless teen, she'd been snatched away by cruel circumstance. Although Meg was badly shaken by the girls' disappearance and feared terribly for their safety, she took a moment to wallow in self-pity. *Why does everything happen to him—and as a result, to me?* And yet this very affinity for trouble attracted her to him like a moth to a flame. Beneath Patrick's craggy features, grim-set jaw and taciturn manner, the waters ran fast and deep—shifting, unpredictable and fraught with alluring danger.

But Patrick's present behavior terrified her. He was clearly still feeling the traumatic effects of losing his wife in such a violent manner. She had read just enough about Post Traumatic Stress Disorder to know that when exposed to conditions similar to the original trauma, its sufferers tend to relive the original experience. She had once suggested a float trip for the two of them and received a flat rejection; Patrick hadn't felt any need to explain why. No wonder Patrick wanted to keep Erin away from the river!

She tried to put these dark thoughts out of her mind and concentrate on the good things in their relationship—his ability to defuse tension over complex issues with a wry comment or a joke, to banish her negative feelings about men and to focus her on the positive. But Erin's refusal to accept her stood in the way. And something he hid deep inside gave rise to an unknown fear. This new outburst topped them all—the worst she had ever seen him.

No matter how bad such days might get for Patrick, though, she had long ago resolved to try making them better.

It was just getting dark. Meg brought in some chamomile tea to calm his shattered nerves.

Patrick opened his eyes.

"How are you feeling?" She set the tea on the end table.

"I was so tired I must've zonked out for a while." Patrick blinked and grinned sheepishly.

"That's putting it mildly. I think the news about Erin really got to you."

"Oh, boy," he moaned, when he recalled Mary's report. "The campers aren't here yet?"

"I think we can expect them anytime now."

"I just know bad people got to Erin and Aliesha. Some pretty desperate folks hang out in those hills."

"Probably no worse than here in the city." She groped for reassuring words.

"I'll never forgive myself if something terrible happens to Erin after I let her go off alone like that," he rambled on. "I wanted to go along to chaperon, like sophomore year."

"They wouldn't let you, remember? Everyone heard about your little roll in the grass with Liza Sharpe."

"She wasn't even going this year."

"I still think you're over-dramatizing the Ozarks' dangers."

"No, I was sure anything could happen—and trouble from an earthquake and overturned canoes seem to be only the beginning.

"I should've known. That professor Iben Browning declared back in the eighties that our region was overdue for a major earth tremor. For a while people believed him. All the building codes were overhauled to place St. Louis in a higher risk zone for earthquakes. Then most everyone forgot about it—until now."

Meg let him ramble on, It kept his mind off worries about Erin, For the moment.

The doorbell chimed. Patrick raced to answer it. Mary Epley stood on the porch with her daughter Kelly, and Cassie. Kelly wore dirty jeans and a tank top, her long hair ratty. Cassie still had on a sweater and shorts. All three looked bedraggled and tired. When Kelly saw Patrick she started to cry.

Still standing in the foyer, Patrick began plying Kelly with questions. "What happened? When did they disappear? Where did you camp?"

Meg stared in bewilderment.

"Our group of three boats with the strongest paddlers got way ahead of the others. We were caught in a landslide. We—"

"Please sit down, so we can sort this out." Meg interrupted and led them into the den.

"There was an earthquake!" Cassie exclaimed. "Giant rocks crashed down into the river and made new rapids."

"Our three canoes were way ahead of the pack. We made it through," Kelly continued. "One of our canoes overturned and they ruined their cell phones jumping in the water to help. We were cut off from them. We figured they wouldn't try to shoot the rapids since it would be dark soon. We decided make camp and wait."

"What happened to Erin and Aliesha?" Patrick asked.

"I'm getting there."

"Well, at that point being separated from the group, was no big deal," Kelly continued. "We knew they'd catch up with us when they came downstream in the morning. But we were alone, and cold. Erin told us to be brave, like pioneers, but it was scary. When the fire died down, the rest of our party, and finally Erin and I, went to sleep."

"Come on, come on. Then what?"

Patrick couldn't sit. He paced as Kelly continued her story.

"When I woke up later, Erin and Aliesha were gone. I heard a scream, so I woke Barb. The noise came from the trail leading to our latrine. We followed it deeper into the woods for about 100 yards."

"When we heard the scream," Cassie burst in, "the rest of us ran up the trail toward the sound. Up there, past where we dug the latrine, was a clearing in the woods. The moon was going down, so it was hard to see. Kelly kicked a big pile of dirt, and a man's hand poked out. Yuck." She made a face. "I turned away. I didn't want to see any more."

"A man?" Patrick froze; his pacing stopped.

"It was awful," Kelly said. "It was a black man. We could see the sleeves of a shirt and a suit on his arm."

"A body, a *dead* body." Patrick stared at the floor, shaking his head.

"Can you imagine dying in your business clothes, with nobody by your bedside to kiss you goodbye?" Cassie said. "And poor Erin and Aliesha were gone."

"Mary, what sense can you make of this?" Patrick faced her.

"About eight this morning we set out to look for the six girls," Mary said. "We saw three canoes beached on the bank and reached their camp. The girls were tired and scared. They led us to the body. We called the sheriff. He knew how to get to our spot by the back roads, and he took over. The sheriff's theory is that Erin and Aliesha saw them burying the body and they couldn't risk leaving them. Here's his contact information." Mary put a slip of paper with the sheriff's name and number on the coffee table. "I told him you'd call."

"My daughter—captured by murderers." Patrick began pacing again. "I offered to chaperone the group. I offered...I forbade her to go."

Erin had been threatened before during their last murder case, but she had avoided harm. This time she'd stumbled into a real mess. And poor Esther Robinson would share their anguish. Who were these criminals, and where had they taken these girls?

There was nothing more Mary and the campers could do. Patrick thanked them and let them go to the Robinson home to report the grim news to Aliesha's mother. He called Assistant U.S. Attorney Adam Reiner, who had led his previous case, at home and told him what happened.

"What? Erin? Not again!" He was pretty sure he had jurisdiction. He assured Patrick that FBI Special Agent Bobbi Romano would be on the case at first light.

After the call ended, Patrick babbled, "I can't face that river. It's all too familiar."

"It's better if you stay here. You can talk with Bobbi in the morning."

"Tomorrow may be too late. The trail will get cold. Meg, you go home. I've got work to do. Just when I thought my life was back on track. After four years, it's all starting again. But you can go home."

"No, I'd feel better staying here, to make sure you're alright."

Patrick called the number Mary left with him. "Sheriff Holland? This is Patrick MacKenna, father of Erin MacKenna, one of the missing girls."

"Yes?"

"Sheriff, you should have called the minute you knew about Erin's disappearance."

"Mr. MacKenna, that's not how we work. We get to the crime scene as quickly as we can, in case the murderers are still in the area, or we'll miss our chance to catch them."

"I feel so powerless. Can't we go to that crime scene and comb the area."

"Sir, it's already getting dark. You can't find the crime scene without me. I've already talked to FBI Agent Bobbi Romano. The next time we can even get to the site will be tomorrow morning. This is a law enforcement matter. If you have her permission, you're welcome to come along. That's the best I can do."

"Thanks, Sheriff."

He hung up and faced Meg. "I'm so torn. I should go with Bobbi.

But a powerful force is telling me to stay away. Why am I so afraid of going out there?

"It probably has to do with that horrible recurring nightmare. Maybe you need to face some old fears, *because* it's on a river."

What if she were wrong? In visiting the banks of another river, he might lose all hope and learn he would never see his daughter again.

Eight

The sun found its way through a missing shingle in the cabin roof and shone on Erin's face. She rolled over in the sagging, lumpy cot, her neck stiff, shoulders sore and back aching. She opened one eye.

Dang! Last night's harrowing ride replayed in her head.

Erin reflected on yesterday's disasters. She had wanted to get these kids from the inner city into a healthy outdoor environment. They were in the outdoors alright, but it promised to be worse than the inner city. Aliesha seemed to sense more danger than she did.

Rising on one elbow, Erin looked over to the pallet, where Aliesha was just stirring. How long had she slept? It couldn't have been more than five hours. With effort she sat up and discovered bruises and scratches from the rope on her wrists. The murmur of men's voices filtered through the wooden floor.

She tiptoed across it until she reached the point where the voices were loudest and sprawled on the rough wood planking. Cracks in the irregular boards varied from just touching to as wide as half an inch. She pressed an ear to the widest crack she could find. Aliesha crept alongside her. Erin pressed a warning finger to her lips.

"What am I supposed to do while you're workin' in the shack?" It was the voice of Momo.

"Lock 'em in the cabin and stay with 'em. Don't let them out of your sight. And no funny business. We gotta deliver these goods in mint condition."

"Hey, what do I look like? A robber, maybe, but no child molester."

Score one for Momo

A chair scraped, and then Jake's muffled voice. "Yeah, Vince will certainly be interested in this find. Wait until I…" The words trailed off, too faint to hear. He must have gone into the kitchen.

"More of this mud?" Jake was back with the coffee pot. The aroma wafting through the crack reminded Erin of her empty stomach.

Aliesha pushed up and stared at Erin.

"You okay?" Erin whispered.

"I was fine 'til I remembered where I am. Shee-it."

"Shh. Listen."

"So what'll you tell Vince?"

"I'll see if he'll sweeten our deal. He can always use good-looking broads in his operations."

"You can't turn them into working girls!" Momo seemed to have a shred of decency

Awful possibilities crossed Erin's mind. Aliesha had warned of being forced to hawk drinks to greasy customers, maybe even forced go into a room with them and… She shuddered and blocked out the image.

"Oh, maybe they'll get lucky and dance in one of his clubs. But I don't think the white gal has the tits for it."

Although sprawled on the floor as an undignified eavesdropper, Erin raised up her torso, and inhaled, deeply offended. "What's wrong with my tits?" she whispered to Aliesha. "My figure's like Mom's. She had gently spreading hips, a tiny waist and a perfect B-cup, without padding. Jimmy says my boobs are more than a handful, and he can't get enough of them."

"They look okay to me," Aliesha said, "too good for the likes of them." She pressed her ear closer to the floorboards.

"Once he gets her hooked he can do anything he wants with her. Whatever he does, he's got to keep them under wraps—they saw us bury the body."

"Well, you better make it quick," Momo said. "They won't look so hot after a few days out here."

Aliesha stood up, furious at the way they talked about them.

"I'm hungry. I'm going down to see what they've got to eat." Erin walked toward the hatch and stamped on it to get their attention

"I gotta get my rear in gear. I'll be along in a few." Aliesha propped herself on her elbows, preparing to face the day.

They agreed to play ignorant of what they'd just heard. Erin slid the bed back against the wall and finally attracted the men's attention. When Momo lifted the hatch, she said, "I want some of that coffee." Erin climbed down the steps with the makeshift chamber pot.

"Good mornin', Princess," Jake said, his voice freighted with sarcasm.

"Good morning, Jake. I need to dump this and wash up. Do you have a bathroom in here?"

"Why of course, my dear. A young lady needs to powder her nose. It's through the door on the left, off the bedroom. And no tricks, babe. I'll be right out here."

Passing though their bedroom she glimpsed two unmade cots like the one above, amid heaps of clothes, a cluttered dresser and a small table with a chair. She squeezed into a closet-sized bathroom and closed the door. A tiny window sat high in the wall above the toilet, a makeshift shower stall occupied the other end and a small lavatory was mounted in the middle.

In the cracked mirror, its silver back flaking off at the corners, her eyes looked puffy from lack of sleep, her hair a rat's nest and her cheeks stained with tears. She opened the single tap and doused her face with ice-cold water. She washed her hands with a dried bar of soap on the sink and, shunning a dirty green towel on a hook, wiped them on her jeans.

She sat at the table. Momo brought them cups of coffee.

"Do you have any milk for this?" Erin asked.

"Do I have any milk?" Jake sneered at her. "Gee, we're fresh out."

"Just asking. I'm hungry and thirsty."

Jake slid a box of doughnuts over to her. "That's what we got. Take it or leave it."

The coffee was burnt but doughnuts tasted good enough. She finished one and took another.

"Momo, your job is to watch them. I'm going to town for supplies and then I have to finish up our order."

"Yeah, bring some grub. And we're almost out of beer."

"If you're going to the store we need a hair brushes and combs, toothbrushes, some shampoo and conditioner, Erin said, "and you should all be eating better. Pick up some skim milk, granola cereal, and some fresh fruit, say, apples, oranges and bananas. And what about lunch? Some wheat bread and sliced turkey would be nice."

"Hey Jake, that sounds great."

"Aw for chrissake. What am I runnin' here, the Ritz?"

Jake left the cabin, grumbling under his breath, "...not a goddamned a baby sitter." He hiked around the side to a trail deeper in the woods. An hour later he came back, loaded some boxes into his car and drove away on the gravel road.

Momo turned on the TV, but allowed them to go above and neaten up their attic space.

As she rearranged the pillow and blanket on her cot, Erin said, "I've thought of questions to ask Momo. Jimmy taught me the army rules. When captured, immediately plan your escape. While we're alone with only Momo around watching TV, we can figure out our plan."

"Hoo-ray," Aliesha said half-heartedly. "They like to do us the way they did that poor stiff."

"I've never heard you talk like this before, in the argot of the street," Erin said.

"Argo? Argo fuck yo'self! It's the only talk they understand. We in deep crap, honeypot."

"They're planning to put us to work in their strip clubs. It might not be so bad. I might like to be onstage."

"No way, José. I'll kill 'em first wit' ma bare hands. You don' know where that leads. They hook you on coke an' pretty soon you gonna be number one ho' in they cat house."

NINE

At 7:30 a.m., after tossing most of the night, Patrick was awakened by a call from Bobbi Romano.

"Thank God you're on the case," Patrick said.

"Adam Reiner filled me in. I talked with Sheriff Jeb Holland at the Shannon County Courthouse in Eminence. Whoever the sons o' bitches behind this are, they'll pay." One of the youngest agents at the St. Louis office of the FBI, petite, sexy and tough, Bobbi had earned a reputation for dogged persistence and taking no guff from anyone. "I'm headed out this morning for the crime scene."

"Bobbi, I'm afraid they'll kill them."

"No, they would have done it on the spot, and buried them too. There's a reason they didn't. I need to inspect the scene of the kidnapping."

Bobbi's jarring use of the word brought home the fact of Erin's abduction. Still, her calm tone reassured him she could manage the situation.

"There's no need to go with you. I can't bear to go to the scene."

"That's so unlike you, Patrick. You've got to come with me."

"Dammit, I can't face it. I'm terrified at what we'll find."

"Nonsense. I'm sure you can handle it. Besides, you're familiar with the river, and you know your daughter better than any of us. I need you there."

"I don't know what I can contribute. One river is like the next—full of trouble."

She sighed. "You're coming with me. I'll pick you up in half an hour."

While he waited, Ed Mossbach called. "Our meeting with Gary Archer is at ten o'clock. Can I come by for you?"

"I'm not going. I'm investigating the scene of Erin's disappearance with the FBI."

"Patrick. I need you in this meeting. We've got to calm Gary down."

"You and Archer go way back. Tell him tomorrow's soon enough."

"Don't push your luck."

"Ed, frankly I'd rather be with you. But the FBI Agent insists she needs me. Just do it!"

Mossbach sighed. "All right, already. I'll inspect the transmission tower site today and drop by to tell him we'll see him tomorrow morning, without fail. And in case you've forgotten, afterwards we're meeting with Marancik, all afternoon."

"Good. I'll need something to keep my mind off this. I feel so helpless, it's unbearable."

Patrick knew Mossbach was just trying to protect their business interests. And he was happy to latch on to any excuse to avoid facing this.

Gary Archer, however, was not so understanding. At nine-fifteen, as Patrick and Bobbi rolled though the town of Cuba, his cell phone rang.

"MacKenna, where are you? You scheduled our meeting. How dare you not show up!"

"Gary, believe me, your project is the most important one on my plate. But my daughter has disappeared. The FBI needs me to go to the scene of the crime. Ed Mossbach is headed for your office right now."

"I thought you were an architect, not a detective."

"Everything changes when you daughter's life is at stake."

"Sounds like your problem, not mine—and I have a few of my own. If you want to remain an architect, at least on my project, you'll get over here and work on it, not later than tomorrow morning."

"As Ed Mossbach has already told you, I can do that." He clicked off the phone.

"Who's that sonofabitch? He was shouting so loud, I heard the whole thing."

"That's the City Administrator of Deerpath. Some fun, huh?"

"Geez, what a grouch. And I thought I had jerks to deal with."

"He feels put upon by everyone and wants the impossible."

"Lot of luck with that one."

An hour later Bobbi and Patrick pulled up to a boxy red brick courthouse in Eminence, the Shannon County seat, just as a tall man in a gray uniform and a Mountie hat climbed out of a sheriff's car.

"Sheriff Holland?" Bobbi said.

"You're lookin' at him." His shoulders slumping, he looked down into Bobbi's car.

Bobbi shook his hand and introduced herself and Patrick. "Where's the body?"

"We have the victim on ice until our part-time coroner can come in today and take him to the morgue." He wiped his wrinkled forehead, already sweating in the morning sun. "I warn you, it's not a pretty sight. He's been shot up bad. I don't know how you'll even be able to get an ID on him."

"We have our ways." Bobbi exchanged a grim smile with Holland.

When he conducted them to the holding room in the basement of the courthouse, she stopped smiling.

"Geez, this is gross."

The close air in the room made Patrick gag. Despite refrigeration, the victim—dead who knew how long?—already contributed to the lingering stench of past visitors, somewhere between skunk and rotten meat.

"Take your time. I've got to go up to my office and get my file." Holland turned and left them with the corpse. Bobbi pulled out her compact high-resolution camera.

The victim was a heavy-set African-American male in a gray suit. He wore trousers with a good crease but wrinkled and soiled beyond reclamation. Bloodstains had ruined the jacket, royal blue shirt and white silk tie. When his gaze settled on the man's face, however, Patrick blanched. The nose, one eye and parts of the mouth had been blown away.

"Bullet entry from the back of the head," Bobbi said. "Rips hell out of the other side."

"Maybe the poor guy never knew what hit him."

"Yep." She sucked in her breath and continued snapping photos.

"Must have been a powerful gun."

"Something that could pump a lot of lead in a hurry, that's for sure.""

"I wonder who he is?"

"That's the sixty-four dollar question, isn't it? You don't wanna know how many African-American males checked out in the region this week. This one's well-dressed. That might narrow it down a bit."

Patrick shivered, only partly from the chilly temperature. He clasped his upper arms with his hands and circled the tiny room, not taking his eyes off the body. In the glare of the room's sole fluorescent light, something caught his eye. As he studied the large bloodstain on the victim's left lapel, he spotted a tiny brass post protruding from the buttonhole. Whatever jewelry it had fastened had fallen off.

"Had enough?" Sheriff Holland rejoined them in the room.

"Thanks for the look," Bobbi said. Let's go inspect the scene."

The sheriff led them back to his car. They wound for a half-hour through woods on twisting, hilly roads.

"Dark gray clouds coming up," the sheriff noted. "This might be the last chance to search the scene for clues before water and wind get to it."

Holland parked on the shoulder. They followed him to a clearing where the girls had found the body. Soil had slid back into the hole when the corpse was removed. Bobbi took more photos while Patrick searched the site, his head down. Holland led them further down the trail to the riverbank to see remnants of the girls' campfire. He pointed just upstream, where boulders loosened by the earthquake had tumbled into the water. Patrick lingered at the riverbank. He was surprised to see new rapids in this familiar reach, making it hard to recognize.

The sheriff led Bobbi back toward the road to show her the tire tracks. Patrick paused alone in the clearing and took a last look around the place where Erin had disappeared. Angry and frustrated, he kicked away a dead branch lying alongside the shallow grave.

The sun broke through the scudding clouds. Something glinted in his eye. He leaned over and picked up a shiny enameled pin with its mounting post broken off—bearing a medieval crest, most probably the one the victim had worn. Ornate plant tracery surrounded a shield divided into four quadrants, alternately black and gold. A closed black fist and two crossed torches adorned the top of the crest, guarded by griffins. At the bottom shone the large Greek letters, AΦA. Patrick studied the object until the car's horn honked to alert him the sheriff was ready to leave. He knew exactly who he would ask about it. He stuck the pin in the side ticket pocket of his blazer and dashed back up the trail to catch his ride.

On the way back to St. Louis, Bobbi called Adam Reiner and set the phone on speaker.

"It's about time you called," Reiner said.

"With what we found out there, you're lucky we aren't still barfing beside the trail."

"Where was the body? How long has he been dead? Did you find the murder weapon?"

"Slow down, Adam. Jeb Holland and his country boys are pretty sharp. They did a good job photographing the scene and handling the body." She described the clearing in the woods, with the body still lying in its rustic grave. "The killers were trying to hide this one where it wouldn't be found. These two campers really messed up their plans. They must've shot him elsewhere and brought the body there, or the campers would have heard it. We didn't find any bullets."

"What else?"

"They made a mess of his head, ambushed him at close range."

"Whew," Reiner whistled. "An assassination."

"With his face blown away, will it be impossible to tell who it is?" Patrick felt light-headed. His breath quickened.

"No, we can use forensics, maybe fingerprints, or even DNA," Bobbi said, "but it will take longer. Maybe I'll get lucky and be able to match up his body with a specific missing person."

"No identification on him at all?" Reiner asked.

"His pockets were empty—no wallet, no keys, nothin', except part of a hand-scratched note in his pocket. All we could make out from the torn scrap was the name Jake and part of a phone number, with the 618 area code—that covers the whole southern third of Illinois. We'll analyze it further in the lab."

"If you could prove they transported the body across state lines," Adam said, "we'd be able to confirm our jurisdiction."

"We can't prove anything until we identify the mystery man."

"Patrick reached into his blazer and produced the fraternity pin. "Will this help"

"Holy crap! Where did you find this?" Bobbi examined the pin.

"Next to the grave. Looks like a fraternity pin," he explained for Adam's benefit. "The post that fastened it was still in the dead man's lapel. I have a hunch Will Bartley will know exactly how to trace it." Patrick said.

"I haven't had a chance to interview the campers yet," Bobbi continued. "Patrick, tell Adam what they said."

"When they got home, Kelly and Cassie, who were with Erin, told me what they saw." He related what the girls had told him about finding the body."

"I've scheduled an interview at Kelly's house as soon as they get home from school. That's about all I have. How about you, Adam?"

"There must have been other places to hide a body," Reiner said. "If these men were from Illinois, other than to delay discovery of the crime, why would they dump an African-American male deep in Missouri's Ozark woods?"

"I sure don't understand it." Patrick was still reeling from his discoveries of the past twenty-four hours. "Maybe it has to do with all the meth labs in rural Missouri."

"Doubtful," Bobbi said, "unless they dropped off the body on their way to a drug pickup."

"Got a better theory?" Reiner said. "This is getting pretty sinister."

"It got damned sinister when they kidnapped two witnesses."

"I have the names of a dozen of people who disappeared around here in the past week. The fact that he's African-American and probably from Illinois might narrow the search a bit. But statistically, ninety percent of the murder victims in this metro area are black."

"I'll have this report completed an on your desk later today, Adam."

"Good. Keep me posted. We'll meet when we've got something."

Bobbi looked at Patrick, who raised his hands and shrugged. "Thanks, Adam."

"Bobbi, keep in touch. I'd say you have your work cut out for you."

Ten

A fresh breeze, redolent of pine and rain-soaked earth, penetrated the chinks in the roof and woke Erin. Dispersing clouds let the morning sun break through to the forest floor. Normally this would be a great morning to be alive.

But Momo poked his head up through the hatch. "Outta bed, you two, and make it snappy. Jake's got a big day and he wants you where we can keep an eye on you."

"Go shoot yourself, Momo," Aliesha mumbled from her pallet.

"You shut up, bitch. Just get up, and don't try any funny stuff," he snarled. "I'm lockin' you in." His head disappeared though the opening.

"That damn Momo needs to take his head outta his ass." Aliesha lifted from her bedroll and leaned on one elbow. "He's so low on this totem pole, they gonna swat him dead like a fly when they through with him."

Erin watched Aliesha fold her bedding. She was made of tougher stuff and knew more about this alternate world. Maybe she'd have an idea of what to do.

"Aliesha, can you clean up your speech? You won't be fit for polite society when we get out of here."

"Ha! You think we gettin' out? You see the way Jake looks at me? He got big plans for me in them clubs. They gonna get me a skimpy, shiny dress and a big bed. They gonna feed me barely enough to keep me alive and then work my ass ten hours a night. My only hope is talk like this and scare the hell outta them johns so they be gentle."

"No! We can't give up. We've gotta resist and fight these creeps."

"Nobody I know ever beat 'em. They got too much money an' lots o' fun and excitement to keep you amused. If you don't play ball they keep you in line with drugs and guns."

"Well, not me! I'll fight them."

"You never tried drugs, did you?"

"Why, no. Jimmy warned me to stay away—and Dad warned me about meth."

"Meth? That's a white man's problem."

"Maybe now, but Dad says it can lead to coke and heroin addiction."

"Oh, yeah?"

"He said the drug economy thrives in the Ozarks because the soils are too poor for agriculture. The only available jobs are serving tourists who come for Missouri's natural beauty and Branson entertainment."

"It was sure pretty out there. I wish we coulda hung around to enjoy it."

"Yeah." Erin sighed. "But tourists only provide work for three or four months a year. The only hope of earning money year-round is an impossible dream—making meth from simple ingredients and selling it for big bucks to everyone else. In winter when the tourists are gone, everyone else is strapped for cash—where's the money for those buys supposed to come from?"

"I get it—bad deal all around."

"Dad said, if the Ozark hills were no good for crops, they sure had been fertile for bandits who produced illegal substances. In the twenties came moonshine and bootleg liquor, in the sixties, marijuana, and now methamphetamine."

"For poor folk, mainly. Not everybody."

"No, it affects the rich, the poor, the educated and the ignorant alike."

"My big sister tol' me plenty. In my part o' town, some girls my age, even younger, do anything for drugs—steal, turn tricks, kill folks—anything at all."

"You mean if we don't cooperate, they could turn us into addicts? We'll never get out of here."

"You got it. You think you too pretty to be their victim. You're one in a million pretty girls. They sell pretty for a livin'. But you won't be so pretty when they get through with you. You get uppity they can mess up yo' face, starve yo' body and break your legs. Best thing is play ball and maybe you get a nice soft job with boyfriends and spendin' money and nice clothes."

Erin felt her stomach drop.

To hear Aleisha tell it, she was being sucked into a whirlpool with no escape. "Look, they didn't find my cell phone." She drew it out of her back jeans pocket. She tried to turn it on, but still got no response. "You know that fan in the kitchen? Maybe if we dry it out while Momo's gone it will work again."

"Yeah, right. An' who you gonna call? Ghost busters?" She burst into hysterical laughter.

"My dad. He'll get the FBI to get us out of here."

"Oh right, like he's personal friends with the cops."

"He is. The police chief came to our Christmas party. On his last case, he worked with the FBI. Special Agent Bobbi Romano is sharp and quick—she has to be twice as good to show the men in her outfit she can cut it."

"If these bastards find that out, they'll kill us. Best bet is, don't tell them about your big-time friends."

"No! You mean we'll be worse off?"

"They're not stupid. They got girls from Russia, Bosnia, and poor runaway kids from the city to sell—easy pickin's. If they knew you were so connected when they found us, they mighta killed us and made it look like an accident. No sense gettin' the FBI pissed off at 'em."

"But they didn't know, and they didn't kill us. Now what?"

"Dunno. We know too much. Everybody knows we're still alive. but still, we gotta chill with the FBI threats. They're packin' too much heat to take a chance."

She wished she could turn back time to last Friday. All her old worries now seemed so petty and small.

Eleven

After Bobbi dropped him at his house, Patrick got in his car and drove downtown to St. Louis Police Headquarters. He'd known Will ever since Patrick was planning neighborhood improvements and patrolman Bartley was assigned to represent the police in discussing neighborhood security measures. Later, Patrick found a way to defuse a confrontation between residents of a fashionable West End district and the city over zoning permission to locate a methadone clinic there. He had forged a compromise in which the clinic was moved to a location near downtown, where transit lines converged and individual homes would remain unaffected by the center's frequent traffic from known drug addicts. Bartley had received a promotion and Patrick made a lifelong friend.

"I know we're long overdue getting together, Patrick, but right now? What's up?"

"It's Erin. She and another girl are missing." He related his daughter's predicament.

"My God." Will told his secretary to adjourn the meeting, led Patrick into his office and closed the door.

"What's going on?" Bartley adjusted his black spectacles and regarded his friend with concern.

"Will, a man is dead, my daughter and the little girl she sponsored from the city are gone, and I'm terrified we'll never see them again."

"Erin sure has had some tough luck," Bartley said. "First losing her mom and now this."

"There's more. The other campers said the body those guys buried was a black man. I may learn more in my meeting with Bobbi and Adam Reiner tomorrow."

"This has been a really bad month for my black brothers. Random drive-by shootings, murders from drug deals gone bad, several good folks taken down. Did you find any clues?"

"The sheriff and the coroner will look more carefully at the body. But I did find this." He reached in the side pocket of his blazer, retrieved the gold and black pin and set it in front of Bartley. "Any idea what it is?"

Bartley gasped. "Where'd you get this?"

"At the burial site. I'm pretty sure it broke off the murder victim's lapel."

"It can't be." Finally, Will let out a breath. He shook his head and his eyes welled with tears. "Alpha Phi Alpha, the oldest black fraternity in the nation, founded in 1916. We can claim Martin Luther King and Duke Ellington among our illustrious members."

"What are you saying?"

"Now a close friend of mine has disappeared. He hasn't been heard from in almost a week."

"Who is it?"

"Caleb—Caleb Mitchom, Mayor of Brooklyn, my fraternity brother at Southern Illinois University. I've been deeply concerned about him. An honest man and a good friend."

"Will, if it is your friend, I'm truly sorry." Patrick reached across the desk and held his friend's arm.

"He attempted to clean up Brooklyn. It made him a likely target of the vice and drug lords over there."

"Bobbi Romano needs you to confirm this. Can you call her?"

"You bet. We'll run down the forensics. If Erin is mixed up with those crumb-bums, what terrible luck!"

"What's worse, Erin's as beautiful as her mother."

"I know. I saw her at your party last year. She's turned into quite a young woman."

The police chief bowed his close-cropped head and shook it. Then he looked up, brightening. "Hey, I do know someone who could help solve this: Burton Scales, an Illinois circuit judge for that district. He has made a personal mission of getting to the bottom of this vicious cycle. He uses his tough love to rescue exploited kids and reform young lawbreakers. He also knows the exploiters." "That doesn't exactly cheer me up. But I'll take anything at this point."

"I'll call him right now and let him know you'll contact him. He can help you understand what Erin's thinking. Here's the judge's number. He jotted on a note pad. Have Bobbi call him, and then you two can go see him."

"Thanks. I need to find my daughter, fast."

Will Bartley didn't contradict him.

Twelve

Ed Mossbach picked up Patrick Tuesday morning. Before going to the city administrator's office, Ed showed him the damage he'd observed at the site of the proposed new police station and pointed out defects in the city hall building.

"The brick and concrete block exterior walls on two sides of the building broke free of the floor slab," Mossbach told Archer. "Walls are disconnected from the roof and floors in some places and are leaning outward, an inch out of plumb."

"Doesn't sound like enough to worry about right now," Archer said.

"If we ignore it, another tremor like this one could be disastrous. Without retrofitting, the whole structure could come tumbling down."

Archer ran a hand through his graying black hair. "Oh, great. Now I need to construct *two* new buildings." Gary loved to wallow in his role as an overworked public servant. Patrick figured Archer had earned his careworn features, baggy eyes and bent posture from a lifetime of dedicated military and public service. He tolerated his impatience, brusque manner and snappish disposition out of respect for the older man's long experience.

"There's more," Mossbach said. "We've inspected the site of the new police and fire station. Your radio tower snapped two of its guy wires and is leaning. On the ground beneath it, an eighteen-inch crack opened up along that suspected fault line. I'm afraid that changes my opinion about the suitability of the site for construction.

Archer's gaunt face turned even grayer; his steely eyes were expressionless. He stared at Ed from his nicked wooden armchair behind a beat-up wooden desk, uncomprehending, and then fixed his gaze on Patrick. "How much is this gonna cost me?"

"Cost *you*? Nothing beyond what the city pays for construction," Patrick said, "except some minor aggravation. We'll help you through that."

Archer sighed again. "We're already over budget, with your latest cost overrun. You knew we had barely two and a half million to build the project, and your estimates are running a million over that."

"Gary, you're forgetting the conversation we had after the police chief added an emergency operations center and the fire chief wanted another equipment bay added to the station house. I predicted a higher cost then and even sent you a memo about it. I suggested the city float a bond issue to pay for the construction. Now you should add the repair of City Hall to the total, all to be repaid with a sales tax increase."

To protect his colleague from himself, Mossbach jumped in. "Now Patrick, remember, you've already considered ways of solving this. As far as repairing this building goes, we can rebuild parts of the leaning walls and tie the building together at the slab edges and the corners. This retrofit will be modest in cost, and it'll buy us many years' additional life for the building."

"I can always depend on old Ed," Archer said, in a lighter tone. "Did I tell you, I've known him for years?"

"Yeah. Where did you guys first meet?"

"We were in Vietnam together," Archer said. "We shipped out with the same unit from Fort Benning, Georgia. We got split up. He was assigned to a different area. I was a supply sergeant. Until we got volunteered as replacements..."

"You guys were all heroes as far as I'm concerned."

"*They* were," Ed said. "I got assigned to a desk job back in Saigon, just lucky, I guess. Gary and the others did the heavy lifting, out in the villages."

"What did you have to do as replacements?" Patrick asked Archer.

"We had to search villages for Viet Cong. The locals didn't care who was running the government, and at least these indoctrinators spoke their own language. But patrol duties were the worst. You never knew where the enemy was coming from, and you had no advance warning. It was difficult and dangerous work, and some collateral damage was inevitable in every conflict. But we stuck together and got the job done for each other's sake."

"I know we're tight on this City Hall site, without much room for expansion," Patrick said, eager to change the subject. "But now that we have to fix the existing structure anyway and the other lot may be unsuitable, I've been thinking it might make sense to expand the existing building in height, with the new city offices above. We can add to the ground floor for the police and fire station and retrofit the basement for the emergency operations center."

"Great, and what are we supposed to do with that pig in a poke we bought—the new site that's now got a big crack in it?"

"Once we get the cracked earth re-graded and the radio tower moved to the City Hall site, it would make quite a nice public park." Patrick grinned. "Maybe those environmentalists who've been saying it's only good for park land weren't so crazy after all."

"Oh right, Mr. Funny Man. Get out of here."

"Look, Gary," Mossbach said, "let Patrick work on this idea for a week. I have an inkling he's right about the costs. It would save you money"

"Do I have a choice? The mayor will need a strategy to put out to the public. I'll have to say we're following yours. You'd better be right, Ed, that's all. I'm about to lose my patience with you guys."

With shaky assurances on all sides, the two escaped from the meeting.

Thirteen

At her corner eatery on the Hill, Angelina stood at her counter and took Patrick's order, while Ed held a table against the throng coming out of the line and swarming to the few available spots. "You guys are late today, Patrick. You usually beat the rush."

"Yeah, we thought about not coming over here at all," Patrick teased.

"But my soup is too good to pass up, right?' Her coal black eyes filled with laughter. "Italian wedding soup today. I put spinach, homemade meatballs and tiny pearl pasta in a chicken broth base with special seasonings."

"You having another wedding?"

"You never know. Gina will probably be next. Isn't she lovely?"

"Right." He grinned. The history of Angelina's ample figure could be documented in each of three daughters making salads and sandwiches behind her, whose classic forms epitomized Italian beauty from teenage through the various stages of courtship and marriage. Her middle daughter, the ravishing Gina, took Patrick's ticket from her mother and called the order to her sisters.

He turned, waved at Mark Hastings, president of his firm, absorbed in conversation with Executive VP Jim Harvey at a corner booth, and rejoined Ed at the deuce he was holding for them by the window. Lively chatter from office groups, construction workers and over-the-road truckers bounced off the embossed tin ceiling, amplified by the stunning daughters' cries of ticket numbers at the food window. The din nearly drowned out Ed's voice.

"Congratulations on the new state contract. It implements that new rule on emergency facilities, the policy we urged the state to adopt." The new regulation required all critical emergency facilities, including police and fire stations, radio towers, hospitals, schools and emergency operations centers, to be housed in earthquake-resistant structures and protected from seismic hazards within five years.

"It makes sense," Patrick said. "If the critical buildings are taken out, the city is helpless after a quake and can't recover. This little tremor may have benefits after all."

"But five years doesn't give communities much time to respond." Ed, the conservative engineer, never shied from the facts, whether or not they were favorable or politically convenient.

"Ed, I can't deal with any of this right now. I've got to find my daughter."

"I know, I'm so sorry. How can I help?"

"First, let's concentrate on helping the clients who have hired us. We helped get the regulations adopted. Let the rest fend for themselves."

"Our plans for the police and fire station will meet the new codes, if they ever forgive me for approving that site with the earthquake fault under it."

Gina, the beauty who had Patrick's number, called it out. He couldn't face her today and sent Ed to the pickup window to claim their lunch tray. Ed set the soup and salad in front of Patrick and attacked his "Angelina's Special" sub.

"How soon can you look at the Deerpath job, so you can tell me if your solution might work?"

"Maybe next week. If I don't get some news about Erin, maybe never. In this afternoon's meeting with the big boss of Gold Coast Gaming about a floating casino, we've got all kinds of jumps to get over—gaming license, financial feasibility, flood protection…"

"Just remember what I told you about putting accessory buildings too close to the river. The Corps won't approve them. They want any structures beyond the harbor line to have open sides, so water will flow through."

"Right now that's the least of my worries. Mark hates this client. He's watching me like a hawk to charge them for every hour I spend on it. He says the only way we want to dirty our hands with the predatory gambling industry is if we earn some of their obscene profits."

"The sooner you can get back to the Deerpath job the better. I promised Gary we'd have a concept within a week."

"I promise." He sighed, wondering, like the guy in the TV commercial: "Denver on Monday, I can do that, New York on Tuesday, I can do that." How in heck he was going to do all that. "All I really want is to get Erin back. I don't know what to do and I don't meet with Adam and Bobbi until tomorrow afternoon."

◊

At ten minutes before two, punctual for once, Patrick knocked on the door of Manny Marancik's suite at the airport hotel.

"You're early."

Patrick barely recognized the man who answered the door. His face was half-covered with shaving cream, but he made out a few familiar features: plucked eyebrows, lifted lids and stretched skin, which kept his eyes wide in a perpetually startled look. He wore shower clogs, gray workout pants, and a sheer undershirt, which showed off well-earned biceps and a waxed, hairless chest. He propped the door ajar with the night hasp.

"Hello, Mr. Marancik," Patrick said. "This is Ed Mossbach, our project engineer."

Marancik nodded in acknowledgment and waved them toward a modern living room sofa and chairs. "Make yourselves comfortable while I finish up. The others will arrive soon." He lifted a razor to his face and resumed shaving as he walked back into the bedroom.

Two beefy bouncer types in identical black suits strolled in. They were soon joined by Phil Swanson, the Las Vegas transplant who'd shown Manny how to set up gaming operations in the Midwest. He introduced the Blues Brothers as an accountant and a road manager. It crossed Patrick's mind that the highway department already did a pretty good job of managing the roads.

Immaculately attired in a chalk-striped navy wool suit of conservative cut, Swanson consulted the Rolex on his wrist. "You're right on time." Patrick introduced Ed.

"A pleasure, I'm sure." Mossbach broke into a silly smile and shook his hand.

"Engineer, eh? I hope you're the practical one."

"He reins in my excesses," Patrick assured Swanson with a grin.

Marancik reappeared in a maroon dressing gown with a black satin collar, burgundy leather slippers and a dotted Swiss crimson foulard, its dimples arranged to bulge just so from the robe's lapels.

"We can meet in here gentlemen." Hands in his robe pockets, Marancik conducted them into a room opposite the bedroom door, where a long table had been set up with side chairs. Picture windows overlooked a lake with three golf greens and a gazebo on individual islands, connected by walking paths and high-arched wooden bridges.

"You play golf?" Patrick said.

"Of course," said Manny, to whom leisure was clearly a matter of course.

He and Ed Mossbach hauled two oversized presentation cases into the room.

Marancik sat at the end of the table and held forth in a nasal voice about the big deal he had just worked to bring in Billy Bob Custer for a casino tour.

"Billy Bob's got that all-girl country swing band of big-boobed, buckskin-fringed chorus girls, and they all travel with him on the road. He's one crowd pleaser, all right. Isn't he, boys?" Manny's high giggle resembled a whinny—okay for a thoroughbred, Patrick supposed—and cocked his head with self-satisfaction. The other staffers in the room nodded, very pleased indeed.

"I hope he's only staying one night at each property," said Swanson.

"Now Phil, be reasonable," the boss whined. "I've booked the same deal as last time."

"That's what I was afraid of. His crew toured on our tab for a month and ate and drank a healthy chunk of our profits."

In prepping Patrick for the meeting, Swanson explained that Marancik was born into a sweet deal—his father was a wealthy entrepreneur in Chicago. Pursuing his lavish lifestyle, Manny had cultivated the friendship of some big moguls in Las Vegas. When several Midwestern states passed gaming legislation, he'd talked his dad into spinning off a gambling subsidiary. Manny had hired Swanson, a manager for one of the Las Vegas operators, to come to Chicago and set him up in the gaming business. Phil had sought to create new casinos in Chicago, Joliet, Bettendorf, Iowa and St. Louis, provided they could get the appropriate state gaming licenses. So far, they were batting three out of four.

Despite Patrick's anxiety over selling his design concept, he was glad the meeting had begun. Erin's absence overshadowed his mood. Even in getting dressed for the day, in his familiar navy blazer and his best khaki dress pants, he missed Erin's scornful review of his fashion choices.

While Phil's coaching had enabled him to prepare a proposal suitable to the gaming market, hiring his firm as their architect-engineer depended on how well they pleased the boss. Swanson's introduction and buildup gave him time to set up two easels for his presentation. Patrick wasn't in a selling mood. His staff's fine artistry would have to speak for itself.

He went through the motions of his carefully rehearsed presentation. Fortunately, his staff's color renderings of the proposed gaming boat would absorb the group's attention and tell most of the story for him. In keeping with the state's restrictive gaming law—a hybrid political compromise—the river craft had to float on the water and look like Missouri's historic river steamboats. This project would be constructed on a cluster of barges. Evoking memories of mustachioed card sharps, stripe-shirted piano players in derby hats and spiffy gamblers, his staff's color drawings had put a cheerful face on the tawdry business of stealing people's hard-earned money.

The six decks of the proposed vessel appeared to curve upward from the waterline at bow and stern. They were lined with carpenter's scrollwork, turned baluster handrails and bracketed columns, marching along in stacked rows. In the night scenes, decks lined with glowing bulbs reflected in the gliding river's surface. Atop the highest level sat the pilothouse. Above its curvy pyramid roof, two great smoke stacks with fringed metal tops spewed fire into the sky. On the stern sat a huge paddle wheel that looked, anyway, as if it could propel the whole works up and down the river. Inside, strapless-gowned women and dapper men pumped multiple slot machines, hunkered over half-round poker tables, gathered around long green craps tables or laughed merrily at bars located throughout the vast cabin. One could almost hear the constant ring-a-ling of the one-armed bandits' electronic wheels and frequent bursts of mad clanging when jackpots scored. The scene had an amber glow, fading above to a blue mist of cigar and cigarette smoke.

Ed Mossbach discussed the site for the future hotel: landside reception buildings, lobbies, a restaurant, circulation ramps and elevators. "Their placement, mooring arrangements and design must comply with river regulations and Corps of Engineers requirements. It will also have to undergo the long process involved in getting their permit approvals. What we've presented here appears feasible on this site," Mossbach said. "It's a good location, on an interstate highway at the river, so customers from both Missouri and Illinois can reach this spot."

"There will be stumbling blocks ahead," Patrick said in wrapping up, "but our firm has the experience to overcome them."

"Bravo!" exclaimed Manny Marancik. "You've captured my vision. Welcome to our project team."

Amusing as it was to watch Marancik's minions jump through hoops to please him, Patrick knew he was merely the latest trained monkey in the show. What was he doing here, promoting a project that would serve no useful purpose? He was more concerned about his missing daughter.

Despite his unease, Patrick took some consolation in making the sale.

Marancik held court, regaling his captive audience with his latest ideas for the venture. "If we can be open by next summer, we'll take full advantage of the tourists and get the kinks out of our operation before the fall season. That's why we've got to move fast."

"We'll go as fast as the regulators allow," Phil Swanson said, filling a much-needed role as governor on Manny's juggernaut.

"To speed up the project," Manny continued, "I've purchased a vessel for us—it's a Great Lakes Steamer." He propped a picture of a short lake freighter on the table, the Northern Star, with a forecastle, a lower middle section and high decks fore and aft. "Now all we'll have to do is float it down from Lake Michigan and set it up on the site. Isn't that amazing?" He giggled again.

Swanson stared at him with a mixture of alarm and disbelief. "You, what?"

"I bought it—it was a hell of a bargain. They've been replaced by container ships. Nobody wants these old vessels anymore."

""But—, but—maybe we don't want it, either," Swanson sputtered, "What are we supposed to do with that monstrosity?"

"What about the design I just showed you?" Patrick said, This project was careening out of control in a hurry. "It's intended to be built on flat barges. We didn't count on the high sides of a lake boat."

"With the design ability you've just demonstrated, Patrick, I'm sure you can handle this one." Manny beamed in Patrick's direction, with a wink that was not returned.

"You can't make a silk purse out of it, either," Mossbach said. "What is the draft of that vessel?"

"Draft, what's that?"

"How deep does the water have to be to float it? "

"Hmm. I have all the specifications right here." Marancik rummaged through a fat file folder. He gave up and offered it to Mossbach, who leafed through the pages for the ship's specifications.

"Ah, here it is—says nine feet empty and twelve fully loaded."

"Well?" Manny looked around for the usual approval.

"The good news," Mossbach said, "is that the Corps maintains a nine foot channel depth on the Mississippi and Illinois rivers year-round. We can probably get it here if we float it down empty in any time but late fall or winter, when the channel could get too shallow in spots. Even then, we might need to remove some of the masts and superstructure to get it under the lowest bridges."

Manny's startled-looking eyes got even wider. "I had no idea," he said, his good cheer deflating like a punctured hot air balloon.

"But the real issue is what to do with it when we get it here," Ed continued. "At the site where you want to moor this vessel there's only about six feet of depth during low water. We figured that at best you could float lightly loaded barges there. We can do it because the gaming commission no longer requires you to cruise during gambling sessions."

Phil Swanson's jaw sagged, and his piercing eyes darted between the speakers like a spectator at Wimbledon.

"No problem," said Manny, whose optimism was no doubt fostered by his ability to throw his father's money at any problem. "We'll just dredge a berth for the ship."

"It's not so easy," the practical engineer replied. "No matter how deep a trench we dredge, the river will most likely silt it up before the first year is out—that is, if we can dredge at all. If not, in the slack water of winter your round-hulled ship would sit on the bottom and list to one side."

"What do you mean, 'if we can dredge at all'?" Marancik's rosy face paled, and the earlier joy of conquest drained from his expression.

"This spot on the river is within the Chain of Rocks, a big river bend with shallow rapids and a rocky bottom which extends southward all the way to our site. We might have to blast it out. That takes a Corps permit, too, since it kills lots of fish, and it would still fill in with silt and mud." In the 1950s, he explained, the Corps had cut a canal bypassing this treacherous rocky stretch of riverbed. To allow ships to navigate the sudden drop in river elevation due to shortening the channel, they built a pair of locks near the foot of the canal.

Manny Marancik was not to be deterred. "How soon can you figure out the cost of dredging or blasting, or whatever we have to do? I want to locate here."

"We'll have to hire a marine company to do soundings and core samples of the river bottom at your site," Ed said. "That part won't be too expensive, and it could probably be done in a couple of weeks. But in the meantime, if we must use this boat, you might want to be thinking about some other locations along the river. For example, the deep channel crosses to the Illinois side opposite St. Louis, where there would be less of a problem floating your lake steamer. Maybe some little town over there wants a casino."

"What about the Village of Brooklyn, across the river and a bit north of the Arch?" Patrick suggested. "They seem to like entertainment venues." Without some positive suggestions this project would be heading downhill fast.

"No damn way!" Manny gave MacKenna a menacing look.

"By the time you fight this odd-looking vessel through the Missouri Gaming Commission—they want it to look like an old fashioned riverboat—you might save time in the long run."

"You don't understand. I don't think they'd welcome such a project at all."

"It's your show. I'm just trying to help." Patrick wanted to add this client to his stable, especially since he paid well. But what was his objection to an Illinois site?

Mossbach broke the tension. "I'll get the detailed costs for this exploratory work and call you tomorrow for your approval. We should be able to get it done for you pretty fast."

"That's good. Get on it right away." Manny rose, and his eyes drifted to the window. The meeting was over.

Patrick stood and began gathering his equipment. He wasn't hopeful. The complications Marancik had just introduced would add costs and even more bureaucratic delays to this project

"Patrick, call me Manny." Marancik put an arm around his shoulder. "I'm really glad Phil found you. Your design ideas are great, and I look forward to our relationship. Next time I hope your gloomy friend here has better news."

Patrick disengaged from his new client's grip. To his relief, Phil Swanson took Manny aside and spoke earnestly with him. Then Swanson turned back and grabbed one of the presentation portfolios. "Patrick, I'll walk you out."

Ed Mossbach followed, hauling the other case.

"Patrick," Swanson said, "I'm sorry. I forgot to mention it to you, but Manny has 'particular tastes,' as they say in Europe, and sometimes he comes on a little strong. He means well, but he often can't separate business from pleasure."

"He's gay? I'm not worried about that," Patrick said, "but he really threw me a curve with that lake boat. I hope we can do you some good on this project."

"He's his own worst enemy." Swanson shook his head.

Patrick wondered what kind of a man he'd won as a new client. Why had Manny reacted so strongly at the mention of Brooklyn? Was he just his own enemy, or did he have others?

Fourteen

Patrick rose early Wednesday for his trip to Jefferson City to sign a contract with the State of Missouri. He missed Erin at the breakfast table. Although she was usually sullen and moody, he longed for her youthful outlook, her companionship and her beautiful face, so like Kitty's. He didn't know what had become of her. She might be hurt or starving, or worse. At least Bobbi Romano was on the case. She was supposed to give a full report of her findings on the murder victim this afternoon in Adam Reiner's office.

To spend a few minutes in Erin's world he climbed to her bedroom. It helped to get the scent of her things and look at her favorite pictures. On her green and white striped pillow sham lay her favorite teddy bear. Such a package of contradictions—part little girl, part grown woman. She had his own analytical skill but tempered it with Kitty's down-to-earth common sense. He hoped she would use it.

Her computer sat on the desk along with the powerful boom box he and Kitty gave her for her thirteenth birthday. Between them was her picture with Jimmy Steele at last year's junior prom. A good foot taller than she, he wore his curly blond hair cropped short, his muscular swimmer's arms and shoulders bulging in a white dinner jacket. Erin's emerald sheath had cost a fortune, but he'd objected even more to the revealing strapless cut. It brought out her glowing eyes and maturing body. Her beaming smile was pure Kitty.

The desktop was littered with her calculator and felt tip pens. Automatically he swept them into her center desk drawer, which was stuffed with papers, photos and dog-eared spiral notebooks. But now he couldn't get it closed. When he opened the drawer again and neatened its contents, he noticed the corner of a sepia drawing at the bottom of the stack. The line work looked like Conté crayon, a medium he'd favored in architecture school for his sketchbooks, with its warm earth tones, ideal for rendering buildings and natural objects. He extracted it carefully to get a better look, trying not to smear its chalky surface.

The red-brown strokes skillfully captured a shapely female odalisque extended on a linear sofa. He admired its artistic effect. An original drawing, it showed real talent. His daughter was a better artist than he'd given her credit for. Then with a jolt he recognized Erin's head as she reclined on the couch in his den. He made out the scribbled notation in the lower right hand corner, "—Love always, J."

Jimmy!

His ears burned with embarrassment, and not only for his accidental intrusion into his daughter's personal space. He was staring at her naked body. A ladies' man when it came to his own desires, Patrick was in perpetual denial of his daughter's blossoming womanhood. His little girl had grown up right under his nose. From the TV shows she watched—Miley Cyrus and the rest—he realized too late he should have known. Weak-kneed, he plopped hard in her desk chair. When, how, how far had they gone? He'd really blown it this time. He reached for his cell phone to call her. Of course. he got her recorded message.

He carefully replaced the fragile drawing in its previous location near the bottom of the stack, arranged the contents so they would fit and closed the drawer.

Her digital clock said 7:35. If he didn't start driving now he would be late for his meeting near Jefferson City.

He arrived at the State of Missouri's Emergency Management Agency offices in Algoa, outside the state capital, ten minutes late. From a large window in the conference room wall he overlooked a sea of empty desks, each with its own computer console. Below, like a NASA mission control room, lay the state's Emergency Operations Center.

"During a disaster," explained Barry Wainwright, director of the agency, "the governor sits in this conference room with his aides and department heads. Our staff at the workstations below take situation reports from all over the state. Technical managers in the elevated control room you see behind the big space relay instructions from the director to the various area desks, monitor and record calls, coordinate reports, assemble videos and keep records of the events as they unfold—whether in forest fires, floods, tornadoes, ice storms, power failures, earthquakes or pandemics—any time the governor declares a state of emergency."

"How can you prepare for so many different types of disaster?"

"That's where you come in. Private firms such as yours all over the state will be helping us upgrade emergency response structures. If a critical radio tower falls over and knocks out the emergency broadcast network; if the firehouses collapse on fire trucks, or if the hospitals are damaged and out of commission, it will be even more difficult for the affected communities to recover. We're beefing up this state's critical infrastructure."

"Yeah, we've been retrofitting radio towers and buildings throughout Southern Illinois."

"That's why we've selected your firm," Wainwright continued. "Earthquake resistant design is a top priority for us, especially for critical structures. St. Louis is separated from most of its surrounding counties by bridges. If all the bridges were destroyed, or even obstructed, in a big quake, the city could become an island isolated from road transportation. Highway 100, Manchester Road would be the only way in or out of St. Louis without crossing a bridge."

"Your experience, not only with upgrading towers, but in retrofitting buildings for earthquake loads, is crucial," Dan Garfield said. As facilities director for the agency, he sat with two of his staffers around the large, square conference table. "We think you're the best qualified firm to do the job in your area. Here's the contract we've prepared for you to sign. It's open-ended, with only your requested hourly rates listed, so fees can be negotiated once we know what's involved in each assignment."

"Fair enough," Patrick said.

"Here, if you'll sign the contract," Wainwright said, "we can give you the first project."

Patrick signed three copies. Wainwright followed and handed Patrick his copy. The deal was official.

"By the way," Garfield said, "I heard about your daughter's disappearance. I'm terribly sorry."

Patrick grimaced at the reminder. "Thanks. We've got the FBI's best people involved, with little to go on so far. I feel so helpless. My life is spinning out of control. We need a clue, some kind of sign, to know what to do next."

Patrick's cell phone buzzed at his waist. "O my God, I have to take this." He listened intently. "Erin? Where are you?" He covered the mouthpiece. "It's my daughter! She's managed to get a call out."

"There's your sign. Keep her talking." Garfield dashed for the control room.

"I don't have much time before they come back," she said, breathless. "We finally dried out my cell phone after it got dunked in the river, Aliesha and I surprised two guys in the woods—Jake and Momo. They're holding Aliesha and me in a cabin somewhere. They work for some guy named Solly."

"Oh my God, have they hurt you?"

"No, but they keep threatening to if we don't cooperate. They're going to get us involved with all of those horrible nightclubs, and I don't know what else."

"You've got to get out of there, Erin. Escape, before they make you do—"

"Dad, I know that! But they keep us locked in and guard us twenty-four hours a day. We're never out of their sight. Our best way to stay out of danger is to do what they say and work in their show clubs, until they get careless and we get a chance to sneak out-"

"No, Erin. Don't fall for it. You can't trust anything they say. You don't know what could happen."

"You've never treated me like an adult, Dad. You'd be surprised at the things I know."

"That's what I'm afraid of."

"We saw them bury a body. They'll kill us before they'll let us go. I was blindfolded, but I know we crossed a river on a big bridge. I'm pretty sure it was the Mississippi and I'm in Illinois. Dad, they're dealing—"

"Dammit, bitch, gimme that!"

"No, Jake. Let go!"

"Now you listen here, 'Dad,'" said a gruff voice. "You stay outta this, or your kid ain't goin' onstage or no place but the river. Wearin' cement shoes. And then we're comin' for you. You got that?"

"Why you no good bastard! I kill you first—" said another voice. Aliesha!

He heard a crash on the line and sounds of a scuffle, and the line went dead.

"NO!" Patrick cried. He was sweating bullets, and his stomach seized up. He could hardly breathe. "They're going to kill her if she doesn't cooperate." He shook his head in despair.

Garfield rushed back into the room. "I recorded the whole conversation. Also I have her location triangulated between three cell phone towers somewhere in Monroe County, Illinois. Too bad it's not one of those newer phones with a GPS locator system. Here's a disk containing the recordings and map information."

"Thanks, Dan. You're literally a life saver."

On the drive back to St. Louis, he called Bobbi Romano at the FBI and relayed the critical information about Erin's phone call, the gangsters' threats and her suspected whereabouts.

"Monroe County, eh?" she said. "That's in our metro area. Let me put my feelers out and see what I can find out. Good work, Patrick."

"Bobbi, tell me there's some other explanation. I saw on the news last week that St. Louis is a center for human trafficking—really?" Patrick knew way too much about such abuses in Chicago.

"Unfortunately the FBI has found, because of our web of interstate highways and central location, St. Louis is a major hub for sex slavery and child prostitution. Their report says that slavery isn't dead in the United States. The FBI estimates that 100,000 to 300,000 children are sold into sexual servitude every year."

"Aw, Bobbi, give me a break. I can't stand this!"

"You might as well know what we're up against."

"Impossible. Kitty and I did all the right things to bring her up properly."

"The report goes onto say that the most at-risk teens, while they can come from good homes, have experienced physical, sexual or psychological trauma earlier in their lives."

"And Erin lost her mother in a terrible accident. We barely survived. She's still grieving over that—for that matter, so am I."

"There you go. Both of you probably experienced serious trauma. It's hard to overcome."

"What if they try to make her do…those things? Jake threatened to kill her."

"Patrick, I'm terribly sorry to bring this bad news, but I'm determined to get to the bottom of this and get Erin back. For your own sanity, you need to keep movin'. Where are you now?"

"In Wentzville, about a half-hour from you."

"Come directly to my office. We're gonna pay a little call on Solly Abrams. He's the Outfit's man in Brooklyn.

"What about our meeting with Adam Reiner?"

"It can wait. Abrams is the one who runs all these rackets on the East Side. Then we'll finish your list of people to see over in Illinois."

Patrick's eyes dimmed, and he struggled to stay in his highway lane. He sweated despite the cool spring day. He opened the car window. Maybe the fresh air would clear his head. He didn't want to learn more on the East Side. But his need to find Erin was sucking him into the maelstrom.

Fifteen

Erin, bound hand and foot to a high-backed wooden chair, sat facing Jake and Momo.

Jake dropped her flip phone on the floor and slowly crushed it with his heel. "That takes care of that. You'd better shape up, bitch, or somethin' like that'll happen to you."

"You know who you talkin' to? She'll fix your ass, you bastards." Aliesha's eyes blazed as she strained against the ropes in her chair next to Erin.

"Boss, I thought you said we had to treat 'em right."

"Vince says he can use 'em. I gotta make that happen fast, before they drive me nuts."

"Use us?" Erin asked again, afraid of the answer. "What for?"

"Oh we got all kinds of jobs. You're too skinny for a dancer, but with that mouth on you, you might just have the right stuff to please the high-priced clientele."

"Oh, God, never! Who do I see about that?" She resented being called too skinny. "We'll see what I qualify for."

"Erin, shut up, or you'll cook your own goose." Aliesha glared at her.

"No! If you jerks think you'll get away with this, you're crazy. The FBI will—".

"Listen here, babe. You'll do what you're told." To make his point, Jake drew a switchblade lighting fast, flipped it open and scratched Erin's cheek. "Maybe you'll have an accident and gash your pretty face, so you won't even qualify for that job. We got others."

"You no good bastards." Aliesha strained mightily against her ropes.

"Easy, Jake. You really want to fight the FBI?"

Momo was smarter than he looked.

"You cool your jets, or I'll remind Vince about your second home at Menard State Prison."

Momo braced his arms on the table, gritted his teeth and scowled.

"Jake, you asshole!" Erin shocked herself with her outburst.

"What's this worth?" Jake yanked Erin's gold locket from her neck, hurting her skin and breaking the chain. Tears and a drop of blood from her cheek fell on her shirt.

"Not *that*!" Erin said. "It was my mother's—" *Dang.* She'd said too much.

"Oh? Looks like gold. I could probably sell it, but I think it's worth more if I keep it."

Erin watched him put it in his back pocket. A lump rose in her throat.

"See, kid, ya gotta play ball around here or they'll take away *all* your goodies."

She stared at the bloodstain on her shirt. What else would they take from her?

"Momo, you got any doubts about your job today?"

"No, Boss."

"Okay, I'm going to deliver our load and have a little heart-to-heart with Vince about these broads. Now you put them up in the loft, stand guard down here and don't let 'em so much as move."

Momo untied them, shooed the girls up the stairs, lowered the hatch, and locked it.

Aliesha collapsed on her pallet, exhausted from their ordeal. Erin lay on the cot, her mind racing. Finally the afternoon heat of the attic, her circular thoughts and her confusion had left her, and fell into a troubled sleep.

◊

Erin awoke with the sun's rays pouring directly through the window in the end gable into the loft, raising the heat in the stale air to an intolerable level. She had to do something to relieve her discomfort. She roused Aliesha from her nest. "Hey you. I'm lonesome. Wake up and talk to me."

"What you got to say that I ain't already heard?" Aliesha struggled to sit up, threw off the covers and cracked one eye open. Despite her extra hours of sleep these days, her eyes were puffy.

"Come on, get up! We need to plan."

She opened both eyes and stared at Erin. "Say what? What we got to plan?"

"Our escape."

"Oh, right, like we gonna get outta here. You see that gun Jake's packin'?"

"No, where?"

"On his ankle—you blind?"

"I didn't notice."

"He'll use it on us as soon as we get outta line. Before that, he'll just whip us with it till we can't scream no more. And God knows what other rods he and Momo keep in that room o' theirs."

"But you don't understand. Jimmy taught me what he learned in Army training. As soon as you're captured, you've got to start planning your escape."

"Oh, sure. Honey, you don't know the score. Soon as they put us to work, they buy us fancy clothes, feed us, charge us rent and run up a big bill. We gotta pay it back on their terms."

"Like, how would we do that, and where would we get money?" Erin feared she already knew the answer.

"Duh. They put us in a club, see. Every night we charge the johns for drinks, and whatever they want to do with us. You don't earn your keep, they like to beat you till you work harder. My older brother told me all about it. "

"No! They wouldn't." Erin shuddered. She thought those places only existed in foreign countries like Russia or Eastern Europe.

"Sure, sure. You fall behind, they charge you interest—you never pay it all back. Pretty soon they got you hooked on crack. You're done for."

"That's illegal. If they force you to do all that, you don't owe them a dime."

"You don't, they cut your face and put you in a cheaper club with johns that pay less money."

Erin cringed and fingered the scratch on her cheek. "But we've got to get out of here."

"What you got to do that's more important than saving your sweet ass? You try to escape and you're dead meat."

"First of all, I've got to help you. I got you into this mess and I need to get you out."

"You, help me? I don't *think* so. You're help-*less*."

"Besides, I've got too much to live for, and so do you. You finish your education, you can get a good job, have anything you want."

"Like what?"

Erin dropped her normal inhibitions about flaunting her good fortune in front of Aliesha and told about her once-charmed life. "For one thing, you can have all the comforts of home—a soft bed, an air-conditioned house and all the foods you love. For me it's California rolls, fresh doughnuts, chocolate marshmallow cookies, caramels and moose tracks ice cream with peanuts and chocolate. They're all bad for me, but could they be any worse than this? I miss my eyeliner, makeup, spring rinse shampoo, a closet full of my favorite clothes, and especially Mom's old car, which would let me roam with all the windows open, free as the wind, in my designer sunglasses and a silk head scarf."

"Wow, sounds pretty nice. No wonder you're sad."

"But you know something? Compared with the fix we're in now, I'd give it all up just to be out of here and free."

"Yeah, I know. Maybe I don't miss those things 'cause I never had 'em, but I sure do wish I could see my momma and brother and sisters. They must be worried sick, not knowing what happened to me."

"At least they'll know that now."

"Yeah? You think your dad will call my mom?"

"Sure, now that we got through to him. He'll get the FBI on the case. I'm telling you, that phone was my lifeline. Kelly and I used to talk or text back and forth on it several times every day. She knows my feelings and can finish my sentences. And dear, sweet, Jimmy."

"You got a boyfriend?" She looked into Erin's eyes, obviously impressed. "My sister Kiesha can't even hold on to one, and she's smart and real pretty."

"Well, I had one until three weeks ago. We had a fight and we broke up."

"Why?"

"I don't know what got into me. That stupid Moira Sharpe cornered him at the winter dance and kissed him with everyone watching."

"Who cares about that? Did he give you money?"

"No, but he took me out to nice places and paid for it. Why?"

"'Cause when they give you money, that means they really love you. Kiesha told me paying for nice dates counts, too."

"I can see that now. That high school stuff seems so petty, compared with real trouble."

"Yeah." Aliesha, fully awake now, stared at the glare from the window.

"I miss my dad." She gazed through the tiny window at the puffy, fair weather clouds in the sky, beyond their prison. "Today I could hear the panic in his voice. If he loses me, he doesn't have any family left. So he overprotects me and micromanages my life. It makes me crazy."

"Micro-what? At least you've got a dad. Mine left when I was ten. He'd bring me my favorite treats and would sit and read to me. I never see him anymore. I guess all your dad's fussin' shows he cares. He just wants to keep you safe"

"I kinda know what that's like, to miss somebody so much, somebody who meant so much to you. My mom died four years ago."

"Oh, girl, I'm sorry."

"What are we gonna do?"

"I don't want to be a slave, 'specially not a sex slave. When Daddy read me black history, I promised myself I'd never…" Tears formed in her eyes, and she sobbed. Erin put both arms around her shaking body and held her tight, stroking her hair and pressing her cheek with her own. Soon her breathing became regular and her body relaxed in Erin's arms.

They were interrupted by the two thugs clambering up the stairs, the clanking of the latch and the racket the hatch made when they flung it open.

"Okay, you two. You can kiss each other goodbye. Party's over." Jake grabbed Aliesha's arm. "We gotta keep you separated. I'm takin' this black bitch with me. "

"No way!" Erin shouted. "She's way under age."

"Tough. We'll let Vince decide about that."

He hustled them down the stairs, with Momo trailing behind.

"Momo, help me tie her hands."

"Lemme go, dammit," Aliesha wailed. Momo tied her wrists in front of her with a rope and knotted a dirty bandanna over her eyes.

Jake and Momo then overpowered Erin and tied her, again, to the same chair. With that, they shoved Aliesha into the car and Jake drove away up the rutted gravel lane.

Now they were in real trouble, separated, unable to communicate and Aliesha headed for a life of exploitation and shame.

She had to act. At least without Aliesha to interfere she could think more clearly.

Momo grabbed a beer out of the refrigerator and turned on the TV. With Jake gone, this might be her last chance to improve their fate,

She strained against the rope. The scratch on her cheek hurt. Fifteen minutes had passed and she was pretty sure Jake wasn't coming back. She wept quietly—she didn't have to fake it.

"What's the matter, babe."

"Momo, I'm in pain. These ropes are hurting my wrists and chair's digging into my back."

"Here, let me loosen them." He came over behind her and untied her wrists.

"Hey, how'd you get your nickname?"

"I hate it. My real name's Mick, for Michael, O'Banion. The boys used to call me Momo after the Big Boss in Chicago, Sam "Momo" Gianacana, He started as a driver. They used it to make fun of me—in Italian it means grandmother—'cause was I so careful. They shoulda appreciated how many times I saved their asses."

Erin smiled sympathetically.

His blue eyes never left her face. "Your hair's pretty, like my daughter's. Last time I saw her she was just about nine."

She looked deep into them. "What happened to her?"

"I don't know. I had to leave, I never found her again."

"Does it have anything to do with that second home Jake was talking about?"

Momo hung his head. "I got sent up. I was drivin' the getaway car for a bank job. The other two guys got into a shootout with a guard. They both died, and so did the guard. I was the one they caught."

"How'd you get mixed up with people like that?"

"My wife lost her job and her insurance. She needed an operation. My cut woulda been at least ten grand to pay for it. Then while I was in the slammer I heard my wife died. Workin' out here, I can't find out what happened to my little girl."

"Gee, that's tough."

Not knowing when Jake would come back, Erin took her best shot.

"Mick, I'm going to have a baby."

"Aw..." He stood up and stared out the window, then turned to face her again. "How'd you get knocked up?"

"I screwed up, that's all. See, it happens to everybody."

"Hey, let's put you on the couch." He walked her over, untied her legs from the chair and helped her lie down. He went into the kitchen and grabbed another beer from the fridge.

"Do you have any milk in there?" she called out to him. "I don't want this ordeal to put a strain on the baby. Besides, it's good luck. In Irish lore, it fends off the Little People's mischief."

"You're Irish, too! Jake doesn't have any milk. He's more worried about his precious crank than feedin' the people around here."

"Crank!" Momo's words struck fear into her heart. Jimmy had told her that was local slang for meth. He learned from his brother about the drug habits soldiers picked up on foreign duty. The methamphetamine epidemic in rural Missouri was all over the news, and it threatened to take out a whole generation of the state's young people.

Hysterical thoughts raced through her mind. Could she trust the food they gave her? They might try to lace it with drugs. Maybe they could inject her with dope while she was sleeping. Then she would be powerless to resist their demands. She remembered what her dad had said once, in his rare, and clumsy, advice about boys. "A horny boy is your slave. You don't need it as much as he does. You've got what he wants, and you can give the orders."

Sort of, she figured, but it was different with Jimmy. She'd already failed that test, but now that she saw where it could lead, she'd be immune to temptation from anyone else. They were in love, and she wanted his baby, either now, if she really were pregnant, or later. Right now she had to take charge of these little boys and steer their lust and greed to her purpose. Despite what her father said, maybe Aliesha's last advice made some sense—she should pretend to play along.

Erin had formed her plan. It should work—*if* she had the guts to carry it out. She had no choice. Even if she couldn't save herself, she had to rescue Aliesha.

Sixteen

A half hour after she picked up Patrick, Bobbi turned off Highway 3 into the heart of Brooklyn, Illinois. "Here, Patrick, I'll give you the full tour." She turned down a main commercial street. On the left behind a large parking lot sat a metal building with a plastic illuminated sign identifying it as "Diamond Club, Home of the Stars, A World Class Gentlemen's Club." A cloth banner bearing the Bud Light logo said, "Cover $10 with $1.99 you call it, Every Wednesday and Friday." In front, a large pillar sign with movable letters proclaimed:

CANDY SWEET, VIVID XXX FILM STAR
WEDNESDAY DINNER INVITATIONAL
FEATURING CANDY SWEET.

Further down on the right, a marquee screamed:

THURSDAY 2 TABLE DANCES FOR THE PRICE OF 1!
FRIDAY HOT TUB PARTY AND
SATURDAY TOTALLY JOSIE

"Totally charming, isn't it?" Bobbi pointed to a half a dozen more such clubs as far as he could see along the street.

"I get the picture." His stomach did flip-flops as he imagined Erin's peril.

"This latest mayor, Caleb Mitchom, had some progressive ideas for the place. He used to be a TV producer in Chicago. He retired to his hometown to try to improve his city. He wanted to develop a festive riverfront, with cruise boats, family entertainment, good restaurants, antique shops and a movie theater.

"In fact," Bobbi continued, "he even had some development money lined up from Edgardo Smith, the retired football star who grew up here."

"The NFL left tackle? Come to think of it, I heard something about it on the news. This town deserves a break."

"If our corpse turns out to be Mitchom, this asshole just set that program back ten years." She pulled to a halt in front of Sol's Adult Novelties and Video. "Here's where we start."

Patrick hadn't entered one of these places since he and his pals had snuck off to the South Loop's last remaining burlesque house and novelty shops during high school. It didn't seem to faze Bobbi.

"You come to these places a lot?" Patrick asked.

"Way too much, I'm afraid. I've investigated Solly on a number of vice charges over the years. We've never pinned a conviction on him—his lawyers have been too clever. But I'm not through with the sonofabitch. "

Walking back toward the front of the store, she nodded toward the only attendant in the place, a girl not much older than Erin, selected, no doubt, to be acceptable to the management. She guarded the exit-only door, the most expensive toys, the batteries and the condoms behind a glass case.

"You're the expert," she said. "How would you rate the clerk at the counter?"

"Mmm. She does have an ample chest, a waspish waist—very comfortable to hold, I'd say. But I don't know about that butterfly tattoo on one cheek and maroon fingernails with lipstick to match. Kinda makes the total effect a bit skanky." They advanced to the counter.

"You in charge here?" Bobbi asked her.

"Yes, ma'am. Have you two decided on anything? She removed an elaborate contraption from the under-counter display. "I tried out this one at home. The pleasure was non-stop. She'll love it, and it's got a special attachment for you, she said, mooning at Patrick. "It comes with four C-batteries. You won't be disappointed."

"Sorry, this is business, not pleasure." Patrick rose to the occasion and winked at Bobbi. He wasn't in the market for a slightly-used vibrator.

"Oh, we're here to do business," she responded. "This one is only ninety-five—"

"Where's Solly today?" Bobbi cut through her sales patter and flashed her badge.

The clerk's mercantile manner faded. "I dunno. Not here. We only see him when it's time to collect the receipts." Her bored, matter-of-fact attitude and her hard face scared Patrick—could this happen to Erin?

"Not good enough, honey. Either you spill his whereabouts or you're comin' with me."

The young woman's eyes widened and her lips trembled. "I'll g-get in trouble. I'll lose my job."

"You're already in trouble, babe. We're talkin' homicide. And frankly, losing this gig would be the luckiest break in your sorry-ass life. What's your name?"

"Jane M-Murphy." Her eyes turned fearful.

"Well, Jane, you tell me where to find the boss and we can settle this peaceably."

"H-his office is in a warehouse. It's up the road," she said, cowering.

"Keep talkin'. We need to find him."

"I've only been there once. It's at Fifth and State in Venice, beside the tracks. There are truck doors on one end and an awning over the office entrance."

"Okay. This better be right, babe, or I'm comin' back for you."

Bobbi followed State Highway 3 to the location in Venice, at the back of an old industrial district. A few junk cars littered the lot, but one sleek black Mercedes sat in the shade of a lone maple. She led the way up rusting metal steps to a faded red awning sheltering a door in the loading dock wall. She knocked. "Solly, I need you."

"Hold your horses, Janie," barked a gruff voice from inside. Half a minute later, the door swung wide and a short, sweaty man, his shirt half unbuttoned, presented a pleasant mien to his visitor. "Oh, it's you." The corners of his mouth turned down.

"Hi, Solly. We need to talk."

"Look, Bobbi, I'm expecting someone. Couldn't we make this some other time?"

"Janie's not comin'. This is my friend Patrick. His daughter is missing. May we come in?"

"Of course Agent Romano, always happy to oblige." He stepped aside and motioned for them to come in. Bobbi led Patrick from the bleak corrugated metal exterior into his domain. Behind the desk a gilded frame displayed an oversized studio photo of a long-legged nude reclining frontally on a velvet couch. Off to the right, behind velour drapes, a four-poster bed was piled high with satin pillows. Bobbi ignored the décor as if she'd seen it all before and took a straight chair in front of the polished mahogany desk. Patrick sat next to her.

"Patrick's daughter Erin and her friend Aliesha were camping in the Ozarks and stumbled on two dudes burying a body. Now the girls are missing."

"I'm so sorry to hear that, Mr. MacKenna. But I don't generally come across missing persons. I suggest you call the police."

"You see, Solly, we thought it might have something to do with the missing Mayor of Brooklyn. Since your last shouting match with him down at the Village Hall, we thought you might know something about it."

"Although we've had our occasional differences over business license matters, we would be the last to wish him any harm."

"As I recall, your most recent application for a club license was pronounced dead on arrival. What's the matter, wouldn't he buckle under to your boys?"

"I don't know what you're talking about. We run perfectly legitimate businesses in this community and offer the highest quality entertainment."

"Of course, Solly. We just came from one of your so-called high-class shops, Solly's Adult Novelties and Video. Just the kind of thing the mayor was trying to clean up."

"That kind of facility, for your information, is provided only as a convenience to our club patrons. It's revitalizing business in Brooklyn, as the mayor wants to do."

"You see, we believe we've found the mayor's body, but two witnesses to his burial ceremony have disappeared. We were wondering if you could shed some light on that."

"I'm, ah, sorry to hear that." Patrick sensed hesitation in Sol's reply. "Are you sure Mitchom is dead?"

"We know a stiff when we see one. He'd be overgrown with daisies by now without these two girls finding him. Now they've turned up missing—Patrick daughter Erin MacKenna, redhead, age 17, and Aliesha Robinson, African-American, age 15. So what do you say, Sol? You gonna help us, or what?"

"I'll be happy to come and identify the body, if that will help. What else I can do?"

"We're not worried about his ID. He's the mayor, for chrissake. It's his killer and the two witnesses we need to find."

"Sorry I can't help you."

"We're still tracking a dozen missing underage girls. I'll be on the lookout, as usual."

"Search away. I'll help if I can." Abrams shifted uneasily in his leather chair.

"Okay, Patrick. Looks like we're done here." Bobbi headed for the door and motioned for him to follow. "We'll see if we can find Jake and Momo." She looked back, inquiringly. "Those names ring a bell. Sol?"

Abrams appeared startled. He assumed a faraway look, as if trying to recall a high school classmate.

"In this area, alive today, maybe on your staff," she offered, by way of clarification.

"Not offhand, but I'll be happy to ask Vince Scullin, one of my top executives. He runs my clubs. Why?"

Bobbi and Patrick exchanged glances. He wondered what duties Abrams assigned him to "execute."

Ignoring his question she handed him her card. "You do that, Solly, and let me know."

Outside, squinting in the sunlight, Patrick said "I know he's lying."

"Me too." Bobbi sighed. "But without proof we can't touch him. Legitimate business, my foot! He's offering debasement opportunities to teenage girls, billing them as dancing stars, hooking them on meth, crack and coke and selling them into prostitution to feed their habits."

Patrick shuddered. He admired Bobbi's frankness, but the content of her charges floored him. If his men had gotten hold of Erin she faced a ghastly fate. They had to rescue her soon, before he got her under his control. "What do you suppose got this guy where he is?"

"I've done some research on Solly," Bobbi said. "He grew up in a rough and tumble neighborhood in West LA, where his mother was forced to move when his father left He admired his father, Ziggy Abrams, a flash-in-the-pan actor, who taught him not to get mad, just to get even.

"He's never known the high-life, only the low-lifes. When Sol made his way up the ranks of the gang, he eventually became right-hand man to Johnny Rosselli, protégé of Chicago gang mastermind Curly Humphreys. Curly called him 'The Hollywood Kid,' a wannabe actor and amateur politician, who probably brought the Outfit more grief than gain. Rosselli, who supposedly talked it over with Mooney "Momo" Giancana, another of the Chicago kingpins, in the post-Capone leadership of the mob, advised Sol to set up in a backwater of southern Illinois. While under the protection of Chicago, he would be free to operate without their constant oversight. He'd be situated in the heart of a vast hinterland—Indiana, Kentucky, Iowa and Arkansas—and just across the river from Missouri, with its treasure trove of wealth in its two queen cities, Kansas City and St. Louis, and its natural paradise and refuge, the Ozarks, where Capone had fled when the G-men applied heat in the '30s."

"He sure doesn't seem like a big shot in the Mob—no bodyguards, none of the trappings of power."

"He's tired and going broke. He's fed up with all the surrounding human wreckage. I think he just wants to secure his wealth and retire." The smooth running nightclubs, she explained, trade in heroin, cocaine, that troublesome new, homemade drug, methamphetamine, and the sex trade, with a constant supply of fresh young talent—nubile young women and beautiful boys, hooked on drugs and then sold to prostitution mills in New York, Las Vegas, Chicago and Miami—had provided him wealth beyond his wildest dreams. But his casino investments in Vegas went sour in 2008, like everybody else's, , and he's scrambling for cash."

Bobbi drove south to East. St. Louis and pulled up in front of a modest ranch home in the Denverside neighborhood. Patrick climbed out of the passenger seat among leafy trees and manicured front lawns. In stark contrast to the burnt-out districts, unpaved streets and trash-cluttered homes in other parts of town to the north and east, this district appeared well-tended, safe and prosperous.

"The best view of St. Louis is from over here." Patrick waved an arm toward the west. "Since no large structures blocked the view across the river, the Gateway Arch and the downtown skyline loomed high above the foreground of well-kept modest homes. "This district has been a showplace of this town for the past thirty years."

She knocked on the door of a neat ranch home. A tall black man answered.

"Hello, Agent Romano. Do come in."

She introduced Patrick and he ushered them into a living room with modern decor. Bobbi and Patrick sat on a tan leather sectional sofa and the judge piled his wiry frame in the single seat around the corner.

"Judge Scales, thanks for agreeing to meet with us on your day off," Bobbi said.

"There are no days off when the well-being of young people is concerned."

"We've reason to believe Patrick's daughter Erin and the teen who was with her have been captured by a drug and prostitution ring that operates from Metro East," Bobbi said.

"Oh, my!" The judge regarded Patrick with concern. "If you'll tell me a little bit about them and provide me with photos, I'll alert police to put out an all-points bulletin."

"I've just sent them to you." Bobbi showed him their photos on her Smartphone.

"So you think they're somewhere in Monroe County?"

"Right. Patrick was in a state meeting near Jefferson City this morning when Erin got a cell phone call through to him. The technicians tracking it there were pretty sure about that."

Patrick described the camping trip, the earthquake tremor, and the girls' discovery of the body and their kidnapping.

Scales reached for the phone on the end table and placed a call.

He covered the mouthpiece and said, "This is Werner Schluetter, Sheriff of Monroe County." He put it on speaker and said, "Werner, how goes the struggle?"

"Win a few, lose a few, as usual, Burt. What's up?"

"Kidnapping victims, Erin McKenna, 17, redhead, fair skin, five-foot-six, and Aliesha Robinson, 15, African-American, five-one, missing since Saturday night. Erin's father is sitting in my living room right now. I just included you in the APB. He was at the Missouri Emergency Management Agency this morning when she called his cell phone. They were able to track her location between cell towers in the eastern half of your county."

"That's a pretty wide area. Any other clues?"

"Sheriff, this is Bobbi Romano, FBI. We're pretty sure she's been captured by people involved with Sol Abrams and his crew. You got any idea if he's working out of your area?"

"Whew," he replied, "those guys are brutal on young girls. We've managed to keep the clubs out of here."

"What about meth labs?"

"Now you've come to the right place. We're watching a dozen locations. We close the labs, but they just pop up somewhere else."

"Keep your eyes open," Bobbi said. "You'll find their photos and descriptions in the judge's bulletin."

"Sheriff Schluetter, please hurry," Bobbi said. "We have no time to waste."

They thanked the sheriff and hung up.

"Judge Scales, I'm upset. She ignores my advice about men. What if she's curious, too? What if she wants to find out what it would be like to show off her body?"

"Even if she realizes what folly that would be," the judge replied, "she might side with her captors. It's called the Stockholm syndrome."

"That's what I'm afraid of. She said on the phone she wanted to play along with them. Her mother died four years ago. She's been rebellious since then against my rules."

"They'll get her either way. If she resists, they'll threaten to hurt her. If she cooperates, so much the better for them. Then they'll hook her on meth, crack cocaine and maybe heroin next, to weaken her will and enslave her."

"Oh, God." Patrick broke into a cold sweat.

If he didn't act fast he risked losing all he valued in the world. In his frantic hunt for his daughter, he would have to neglect his clients and could ruin his career. Moreover Erin herself, the only other survivor of his once happy family, could perish, or even worse, be sold to human traffickers as a slave. His ordered existence had been disrupted, first by nature and then by these heartless predators.

SEVENTEEN

A wailing stretch limousine followed a hearse up the narrow lane, and both squealed to a stop opposite the gravesite, fender flags flapping, yellow blister light blinking, its siren dying with a growl. A black-capped chauffeur stepped out and opened doors for the family of the deceased. Cab Constable, a dashing African-American of about forty, emerged from the hearse and guided the family toward the grave. His family owned a chain of funeral homes, the area's most successful black-owned business. He had parlayed his prestige into politics and been elected mayor of a large East Side city. He directed the placement of a lustrous gray metal casket to graveside. A black-robed preacher arrived, surveyed the gathering and leafed through his bible.

A spring storm had blown through overnight, bringing in a blustery April Friday. As the cloud bank receded in the east, the sun winked though remnants of gray hovering overhead and shone on the bluff-top cemetery of Jerusalem Missionary Baptist Church. A crowd of mourners in their best attire—the men in immaculate black suits and ties, the women in elegant dresses and all shapes of exotic feathered and beribboned hats—stood facing a choir of stolid black women, wearing modest caftans and robed in royal blue, bracing against the stiff breeze. The strains of "Swing Low Sweet Chariot" floated down the hillside as Patrick and Meg approached.

Mrs. Mitchom, in a dark suit over a white blouse with tailored cuffs and collar, stood with her two children near the front of the group. On her head she wore a kerchief fashioned from a dark paisley scarf. Abraham, who looked about ten years old, clad in a navy blazer and slacks with a clip-on tie, stood like a brave little man, looking up at his mother for clues about what to do. His slender adolescent sister, Jacqueline, as pretty in a pale blue dress as her namesake, shivered coatless and gazed teary-eyed at her father's casket. A lump formed in Patrick's throat as he recalled Kitty's funeral and the terrible void thirteen-year-old Erin had faced at the loss of her mother. Like Jacqueline, his daughter Erin had gotten bum breaks.

The reverend gave a fine eulogy on Mitchom's achievements and aspirations. After the prayer for eternal rest the choir launched a soulful rendition of "Amazing Grace." Patrick tried to say a silent prayer for Caleb Mitchom, for Erin and for himself—all in desperate need of help. Patrick wasn't picky. Aid from above would be fine.

The keening behind the pastor conveyed their collective grief for the sacrifice of another victim of the urban wars. Caleb Mitchom had been part of the solution. Now there were fewer to combat the many problems he left behind. The choir bore witness to the efforts of the community's most solid citizens, its powerless men and an army of long suffering women, who had spent their meager earnings from menial jobs, relying on their devout faith to survive and persevere. Like a Greek chorus, they offered ironic commentary on the state of civic affairs.

In the Metro East community, news of Erin's plight had preceded Patrick. When he stepped forward and introduced himself and Meg to Mrs. Mitchom, she offered him her condolences first. "Your daughter doesn't deserve this, Mr. MacKenna. You must catch these criminals and bring them to the bar of justice."

"I'm trying, Mrs. Mitchom. But you've paid too much. Your husband will be sorely missed in Brooklyn."

"We have a common cause. I think the crimes are related."

"You do? For both of our sakes, I need to solve this. Did he have any enemies?"

"There were the sexual exploiters. He wanted to shut them down. But they're controlled by the Outfit. Caleb recognized some of them from our Chicago days."

"Was anybody else out to get him?" Patrick asked.

"Most certainly. Besides the owners of thriving clubs, he had to fight the casino operators and the wealthy developers who wanted to put a casino in Brooklyn."

"Yeah." Patrick brooded on the fortunes of a few and the misfortunes of many. While the big operators were awash in obscene wealth, here was the impoverished community these leeches sucked dry. The coffin held this family's breadwinner, who wanted to put a stop to it.

Mrs. Mitchom introduced them to the portly Pearlie Harrison, chorus director and prominent crusader for better housing, crime prevention and basic police and garbage collection services. "Mrs. Harrison raised ten-thousand dollars to buy the best funeral that Constable Chapels could provide. I'm so grateful."

"We owed it to him," said Mrs. Harrison, forming her words precisely. "Mr. MacKenna, we really appreciate what you're tryin' to do. This situation is very unfair to us citizens. A lot of businesses would like to be here but don't want to come because of the crime. The politicians and those who are in power don't seem to be takin' this very serious."

On their way back to the car Meg asked Patrick, "What's this Outfit Mrs. Mitchom was talking about?"

"Organized crime. That's the new Chicago term for the Syndicate, first formed by Al Capone, allied also with the New York Mafia, whose East Coast alliance they called the Commission."

"They're involved, too?"

"It's part of their history, dating back to the nineteen-fifties, when the FBI put the arm on the New York Boss of Bosses, Godfather Paul Castellano. He had maintained an uneasy peace with all factions of the *Cosa Nostra*, their informal name for the mob, Italian for "our thing." His sense of honor among criminals, he explained, caused him to spurn victim crimes such as drug dealing, prostitution and pornography. But his traditional sources of cash for daily operations—the numbers racket, union payoffs and small-time gambling—were drying up.

"When the law put the sting on the big boss, one of his dons, John Gotti, gained influence, and his side of the business grew, with the rackets which victimize people—gambling, drugs, prostitution and human trafficking—the kind Abrams is conducting on the East Side.

"Amateur meth makers popped up everywhere," Patrick said, "and the supply of marijuana, cocaine and heroin from Mexico and abroad flow freely, to meet insatiable American demand. With the unregulated nature of the internet, porn became a multi-billion dollar industry. This enterprise in turn has provided funds and promotional channels to fuel global sex trafficking, affecting even the smaller Midwestern communities, such as Brooklyn. Victim crimes are back, with a vengeance."

The funeral cars tore away from the cemetery, lights flashing and sirens blaring. Cab Constable made sure Mitchom went out with a flourish. The mayor of neighboring Brooklyn was supposedly allied with the other Metro East mayors in their war against crime and corruption, after all, and it figured he would be pleased to honor him. After all, Constable had been willing to roll out the full treatment— for ten-thousand dollars. As he headed back over the bridge to Missouri, Patrick wondered whether today's service for a fellow mayor might be especially poignant for Constable, or not.

◊

Later that afternoon, Patrick fumed as he left the office of Dr. Annette Richards, Superintendent of the Missouri School for Special Students. Preoccupied with Erin's latest dilemma, he now had to deal with a dissatisfied client. Rite-Price Construction had submitted yet another change order, this one demanding an additional $5,500 payment for extra lengths of sewer pipe to carry out the plumbing relocation shown on the plans, claiming the handicapped toilets, though correctly shown to scale and typically not dimensioned on the plans, had longer plumbing runs than they anticipated in their bid. Beside the extra pipe, the contractor claimed this change required more concrete demolition, more patching, more restored floor tile Most good contractors would provide these obvious parts of the job without question, but not this one. Building renovation projects were unpredictable enough without these bandits. But chiseling contractors usually won such battles with state government, making the architect look bad. Rite-Price, indeed. For whom?

The historic handicapped school complex, which had suffered repeated expansions over the past century until it almost filled a city block, was being renovated—again. This time he had designed the remodeling of dormitories built in the 1950s to add accessibility for even more severely handicapped babies of parents addicted to crack—some of them deaf *and* blind. Dr. Richards objected to this changing mission for her school. Without its Braille, urban navigation and self-sufficiency skills, where could the able blind get training, as they had done here for a hundred years, to be useful, contributing members of society? But political opponents didn't care and wanted either to convert the place to a nursing home for these unfortunates or to close it down.

He climbed the worn marble stairs, their treads cupped by generations of students' feet, and walked down an abandoned corridor in the sprawling complex, toward the second floor and the newer dormitory wing. He planned to take measurements and make his own estimate of the lengths of sewer pipe. At least he would dispute the claim and reduce the extra payment the state would have to grant.

A faint cry intruded on his thoughts. "No, please don't. It's not right," a young girl pleaded.

Ahead he saw only the empty hallway, its wall lockers extending in converging lines to the stairwell entrance in the distance. A few hanging globes, an anemic exit sign, one of its bulbs burned out, and glare from the glass beside the distant doorway cast a faint gleam, reflected in the polished terrazzo floor. As he continued up the hall in the half-light, the voice became more distinct.

"No, no. I told you last time, we can't do this."

It was the voice of a young teen, He quickened his pace down the hall.

"It's all right. Just be a good girl."

"No not that. They're lace. Mama gave them to me for my birthday. She'll kill me."

"It's all right. It feels so good. You'll see."

Breathless, he arrived at the intersection of a side corridor in the rambling complex.

"No, it's wrong. It's a sin." She was begging now.

As he rounded the corner, he had no doubt about what was going on. A push broom with a brush three feet wide leaned beside the entrance to an unused teacher's lounge. Through the half open door he could only see chairs around the end of a table and a sink counter.

"It's wrong. I'll burn in hell. Don't. Stop."

"It's okay, it's okay, Lucy dear."

He peered inside and froze in his tracks.

"No, no. NO!" she screamed.

Patrick lunged through the opening, and forced himself between a girl sprawled on the couch and her assailant, a half-naked, pot-bellied janitor, sweating with lust. He pushed the man back so hard, he stumbled and fell. He scrambled to his feet and lashed out with both fists against Patrick, who was taller, stronger and unhampered by tangled trousers. Patrick merely stepped back, gripped both of the man's upper arms and shook him.

"Want do you mean taking advantage of this defenseless girl?"

"I didn't think it would do any harm," he sniveled. "Lucy needs some lov—"

"You didn't think at all, you son of a bitch!"

The man hung his head, and continued blubbering. "Please, please don't tell anyone. I'll lose my job."

"I should hope so! You aren't fit to be anywhere near children." In fury he pushed the custodian away The astonished pervert tripped over his dropped pants and fell backward, hitting his head on the terrazzo floor. His body went limp.

The unfortunate Lucy could not see his defeat, nor did she realize the attack was over. She continued her protest. "It's wrong. Don't. It's wrong, it's WRONG!"

"It's okay, honey." Patrick said. "I knocked him down. We'll see that he never bothers you again." He sat her up on the couch. She scrambled to raise her lace panties from around her ankles and caught her breath.

"Who...are you?" The girl could have been no more than fourteen, chubby, in a turquoise polka-dot dress.

"It's all right, dear. My name is Patrick MacKenna. I'm an architect working on the school building. I just happened to be inspecting construction and I heard you screaming."

He wasn't thrilled about provoking Annette again, but he called her on his cell phone and had her summon security.

Five minutes later Dr. Richards entered with the institution's sole watchman, who doubled as a crossing guard for blind students arriving by school bus and patrolled the vast, half-vacant complex, an exercise in futility at best. Soon they were joined by two policemen. Patrick explained what had happened, while the cops made the janitor pull up his pants, handcuffed him and took control of the scene. Then Annette conducted Lucy to her office to call her parents and attend a hastily arranged session with the therapist. She thanked Patrick for his intervention and mercifully allowed him to escape at last.

Anger burned into his stomach like the bleeding ulcer he felt sure would develop. He thought of Erin's current peril, at the mercy of her kidnappers. Like this blind girl, innocent children, unaware of the dangerous predators lurking everywhere, were falling prey to them every day. How would society's youngsters, some getting their only moral guidance from the mass media, ever escape all the social misfits who found them within easy reach? What ever happened to the responsibility people used to take for each other's sons and daughters when they were out in public? And who would look out for Erin now? Like the poor blind girl in the deserted school wing, she was hidden from the protective view of passers-by. In the face of such blatant disregard for the innocence of children, how could decent folks ever regain control?

Eighteen

The morning sun streamed through the dormer window. Erin rose and checked the nails in the sash to see how hard it might be to break out. If she had the time and tools, and if she dared, she felt sure she could work the nails loose, swing to the front porch roof and slide down a post.

Momo was outside, gathering fallen branches, cutting them up and stacking cord-wood for their stove. He finished a stack of wood and headed into the forest again to look for more branches. When she got to the bottom of the stair, Erin checked the door, found it locked and tried the windows. She rechecked the location of the hammer and a screwdriver in the kitchen drawer. If Momo returned to find the cabin empty, he would be in trouble with his bosses. She wasn't ready to throw him to the wolves. He offered her only hope of lenient treatment. Even if she escaped, she'd been plunked down in unfamiliar woods, and her captors might find her faster than she could elude them. She would be worse off than before.

But the real obstacle to her running away was Aliesha's predicament. If she left now, without penetrating deeper into Solly's world, she could never rescue her. Aliesha, stuck living in a bombed-out neighborhood. never had the breaks she had. When Erin was fed up with the world and its problems, she could retreat to a safe environment and relax. Here was an innocent girl with a future. She was only fifteen, definitely too immature-looking for any glamorous job these thugs might have in mind. They'd surely put her to work hustling watered down drinks to johns and then make her rent her body to filthy, desperate men. The thought of her enslavement by these criminals, condemned to a life of gratifying the lust of strangers, was unthinkable.

And likewise, Erin owed it to her parents to carry on with the life they intended for her. All the good things that had ever happened to her were because of her parents' efforts to ensure her success and happiness. With people all around her now who couldn't care less whether she lived or died, except perhaps Momo if she were lucky, she realized her father's love was a treasure she had up to now taken for granted. Even in her short phone call with him she heard desperation in his voice, a flood of relief when he heard hers and the urgency of his questions about her welfare and whereabouts. Maybe even judgmental Meg wasn't so bad, even though her attitudes seemed way too last-century for someone so young. At least she said she wanted the best for her.

Despite their tiff, she still tingled with memories of Jimmy. Her body craved his perfect chest, powerful arms, soft lips and gentle touch. Her heart longed for his steady hand at the wheel, his confidence in the face of challenge and his gentle reassurance, when her outlook looked the bleakest, that everything would be all right. And now she really needed him—not as a trophy to show the kids at school—but for his support, help and maybe even rescue from her dire situation. Given half a chance, she knew he could and would brave anything to save her from these worthless thugs.

But how could she tell Jimmy how she felt and get him to come and help her? The people around her were the only ones she had to work with, that she could even hope to influence. She had to win them over.

She considered Jake. He seemed to be a hardened criminal, driven by greed. He knew how to make methamphetamine. But to do this he needed Solly Abrams, the dealer who mainstreamed it into the drug network. Jake seemed to be a free agent, apparently not involved with Solly's night club and prostitution rings. So far he hadn't tried to hook her with drugs and force her into the sex industry. Instead he was using her as a negotiating chip to gain favor with Solly in his drug deals. Was he behind on shipments? If so maybe she could use her bargaining value to hold out for a better job, rather than be a sex slave.

Momo, on the other hand, was a gentle gangster. Appealing to his softer side, perhaps she could use this relationship to her advantage. Could she get him to risk Jake's disapproval and even the chance of being returned to prison by doing her more favors? She resolved to try.

When Momo came back inside, he grabbed a beer from the fridge and a bag of corn chips and settled in the ragged easy chair facing the TV.

"You should eat better," she said.

"Oh, sorry. You want some?" he said, as he offered her the open end of the bag.

"No, thanks. You know what I mean. Healthy food."

"You heard what Jake said. No dice."

"He's gone now. Why don't you do that shopping we talked about? It looks as if I'll be living out here for a while."

"Don't count on it. Jake wants to turn you over to them as soon as possible."

"But we don't know when. In the meantime this bad food is unhealthy for my baby, and it's ruining my looks—not even Jake wants that."

"I don't dare try it. Jake would kill me if he found out."

"Your bosses will approve when they find out you're treating me right."

"Where am I supposed to shop? Jake has the car, and they don't exactly have Wal-Marts out here."

"They ought to have all of this at that little store just up the road." She handed him a list, including yogurt, granola, wheat bread, turkey, light mayonnaise, skim milk, lettuce, tomatoes, apples, oranges and bananas. "This will hold us for a while," she said.

"Okay, babe, I'll give it a try." Momo stuck the list in his pocket, went out the door and turned the key in the lock.

Phase One of her plan was working. She was starting to get things under control. Momo was cooperating. Now for Phase Two.

Her only way out, as she saw it, was risky, and disgusting. She wondered what it would be like to display her body to lots of bug-eyed, horny men. She might not have long—if she were pregnant, in a couple of months the baby would begin to show, and her chance to try it would be over. Her father had tried to shelter her from it. Maybe she wouldn't be so bad at first, and then she'd have more freedom, and a better chance to escape. She'd pressed Jimmy about his surreptitious trips to East St. Louis and Brooklyn's strip clubs with his friends. He had described the shows, with music, lights, costumes—small costumes, mind you, which were soon shed to reveal all—and had said it was okay, no big deal. The girls said they enjoyed it and even made good money

In fact she had little choice. Aliesha with her street smarts, was probably right. Assuming she couldn't make a clean escape—and it seemed unlikely—she had to play along. If they gave her a chance, she had to take it. It would be her only hope of finding Aliesha and rescuing her. If she failed to get that job in a high-class club, she had no illusions. She shuddered to think of it.

◊

Momo returned with most of the items on the list, a couple of pizzas and, of course, more beer. He let her prepare a salad in the kitchen, and she ate an apple and drank some milk. She decided on sliced chicken sandwiches for lunch and started to make them,

While she was still in the kitchen Jake returned. "What the hell are you doin', broad?"

"Making you a decent meal, for a change."

"Since when don't we eat right?"

"Since always, I guess."

"Where'd we get all this rabbit food? Momo, you helpin' this bitch?"

"Erin's tryna keep us feed us better," Momo said.

"I asked Momo to buy us some healthier food. You need to forget the Big Macs and fries and eat more chicken and pork, as well as fish. Maybe you could catch some in the stream."

"Prob'ly oughta fish upstream, though," Momo said, "far from the meth factory."

"Meth factory?" she said. "That's *really* unhealthy."

Jake whirled toward Momo. "You shut your trap! She doesn't need to know anything about that. And you left her alone in the cabin. I told you not to leave this place."

"Sorry, Boss. But see, she was good. She didn't try to escape."

"You're damn lucky she didn't." He turned back to Erin. "That does it. You can't stay around here anymore. I had a little talk with Vince today. He says he's gonna give you a tryout."

"For what? If you think I'm going to—"

"Cool it. Vince wants to see you dance. If you can't, he'll find you somethin' else to do. I've had it with babysittin' broads."

"A tryout. Really?"

"Don't get your hopes up. Tomorrow we're gonna take a little ride to town so he can see if you got what it takes."

What if and this wasn't a stage tryout? There was only one way to find out.

If it was, was she deficient in a couple of key areas, breasts and hips? She might be too skinny for the job. She was afraid find out what other jobs Vince had in mind.

PART II: COURTING DISASTER
NINETEEN

Erin awoke early, groggy from a restless night. Hoping she could add some art to her act, she had rehearsed the best moves from her high school dance troupe on tiptoes, trying not to thump on the thin plank floor. She had lain awake on the hard, narrow cot in the stuffy attic for hours, going over dance moves a hundred times in her head. As she washed in the primitive bathroom, she peered at her image in the cracked mirror. Her puffy eyes, tangled hair and crabby mood didn't bode well for what would have to be a sparkling performance.

With Aliesha gone, Erin missed the chance to discuss their plight, commiserate and plot with her. She had no clue where they had taken her. At about ten Jake made Momo tie Erin's wrists in front of her, trundled her into the car, which she could now see was a dark blue Buick Riviera with a flaking blue leatherette hardtop, and put on the blindfold.

"Do I have to wear that thing?"

"It's just to protect your eyes, my dear," Jake simpered like Red Riding Hood's wolf.

"Sorry, Babe." Momo tied the bandanna loosely and eased her into the back seat.

They bumped down the gravel track on the vintage auto's worn-out struts, bounced onto the pavement and glided more smoothly on the two-lane road, the car rocking when cars passed coming the other way. Soon the air from a slit in Jake's side window seemed cooler, as if off the river. After about half an hour, they slowed and stopped occasionally for red lights, as the hum of traffic suggested they'd arrived in town. Vince turned into a gravel lot and crunched to a halt.

When Jake helped her out of the back seat, Momo removed the blindfold and untied her hands. They were on a commercial street, with pole signs in front of plain, corrugated metal buildings. At this hour very few cars occupied the large parking lots in front of each business. On the sign directly above her she read the words, KITTY KAT KLUB, in fat letters tilted at odd angles, curving above a whiskered black cat logo, outlined in unlit neon.

They entered a large, dark space, with small cocktail tables and chairs arranged around a curved stage that thrust forward into the seating area, edged by a low brass railing. Two shiny brass poles were positioned along either side of the platform, with one centered downstage. Smoke from the rehearsal pianist's cigarette swirled in the beam of a dim work spotlight. A girl in almost nothing strutted across the stage, her bottle green bikini top and bottom glittering, in matching spike heels. She had pale long legs and blonde hair cascading to her shoulders.

Erin's heart beat faster as she sniffed the odor of smoke mingled with stale beer, and the fresher scents of lime and tequila from the bar, as a chunky, bald bartender in an unbuttoned black vest shook a mixer of margaritas for the evening crowd.

A gruff voice materialized from a rear table somewhere in the darkened void. "Okay, let's see your stuff. Hit it, Leo," he said to the rehearsal pianist.

The blonde nodded to cue the piano player, the floodlights came up and the dancer pranced to the center pole, where she gyrated to the tune of "The Stripper." First she engaged the pole with a trim ankle and calf and with one hand launched herself up a couple of feet and began a slow spin to the floor. She bumped twice to the beat as the melody broke into its final chords, stepped away from the pole and shed her top. As she ground her hips she toyed with the last remaining triangle of fabric below. When she spun for the third time she was totally nude.

Whoa, she's beautiful. Erin feared she would never make it in this league and despaired of what these men would do with her. On a brighter note, however, her breasts were smaller than Erin's.

"Sweet," Vince said. "Roxie, tell her to take a break and come back in an hour, when Solly comes by."

"No way, in hell, Vince," the woman said. "We've got enough blondes."

Erin's heart sank. If this attractive, talented dancer wasn't good enough, she had no chance. As her eyes adjusted the gloom, she made out a more voluptuous blonde with a clipboard and pencil sitting beside the man with the brusque voice.

"We never have enough blondes. Guys drool for them."

"Look, Solly doesn't want any more. What he says goes."

"Mighta known." He looked away from her, cutting his losses.

Erin quickly got the picture.

Roxie climbed the stage steps and spoke in stern, low tones to the bewildered girl. In the brighter stage light, Erin could see that the two women, while different, were equally attractive. The more mature Roxie, even in her tank top and rehearsal shorts, displayed full curves, a tiny waist, long, shapely legs and delicate features, while the aspiring dancer, slim and willowy, had a youthful glow. Clearly disappointed, the girl slunk back into the wings.

"Who else we got?" Vince asked as Roxie returned to her seat.

Jake stood up and approached the table. "Here's the little cutie been coolin' her heels at our place." He beckoned Erin to follow

Erin obeyed. She'd never realized Jake had such admiration for her.

Vince looked her up and down. Although she had done the best she could with her hair, she still wore her camping jeans and polo, by now smeared with several days' dirt.

"You been treatin' her rough? She's a mess." He glared at Jake and Momo.

"No, Vince, honest. In fact, Momo has been real gentle with her."

Momo's face showed surprise at the compliment.

Erin stared at the floor, embarrassed by the sudden attention to her disheveled state.

Roxie rose and placed her hands gently on her shoulders. "You poor dear. These shitheads don't know how to treat a woman. What's your name, sweetie?"

Despite her coarse language, the gorgeous woman's tone seemed sincere and salved her bruised feelings. Jimmy had told Erin that strippers all had fake, exotic names. While waiting she had prepared something kittenish she figured would fit in well around here.

"Felicia Vermeil," Erin manage to squeak. "Call me Fifi."

"Perfect!" Vince boomed. "You'll have to excuse these ruffians. Roxanne will take you under her wing and help you clean up."

Roxie looked down at Vince. "You know what we got here?"

"I hear ya. We've been lookin' for a young redhead act for a long time."

"Vince, you ain't seen the half of it. She's a real hottie."

Erin grinned with relief.

"Okay, okay. Can you fix her hair, give her a costume and find her some music?"

"You got somethin' to do for half an hour?"

"You kiddin'?" Vince sighed. "If I didn't do mosta the work around here, we couldn't even open the doors. Besides, Jake and me got business to attend to." He called to the pianist. "Take ten, Leo. Then go find out what Roxanne needs." He offered Jake Roxie's chair and turned away.

"Come on honey." Roxie led Erin toward a door to the backstage area and whispered to her like a gleeful co-conspirator. "We're gonna knock Solly's socks off."

"Solly?"

"He's the boss, and a personal friend o' mine, very personal, if ya know what I mean. But after this, he'll owe me big time."

Roxie took Erin to a room with five unoccupied stools and a makeup counter along one wall facing a row of mirrors outlined in lights. She sat down at one, motioned for Erin to take one next to her, and talked into the mirror.

"Look, honey, when I saw you I flipped."

"But Roxie, I've been kidnapped, along with another girl from the city. What's going to happen to us?"

"I don't know, hon. We're all in this together. But right now, for some reason, these dudes are watchin' you like hawks. They won't let you out of their sight, that's for sure. I'm sorry, but there's nothin' I can do about it, 'cept make damn sure you get a good job at this club. You do what I say and I'll see to that."

"Are they really going to give me a chance?"

"It's a cinch. We've been lookin' forever for someone just your type. Now, take off your shirt."

Erin was shocked. She only got this kind of request from her doctor. But this was sort of a physical exam, and in this alternative universe she figured different customs applied. She pulled her d polo over her head, and turned to look at Roxie. "Everything?"

"Might as well. Let's see what ya got."

She complied and glanced up shyly at Roxie.

"Oh—my—God. Young, red hair, pale skin, freckles. Lots of men out there will go ape over you."

She looked at herself in the mirror to see what Roxie saw. Her face and neck reddened with shame. "I'm so dirty. I'd give anything for a shower."

"Right in there, honey. Here are some towels. When you're done, we'll work on a costume and a dance routine. I've got a humdinger of an idea."

The water pricked her skin like a thousand needles, arousing in her a feeling she hadn't had since her night with Jimmy. Dried off, wrapped in a bath towel, her head turbaned, she glowed with pleasure and wondered if she could fake being a glamorous "artist." Taken aback by the lights, music, make-up, sexy costumes and theatrical smells, it was no wonder naive girls were seduced by this "glamorous" world. But she felt safe with Roxie, who knew a lot better than she how to make these uncouth men toe the line. Back in the dressing room, she wanted to tell Roxie more, but it would have to wait. Right now they didn't have much time.

"That's better, sweetie. Now let me tell you the score. If we do this right, I'll win some points with Solly, and you'll get your name in lights. Like I said, he's been my boyfriend for a long time. Lately though, he's' been hitting on my girls. I need to stay in control here, or morale drops and the whole show goes flat. First of all, my girls have never had to put up with harassment from the boss, and we're not gonna start now. Second, I'm his main squeeze, and he'd better not forget it. Now here's what we do."

Roxie led her to a rehearsal room set up like a stage, complete with mirrors on the walls and three poles. and left for a minute, reappearing with several items of clothing, which she instructed Erin to put on.

Erin had deep misgivings about performing. But the alternative, if she didn't succeed in this audition, was grim indeed. She had a beautiful body. By showing it off, she might just be able to save herself. She could also stick around long enough to find her Little Sister. She had gotten Aliesha into this. She had to get her out.

Roxie sat her down opposite her at at a desk with a disk jockey's turntable and explained her vision. "Leo will introduce you as Fabulous Fifi, the Marmalade Cat Girl, and play these recordings. I'll coach you on the dance routine as we go."

Bolstered by Roxie's encouragement, Erin ventured onto the rehearsal stage in five-inch clear plastic talons and her red fox fur wrap. She twirled to the intro music of "The Cat in the Window," by Petula Clark, a sultry song about a cat that wants wings so she can ride to a rainbow. Her long legs in mesh, cat ears atop her wavy flaming hair, she wore a feathered emerald mask with the slits for her eyes outlined in yellow and green. Timidly at first, she strutted across the stage, twirled and flashed some creamy white skin through the opening in the wrap. To her relief, Roxie said, "Here's where the lights will dim and redden." She hoped they would conceal the mortified flush she felt all over her body.

"Okay, now the lighting will change. She switched the music will to Bobby Rydell singing "Alley Cat." She stepped out the moves and Erin followed. Getting into the spirit, she bobbed her head teasingly, turned away and tossed the wrap aside, revealing, when she faced the front again, a vermilion-sequined top and a matching sequined G-string. She grasped the pole, hosted herself up in a graceful ballet pose, one knee bent and the other leg thrust outward, and lowered herself, spinning slowly, to the stage.

"Perfect. Now the lights will glow pale lavender, to bring out the reds of your costume and hair. You'll step into the beam of a white spotlight." She played "The Cat's in the Cradle," by Harry Chapin. "Now jump up and grab the center pole with both thighs and shimmy down, making love to it, and spin away, with your back to the room and remove the top."

Erin twirled, reached in back of her and undid her strap, baring her back, and spun to face the tables, cupping her top. She inclined her head, as if to ask if she should expose more, and spun again.

This song concerned a neglectful dad who keeps promising his son he'll get together with him, and only too late realizes he's missed his son's childhood and the chance to know him. She could relate to this one, and she put her heart into it.

Erin gulped and drew a deep breath. At Roxie's nod, she dropped the sequined bra and twirled it in triumph. Turning her back to the room again, she hesitated, unfastened her G-string and turned to face Roxie, completely nude, clad only in her mask, kitten ears and high heels, with only her own red-orange hair for modesty. The softening curves of her changing body only enhanced the effect.

"Here's where the stage lights fade to black. You gather up the bikini and the red fox fur, spin away and race into the wings."

"Did I do okay?"

"Fantastic, Frlicia. As you may have noticed, I decide who goes into the show, and you're in. Now let's do the audition, really just a dress rehearsal."

"More like an un-dress rehearsal."

"Good one! Ha-ha. We're gonna get along great!"

A half hour had elapsed and they were ready. Roxie led Erin to the wings backstage. Solly. Abrams, who had arrived during their rehearsal, stood at a table in the corner conferring with Vince Scullin. He spotted them in the wings and grinned. "What've we got, here, Roxie?"

"Our new redhead act. You're gonna be blown away!"

"So I see. I can't wait." Solly rubbed his hands together in eager anticipation.

Glare and a clatter at the door announced a new arrival. Bobbi Romano pushed into the darkened interior. As Bobbi approached, Solly compressed his lips in a grimace. "Oh, crap," he muttered, and slunk in the darkness toward the rear door.

"Bobbi Romano," Vince gushed. "To what do I owe the honor of this visit?"

"Can it, Vince,. Bobbi squinted as her eyes adjusted to the gloom. "Solly may have told you I was coming. I asked him the other day how it happened that your do-gooder mayor has left us for a better place. He didn't seem to know much about it, or your underage dancers. I thought I'd better talk to you."

"I've heard he's missing. Now he's dead? How sad for him and his family."

"You're all heart, Vince. You wouldn't happen to know anything, would you, about his disappearance and untimely demise?"

He met Bobbi's stare and leaned forward, both hands on the table. "I'm as baffled as you are. I never agreed with Caleb Mitchom's policies, but he was getting rid of the seamier clubs and actually making business better for us. I'm shocked that someone would just up and kill him. His killer would be so easy for you guys to trace."

"Yeah, yeah. Well, either lucky or unlucky for you, the medical examiner may get to the bottom of that one without my help. I've got a different mission today.

Saved, for the moment. Erin's chest pounded so hard she thought she'd die of a heart attack. She was torn. Part of her wanted to escape through the front door, but she feared for her life.

"By the way, where's Jake?" Bobbi asked.

"I sent him back w—"He interrupted himself. "Jake who?"

Erin hesitated in the wings, listening. Bobbi was in the club, no doubt looking for her! *Dang, now what?*

Her knees felt weak. All she had to do was to alert Bobbi and perhaps save herself. But she'd already seen Jake's vicious side. What about that gun he carried? The result was unpredictable. If she revealed herself, she was terrified the men would start shooting, or at best hold her hostage. She did *not* want to be the focal point of a hostage crisis. Without her presence Aliesha might be shot, or made into a sex slave. Erin would not be spared either. They would care less about her talents than the damage she could do to them as a witness. She figured for now she'd have to lay low.

Roxie hustled Erin backstage. "Solly left, and Vince will deal with that detective. Don't worry, we'll get you back here at seven for a dress rehearsal. We'll have plenty of time to perfect your act."

Embarrassing as it would be, this was the least of Erin's concerns.

TWENTY

At noon Saturday Patrick answered the phone. It was Aliesha's mother.

"Hi, Esther. Not working at the hospital today?"

"Oh no, Mr. Patrick. I'm not, 'cuz I got wonderful news! Aliesha escaped to my brother's house in East St. Louis."

"What the— She escaped? When? How?"

"Yesterday. She outfoxed them. My brother just brought her home.

"My God! Wait until Bobbi Romano hears about this-"

"I'm fixing a special dinner for her. What a celebration we're gonna have!"

"That's terrific! I'm so relieved. I'm sure you'll want some time with her, but when could I see her? I'm desperate to get more information about Erin."

"Of course. I rearranged my schedule to take care of her for a few days. I've got to pamper my baby."

"Can I come right over?"

"I'm sure she'll want to help you find Erin. Here, I'll let you ask her yourself." She paused while she handed the phone to her daughter.

"Mr. MacKenna? Oh, I'm so glad to talk to you. Erin saved my life. I'll never forget it."

"Is she okay?"

"She was fine when they dragged me out of there yesterday. They separated us. But she's still in danger and needs our help. I have so much to tell you. "You could come over here. Momma wants to keep me close. Please hurry."

"I'll be there in half an hour."

He wrote down the address, in the reviving Hyde Park neighborhood north of downtown.

"Tell your mother I'll have to bring an FBI agent with me. But Bobbi's nice—you'll like her."

He ended the call and located Bobbi, wrapping up her week's reports at the FBI office.

"What's up, Patrick?"

"I'm headed over to see Aliesha, at her own house on the North Side."?

"She escaped? Holy crap! Right now?""

"Yes, and yes."

He gave her the street address. "See you then?"

"I'm on it. See you soon."

Patrick parked at the curb and walked up steps to the end of a two-story porch facing the side street, its sloping roof transitioning into a steeper half-gable over the main structure. The Robinsons' house was of the historic flounder style, sometimes called a half-flounder, a type unique to St. Louis. Narrow, two-and-a-half stories tall, it was shoehorned into a frontage only 30 feet wide. A working class home, its decoration was limited to segmental arched windows and a corbeled brick cornice. He turned toward an entry door on the porch along the side street.

Esther Robinson answered the bell. "Oh, Mr. Patrick," she exclaimed, "how good to see you, especially now!"

"Under much better circumstances than before. You have a beautiful home."

"Mr. Robinson and I were very proud of it, before we separated." She heaved a sigh.

Bobbi had arrived early and was seated on the flowered couch.

Aliesha, whom he had just met before the camping expedition departed, threw herself into his arms. "Oh, Mr. MacKenna. I'm so glad to see you! My sister and brother, Kiesha and Bruno are at school activities today. You know Momma, I guess. Here, you can sit next to Agent Romano. Oh, you won't believe all that happened! I'm staying home this week."

"Right, right. Aliesha." Patrick said, interrupting her frantic speech, "I think the best thing would be to slow down and catch us up a bit."

"When did you last see Erin?" Bobbi asked.

"Yesterday, when they separated us at the cabin and tried to take me to one of their horrid clubs. When I left, Erin was fine and unhurt. But I'm really worried about what they'll do with her next."

"Why don't you start at the beginning," Bobbi said, "and tell us the whole story of your camping trip, from the time you arrived at the river, until you escaped from your kidnappers. Take your time, We've got plenty of time to listen. We need to know everything that happened, in order to help Erin."

"Oh, dear," she said. "I felt so many things. I was happy, panicked and then sad. Momma won't approve of some of the things I said when I was upset. I got so angry, I lost all the breeding she taught me."

"That's okay honey," Mrs. Robinson said. "They's nobody here but us chickens. These good folks are tryin' to help you and find Erin. Just tell it like it is."

Aliesha took a deep breath, sat up in her chair and began.

"When we got to this place called Akers Ferry, the canoe rental guy said we'd have lots of fun out there. If anyone got hurt, we could call him on a cell phone, and he'd pick us up. We didn't know our phones wouldn't work."

"He tried," Patrick said. "I guess he couldn't predict everything."

"He told the kids in the first four canoes to shove off. As we were on our way, Erin taught me some cool paddle strokes and we just glided. It was so beautiful!"

She rehashed the other campers' account. But she added their capture at the burial site, the harrowing ride to the cabin in the woods and the way she and Erin had been kept prisoners.

"Who were these two characters?" Bobbi asked.

"Momo, the driver, turned out okay, for a murderer. Erin got him to do favors for us. Maybe before it's all over he still can help her. But he's a parolee, and Jake's got his number. Jake is the little boss, but Solly is over him and Solly's in trouble with the big boss somewhere. They don't produce enough junk."

Do you know where you were?" Bobbi asked.

"No. We were both blindfolded," Aliesha said, "so we never saw how they got to the cabin."

"If we knew that," Patrick said, "we could round up these creeps and most likely find Erin."

"Someplace south of East St. Louis, I know that. On my last trip I peeked out of my blindfold and saw we were on a two-lane road in the woods. Then it got near the river. Yesterday, when Jake took me to that crappy town of Brooklyn. I was through with Jake's screwin' over us. The minute he opened that car door, I jumped on his foot and ran. Man, did he howl!"

"Aliesha, watch your language!" Mrs. Robinson warned.

"It's okay," Bobbi said. "She can't shock me."

"Where did you go?" Patrick said.

"By the time Jake could limp again and start chasin' me I was two blocks away down the alley. I called my uncle's house in East St. Louis, and he came and got me."

'Good thinking, Aliesha," Bobbi said. "You probably saved your life."

"You poor dear. Poor Erin!" Mrs. Robinson shook her head.

"What do Jake and Momo do out there in the cabin?" Bobbi continued.

"Besides breaking' down chicks and selling 'em as whores? Hell, they only do that for they own fun and pocket change. He works in some kinda shed further up the trail, making meth and who knows what. They got some big drug deals goin' down. Jake talks about some huge shipment comin' up. Jake's way behind and he's pissed all the time—if he don't deliver he and Solly are dead meat."

Patrick stood and paced. "Dammit. Bobbi, can't we get these pervs before it's too late?"

"I tol' Erin, she better play ball, or they swat her like a fly. Her best bet is make nice an' pretend she gonna be a big star, 'til she gets her chance to split that sorry scene."

Patrick, Bobbi and Mrs. Robinson exchanged wide-eyed stares. No one spoke for a long time, as they coped with Aliesha's revelations.

"Thank goodness you escaped, Aliesha. This is valuable information, and I think we can find her. I need to fill Adam Reiner in on this as soon as possible."

"But what about Erin?" Patrick said. "We have no time."

"Look I know there's more to learn here." Bobbi stood and grabbed her case. "But I've got to run down these new facts this afternoon."

"Thanks for sharing your daughter's time with us, Mrs. R." Patrick said. "I know how precious it is to you."

"That's okay. I got all week. She missed so much school already, a few more days can't hurt. Besides, my baby and me got some serious catchin' up to do." She looked ominously at her daughter.

"Take it easy on her, Mrs. Robinson," Bobbi said. "She's been through a lot, and she was very brave and smart to escape. If we can put our heads together some more, I'm hopeful we can get everybody back home safely and catch these criminals before they can do more harm."

Bobbi turned to Patrick. "You need me for anything else?"

"No, thanks," Patrick said. "I've got some research of my own to do this afternoon. Thanks again, Aliesha."

"You know," Aliesha said, "it's kinda funny. Here Erin wanted to help us kids from the inner city get into a healthy outdoor environment. We were in the outdoors, alright, but it scared hell outta me. Around here, we only get a drive-by shooting every once in a while. This is way tame compared to life out there in the wild."

Twenty-One

On the warehouse parking lot, Roxie stayed in her car for a moment in the hot sun, while she puzzled how to approach Solly about her latest purchases. She didn't need a big scene right now. She was just trying to do her job. She tried to look at it from his perspective.

She feared she was losing Solly to younger, prettier girls. Maybe Erin would win him. She glowed with the pure innocence of youth. How he must miss those youthful days, when he felt powerful, invulnerable and capable of attracting any woman he wanted. Before the gangs, paybacks, treachery, killings and revenge. Maybe this miracle she'd placed before him promised to fulfill a need Solly sorely missed and Roxie could no longer provide. It could all happen in a flash, in the space of this kid's splendid ten-minute performance. In hopes of winning him back for herself she'd done her production job well—too well. When he got his first glimpse of this girl in her scanty kitty costume, she could see he was smitten. Not since his Hollywood days had she seen him so inspired—and horny.

Roxie opened her car door to escape the suffocating heat, took a deep breath and removed her packages from the back seat of her battered Chevy. She clambered up the iron steps, worked the handle of the warehouse door with her free hand and burst inside with half a dozen bulky packages. Sol Abrams sat at his mahogany desk studying Erin's picture on her "Missing" poster. Something in his eyes told her the girl aroused him and challenged his manhood. A chance to feel young again. The ferocity of a big cat. Satiation of his hankering for new experience. Solly hastily stuffed the poster into his top drawer.

"What the hell? Where did you get all that?"

"Big deal. I went shopping—show costumes for the new girl. What if I *had* gone to Frontenac Plaza? It's a cinch *you'd* never take me."

"Aw, look baby. You done great. The shows are fabulous. Without you, I'd be—"

"Yeah, you say that, but, speaking of shows, you never show *me*."

"Honey, lately everything is coming apart at the seams. That double-cross a few years ago by that black mayor of St. Louis and some Detroit mobsters cost me my six-million-dollar Vegas investment and all its earnings. I've been under pressure ever since the financial markets turned sour in '08. All the big Vegas hotel casinos headed south, mine right along with 'em. Ever since, I've been in a cash flow squeeze. Now we have to get by on the juice loans, drug deals, local gambling and the sex trade."

She knew Solly was falling seriously behind. He was even thankful that this young redhead had fallen into his lap. He was eager to capitalize on his rare find. Plus, there was a personal benefit he had yet to enjoy.

"I got a lotta problems lately," he continued. "The boss up in Chicago is houndin' me for cash—that damned McGurk, his enforcer, is movin' in."

"Don't you dare make me entertain him again," Roxie said. "Last time he came to town, he sopped up your best liquor, abused some of my best girls and threatened to kill me. With that razor-sharp blade he draws on any pretext, he might ruin someone's looks. I was even afraid he was going to use it on me!"

"Okay, okay. I know I been neglecting you. When all this blows over, why don't we take a little trip. Vegas, maybe even New York? We'll get you some new threads—Bonwit Teller, Nieman Marcus, Saks—the works!"

"New York? Really? Could we see a Broadway show? I've always wanted to go."

"Sure thing, New York it is." He checked his Rolex. "I gotta run—call on my overdue accounts. These delays are killin' me, maybe sooner than you think."

He dashed out the door.

Roxie laid her packages on the bed, opened each one and hung the stylish, skimpy costumes in the wardrobe. She couldn't wait to get Erin over here to try them on. She wanted her to have some nice costumes, even if she'd only have to take them off. She'd always believed that a beautiful package adds even more value to a fabulous gift inside. Mainly, she wanted her new star to feel good about herself. Maybe after tonight's debut, the poor kid would have some more freedom to enjoy her striking beauty.

Solly started his engine. She crept back into his office, sat at the mahogany desk and began opening drawers. Lower right, his snub-nosed .38 automatic, two boxes of ammunition and a switchblade. Lower left, old Playboys and other girlie magazines, condoms and Viagra. Upper left, files. She'd have to study those someday to get Solly what he deserved. Center: there it was. Behind the pencils, pens erasers and paper clips lay Erin's "Missing" poster, but not Aliesha's. "The bastard," she muttered. In the pencil tray lay a red thumb-shaped object. Sliding a button on it exposed a plug for a computer. She had a hunch, took it, rolled the picture and put them both in the pocket of her skirt. When she heard Solly pull out of the lot, she grabbed her keys and purse and dashed to her car to follow him.

Twenty-Two

In the cabin that afternoon, the minutes ticked by as Erin waited anxiously for opening night.

She was surfing the few TV channels they received in the woods when a black Mercedes parked in the gravel lane. She heard a knock on the door and the key turn in the lock. Solly Abrams poked his head in. It was too late to find a place to hide. She had to play this cool.

"Hello Felicia," he said, "I'm Solly Abrams.

"Why, Mr. Abrams, what a surprise!"

"Call me Solly, baby. I just came by to compliment you. That detective burst in and I didn't get to see your audition. I'm sorry we had to postpone it. But Roxie has starred you in the show. I couldn't wait. I had to see more of you. You're fabulous."

"Roxie should get credit for that."

"For the costume, maybe, but the beauty is all yours."

Erin frowned. Despite his balm to her hurt feelings, she didn't consider it an apology for the rough treatment she'd gotten since she was carted off.

"I gotta get you outta this hell-hole. How'd you like to come live with me?"

How could she repel this powerful monster, yet not anger him further? "Oh, Mr. Abrams, I couldn't. My father would never forgive me."

"You don't need to ask Daddy anymore. We're gonna pay you a nice salary. And you'll get big tips.

"Babe, I'll set you up in a ritzy place, get you a fine wardrobe, whatever you want. Besides, the Kitty Kat will be so much classier than any of my other clubs."

Solly's offer might have been tempting to other girls, sweeping away their inhibitions and introducing them to forbidden pleasures. It appeared to promise glamour, a bit of fame, a chance to make her talents and assets shine and finally to have that freedom from their parents' stern objections to the exciting life he promised. But the veiled threat that he could send her to one of his "other clubs" couldn't be good.

For maybe a second it crossed her mind that to accept might show her father she was an adult, outdo her stylish and sexy peers and overcome her shyness all in one grand gesture. But was it more important to get even with her father or not to disappoint him?

She looked down at her filthy jeans and shirt, so stiff with dirt she could stand them in the corner of the room at night. His offer, so far out of the question, would end this. As for man potential, he was too fat, too old and way too unctuous. Compared with Jimmy he was hopeless. Even hunky Momo would be better. She had to be firm, no matter what the risk.

"Thanks. It's very flattering, but I can't."

"You'll change your mind. Let's see how you feel after your grand opening tonight. You'll love it—the music, the lights, the beautiful girls—and you the prettiest one of all."

"I'm excited about it," she lied. "I'll do my best."

"You'll change your mind—you'll see." Solly spread his arms and reached for her. She dodged his bear hug, and he landed only a peck on her cheek.

He spun around, and waved cheerfully back at her as he went through the door. He turned the skeleton key in the lock and departed in his car.

She shook with outrage. No wonder so many kids were victimized. Add the threat of debt and the hunger for drugs and most girls, even grown women, would be helpless. She paced around the cabin floor, reeling with roller coaster emotions, until she collapsed weak-kneed on the couch. First a victim of rough hoodlums, she was now the focus of a carefully plotted seduction.

Absorbed by these worries, she was surprised to hear another knock on the door. *Dang.* Was Solly coming back for another try?

"Hey, it's okay, it's me," said a woman's voice. Again the key turned in the lock.

"Roxie! How did you even find me? I didn't see your car."

"I followed him out here, hid my car in the woods by the main road and hiked in." She was sweating from her walk.

"Well, sit down. I'll get you some juice." She walked to the kitchen ell, her mind racing What had she seen or heard? If Roxie found out about Solly's faithlessness in his pursuit of her, she'd be angry as a hornet.

Erin handed her a can of the apple juice Momo had bought, trying to sound casual and hoping her trembling limbs didn't give her away. "Momo's working in the shack, and I'm bored out of my gourd. We've got a few minutes until Jake comes back."

"Well, I'll make it quick, then." She sat cautiously on the worn-out couch. Erin took the once-matching chair.

"What's going on?" she asked, waiting to hear Roxie's version of events.

"Nothin' good. Solly's got some nerve propositionin' you. I saw and heard everything." She pointed to the window behind the chair where Solly sat.

Oh, man. Now she couldn't even hide his treachery from Roxie. Erin felt ashamed. "You might as well tell me the gory details."

"I smelled a rat. Besides, I needed to confront Solly about his moves on my dancers. And there was this new matter that came up today, when that FBI agent barged in after your act. So I decided to follow him. But when he made a beeline for you, I was floored. The nerve!"

Double dang. Now, besides her worry about Solly's infidelity, Roxie knew Bobbi really was hot on her trail and soon to find her. She began to fidget.

"So I waited in his office in the old warehouse where we live until he left. I looked for that paper Bobbi gave him." She held out the poster with a blowup of a girl shimmering in her knockout sheath on her young body, with perfect legs, a carnation corsage on her wrist and her long hair caught up in a fancy twist on top of her head. "She's a dead-ringer for you."

"My prom picture!" She sighed. "They cropped out the best part—Jimmy."

"Well, I caught my breath. Hair: red, Height 5' 6", Weight: 125 pounds. No question about it, my new star Fifi was the famous, missing Erin MacKenna!"

Dang again. Busted. "Yup, in the wrong place at the wrong time," Erin said, "while Jake and Momo were up to some serious mischief in the woods."

"I decided my showdown with Solly could wait until another day, but I tailed him and here I am.

"I need to warn you. Let me tell you what happened to me. You've gotta play ball with these tough guys. You'd be amazed how much power they have over ordinary, decent people. There are addicts everywhere."

"Really? I wouldn't have run across them. Most people we know have good jobs."

"You might not recognize them. Sometimes these addicts keep working—they need the money to support their habits. For people like me, the three most important things in our lives, besides using meth, are money, sex and power. It's not just limited to poor people, or those stuck in the Ozarks unable to find a job."

"Come to think of it, I read about a bank teller who had been embezzling from her customers for five years when she got caught. What tipped them off was that one day she put all the big bills from the cash drawer into her purse and stuffed her envelope for the day's receipts with recycled paper. She thought she could get away with that."

"That's what happens. You need more and more money to feed your habit and become crazed with your own power. Some hallucinate and think they're invulnerable, like the drugged-up kid who jumps off a building because he thinks he can fly.

"For the men, and even some women who cook the meth," Roxie continued, "it's a power trip. They can keep people in fear and keep them coming back, because they've got the money or the drugs they need. I'm always having to bow down to the power. For a while the sex was fun, and then it got to a point where I was afraid to say no. I was afraid not to be involved in it because of the consequences.

When you're into methamphetamine—even if you know right from wrong—you get roped into a whole new sexual world."

"I thought I could be strong and resist. I guess not."

"Believe me, you become powerless. I got scared in a hurry. And it's everywhere—in Illinois, in the Ozarks, on the streets, in nice parts of St. Louis."

Erin knew she'd made the right decision. Now she had to plan her escape. But what could she do about Roxie, who had good reason to get her out of the way, just to hold on to what she had with Solly?

"I guess it's a big letdown when your boyfriend puts a move on another girl, huh?" Erin said. "You heard me tell him I wouldn't have anything to do with him?"

"Oh, sure. That pig. I've all but lost Solly. Now I want to ruin him. With you here, I've got enough evidence to put all these guys in the pen. We'll figure out our strategy after the show tonight." She was determined to carry out her plan.

"I don't blame you," Erin said. But she didn't share Roxie's lust for vengeance.

"So that's my story. The boys will bring you over tonight. We've got to act like nothing is wrong. You'll make a big splash. I've got to get back before Solly misses me. Sorry I have to lock you in again. But in case anything goes wrong—anything, you hear?—you call me if you need me. Find a pay phone, or steal Jake's cell phone if you have to. Here's my cell number, understand?" She wrote her number on a slip of paper and handed it over.

"Wait. What happened to Aliesha?"

"She's gone. Solly said while Jake was taking her from the car to the club, she stepped down hard on his foot—you know the arch, where it hurts like hell—and she ran away down the street. Jake was no match for her. She ran faster, ducked into an alley and got away."

"I hope she's okay." Erin expressed concern, but felt a surge of relief.

Roxie turned toward the door. "Oh, while I was rooting around in Solly's desk I found this. Maybe you know what is and how to use it." She handed Erin a red object no bigger than her thumb with a retractable metal tip and a ring for attachment to a keychain.

"It's a flash drive," Erin said, trying to sound casual. Her heart beat faster as she took it from Roxie. "Solly probably keeps a list of his girlfriends on it."

"Good, now maybe he'll have to keep his flashlight in his pants."

"Flash *drive!*" Erin said. "It's a computer part."

"Whatever it takes to keep Solly's part supplied, huh? Ha-ha."

They laughed until Erin made her unladylike snort, and laughed some more, relieving the tension. Erin put the paper and the flash drive in her jeans pocket.

"Thanks, Roxie. Good luck. I'll get in touch if I need help."

Roxie left and turned the key on the outer side of the door.

Erin poured herself a glass of milk in the kitchen and sat at the table with a box of Pop Tarts, eating them cold, one, after the other, to console herself. She was upset about the way this was going.

First, she felt sorry for her dad, who must be frantic by now. For the moment she forgot her father's criticism and harping over her bad habits and her choice of friends. She recalled his wisdom and his willingness to share it with her. Turned out he was right about the dangers of the Ozarks.

Then, she ached to see Jimmy. Even if she managed to get out of here, would they get together again? She was so confused. If she hated him so much why couldn't she resist the urge to put her head on his chest, wrap herself around him and hold on tight for reassurance and comfort, to kiss his smooth, firm lips and draw from his inner strength? When she looked into his steely blue eyes, she could see infinite depths. Maybe Kelly was right when she said, just before she'd fallen asleep in the pup tent, "You two are so far gone you don't even know it."

That's why she had to see him, had to have it out with him. Right now she wasn't even sure she could look into those eyes. They would make her furious, showing his unyielding determination to chart a life in the Army that would take him away from her for long periods, maybe forever. Did he hurt as much as she did over their breakup? He'd learned about drugs through his brother's Army buddies. Would he use them to ease his pain and become an addict?

Like me. Her body stiffened; she could barely lift an arm. If she couldn't escape, what would life in this so-called glamorous world be like? Would she get hooked on drugs, too, and glide down the slippery slope to personal ruin?

If she made her debut tonight, would they whisk her away to another location? Maybe it would be more luxurious, although she doubted it, but certainly more secure—a satin prison. Maybe even with a bodyguard, in the literal sense—to make sure her precious body was available for the next night's performance.

Now that Aliesha had escaped, she had no reason to stick around. Right next door to Brooklyn were her uncle and cousins in East St. Louis. All she had to do was call them and she would be in good hands. It was likely she'd made a clean getaway. The last obstacle to her escape plan had been removed. There remained only to decide and act. Tonight would be too late.

She had to do something, fast.

She couldn't count on any help from Roxie. In fact, if she found out, she would complicate things and call in reinforcements to keep her. Besides, with Solly's change of heart, Roxie had as much reason to get Erin out of the way as any of them. These creeps were going to jail anyway, whether Erin helped Roxie get revenge or not.

If she could get her hands on a phone, who would be the best person to call? If she phoned Bobbi Romano, it might take too long and she couldn't control what would happen. The local cops might want to be involved and the whole thing could turn into a fiasco, which might make things even worse for her, or even get her killed.

Her thoughts turned again to her first love, Jimmy. Erin blinked as a drop of cold sweat from her forehead dripped into her eyes. Suddenly thirsty, she lurched toward the sink and filled a coffee cup from the tap. Her hand trembled as she lifted it to her lips. Soon her whole body shook and her teeth chattered she re-crossed the filthy floor and collapsed on the overstuffed chair, weak and nauseous.

What have I done, she thought, turned my plans, my hopes, my life over to these thugs? She sat for a long time, as images from the past two weeks raced by her like scenes from the window of a speeding car. The earthquake, their party separated, the burial in the woods. She had been snatched from her world to a new one, with the bizarre glitter of sleaze. Tough guys, scared of even tougher ones, living in terror of others.

It was time to bolt.

She reached for the arms of her chair, raised herself slowly to a standing position and took her cup back to the sink. Absently, she opened the drawer. There lay the hammer and screwdriver.

Her body knew what to do. But her brain warned her—first, make some arrangements

TWENTY-THREE

When he returned from the Robinsons' house, Patrick realized he had neglected the Deerpath City Hall project for several days. He was way past the deadline he'd promised to Gary Archer. Desperate as he was to get back to his daughter's case, he thought a couple of hours spent on a Saturday afternoon finishing his new design concept for the existing city hall would pay off. It could confirm the new idea's feasibility sufficiently to show the city administrator. After an hour and a half of energetic sketching and calculations, he confirmed that they could build a functional expansion of the complex, while fixing the building's earthquake problems. As he predicted, the idea would also save money, maybe lots of it.

He rushed out to the existing city building to verify some dimensions and details of the existing structural systems. He climbed a stepladder in the Deerpath City Hall, measuring the span, length and depth of a steel beam that would have to be replaced.

His cell phone beeped. Twisting his way to a sitting position on top of the ladder, he listened as Bobbi Romano reported in her rapid-fire style. When she left the Robinson home she had visited Abrams's club and talked with his club manager, Vince Scullin.

"He claims to know nothing about who's holding Erin captive, and where. I don't believe him. Look, I need more information about Erin. Do you suppose I could come over and look at her notes, her computer, see her room? We know a lot more about her state of mind after talking to Aliesha. Maybe we can put some facts together."

"Sure. I'm about done here at City Hall. Can you meet me at my house in about half an hour?"

"Check. See you then."

As Patrick hung up his jacket in the hall, the front door chimed and he let Bobbi in. "That was quick."

"We've got no time to waste. Now could I see her stuff?"

Patrick led to Bobbi upstairs to Erin's room. He indicated her computer on the desk.

"First, you need to see this." He removed the sepia drawing from the drawer. "Jimmy must have done this—look, he signed it." I would never snoop on her, but since she's been gone so long I missed her and sat for a while up here. I came across this by accident."

"She's so beautiful." Bobbi cried out. "We've got to get her out of that den of perverts. They had been auditioning new girls. They shut it down when I arrived. She might even have been there and I might have rescued her. I was so busy threatening them, I missed my chance."

"Hey, that's not all bad, you know." Patrick broke into a grin "So you're human, big deal."

"Still, Erin is in great danger, all because of me.

"Think. What would be their next move?"

"Oh my God! Maybe she'll have her debut tonight."

"There, see? You'd have had to wait for backup anyway. You can still move in tonight when the show opens."

"Right, with a SWAT team. Now I can prepare the warrants. Patrick, I almost lost it,"

"But you didn't." He looked deep into her coal black eyes with new respect. "Get busy and plan your operation."

Bobbi left as quickly as she'd arrived.

Patrick sat in the kitchen, let Parnell out for a rare daytime romp in the yard and poured himself another cup of coffee. For the first time he felt he knew the mysterious, inscrutable Bobbi Romano. On the one hand, she was right more often than not, had her heart in the right place and had proven time after time her determination and skill in bringing wrongdoers to account.

Her working style, however, was the opposite of his. She was missing important information because she had no inkling of a scenario, like the one slowly forming in his mind. It was time to test his own theory on Erin's kidnapping and the plot to get rid of Caleb

Mitchom, Mayor of Brooklyn.

Tonight would be too late. Erin was falling under their influence. Maybe they had already drugged her. He had to act right now.

It was already three p.m. Patrick grabbed an apple from the kitchen, drove downtown and crossed the interstate bridge to Illinois. He pulled into the Kitty Kat Klub parking lot.

NEW XXX SENSATION
FIFI THE MARMALADE CAT GIRL
DEBUT TONITE

Furious, he pushed through the entry door. It took a minute to make out shapes in the darkened interior.

"We're closed," said the bartender in rolled sleeves.

"I need to see Vince Scullin," MacKenna said.

"He ain't here."

A tall muscular man materialized from the gloom. "I'm Scullin, Who are you?"

"MacKenna's the name. I'm looking for my daughter, Erin."

"Erin MacKenna? Nope, never ran across a dancer by that name."

"You sure? Petite redhead, green eyes, about five-foot-six?"

"Look, I dunno where they took her. You'll have to ask him." He pointed to a table hidden in a dark corner, where a big man sat with a shapely blonde.

Patrick approached the pair and caught snatches of their conversation. They were arguing.

"You'd better shape up, Solly, or your whole show's gonna fall apart."

"I can explain ev—" He noticed Patrick approaching the table and put a restraining hand on the woman's arm.

"Why, Patrick MacKenna. What a pleasant surprise!"

"Save it, Abrams. Where's my daughter?"

"Your daughter? I don't even know her. Roxie, if you would talk to this gentleman, I'd appreciate it. He's a friend of Bobbi Romano. I've got an urgent meeting to attend."

"For your sake, I hope it's with your lawyer," she said.

Abrams retreated toward a back door, leaving Patrick facing Roxie.

"MacKenna, eh? Are you Erin's father?"

"How did you know?"

"We had a visit from the FBI." She glanced toward the rear door where Solly had made his exit. "That creep. I hope he gets what's coming to him."

"Yeah." His gaze followed hers.

"I'm Roxanne Smiley." She smiled.

Right, and I'm Mickey Mouse. "Where's my daughter?"

"Waiting in the woods, I guess. She's about to make her stage debut tonight."

"Fifi, the Marmalade Cat Girl? Why you—" Patrick clenched his fists at his sides. "Where is she?"

"Your daughter's fine, or at least she was an hour ago. I'm tryin' to help her."

"Where are you holding her prisoner?"

"*They* are, in a cabin way out in the woods. I was trying to spring her free, or freer, anyway, to be a dancer, so Solly and the boys wouldn't sell her to the sex trade. Then Solly turned on me." Her voice broke and her eyes filled with tears.

"Did they think they could get away with that?"

"Turning on me? Ha!"

"No, the other thing."

Roxie heaved a sigh. "They do it all the time."

"What about Aliesha Robinson? What happened to her?" He played dumb, to see what else he could learn.

"She flew the coop. Whadda ya think I am, the Bureau of Missing Persons?"

"Hey, I'm trying to get these girls back."

"Okay, okay," she said. "Aliesha bolted outta the car when Jake was bringin' her here. Practically crippled him in the process. Maybe she's called home by now."

"Thanks. I'll check it out."

"I'll help you if I can. What else do you need to nail these guys?"

"First, do you know a guy named Manny Marancik?"

"Manny, Manny—not Maran—whatever, but I do know a Manny Markey. The boys call him Fanny Manny."

"What boys?"

"It's kinda disgusting, really.

"He's gay?"

"Yeah. I hooked him up with this guy that keeps him supplied with beautiful boys."

"He sounds like the guy, alright. Oh, boy." He pursed his lips.

"Right on."

"I don't care about his sexual tastes. Who arranged it?"

"If I told ya I'd have to kill ya—ha ha." Her hollow laugh hinted she was kidding—on the square.

"Help me here, please."

"My source—anonymous, mind you—says this Manny guy tried to get permits for a floating casino boat on the Brooklyn riverfront last fall. He was turned down cold before it could even get to a council vote. That's why nobody knew about it. Manny took it kinda hard. Is that your guy?"

"Sounds like him. Now he's trying to moor a nine-foot-deep lake freighter in six feet of water on the other side of the river."

"Whatever floats his boat—ha ha."

Another one of her classic gags.

"Thanks, Roxie. This may help us catch these crooks. But can you take me to the place where Erin's being held?"

"God knows I got nothin' left to lose around here...except my life, for what that's worth." She sighed.

"Hey, we're trying to keep people alive here."

"Lotsa luck with that one. I'll be happy to help, but I gotta make it quick."

"Please, I'm desperate to locate her."

"Okay, I'll draw you a map to the cabin." She sketched for a moment on her clipboard. "See, you get off 255 where it says turn for Columbia and stay on Route 3..." She talked as she drew. "You turn south on this gravel lane into the woods."

"I really appreciate this."

"Hey, anything for a good kid and her dad. Now I gotta make tracks—and cover them up—ha-ha. Also, the Outfit has a secret operations center in the basement of an old office building in East St. Louis. They're almost never there, but Solly might take her there for a while, while he reviews his operations. You wanna check it out?"

"Can you take me there?"

"If we make it quick. I can show you where to get in, but you're on your own to get out."

"Let's go."

Patrick pulled out of the Kitty Kat Klub's parking lot behind Roxie's car and followed her slowly up the street. Absent their night time glitter, the rubble-strewn parking lots, corrugated metal buildings and high-rise signs were an eyesore. Caleb Mitchom wanted to replace these tawdry attractions with family oriented shops, a department store and maybe even a health club. If his luck hadn't run out, he had a good shot at cleaning up this cheesy excuse for a business district.

He wondered if a businessman trying to appear legitimate would pull a stunt as obvious as murder. Even if someone like Abrams did order the man killed, he would never have anyone close to him do it. He would have to have another, stronger reason than to make his sleazy nightclubs a bit more profitable. So far he didn't have a shred of solid proof as to who might actually have committed the crime.

.

He followed her as she drove south on Illinois Route 3 and east on Missouri Avenue to Collinsville Avenue, the heart of old East St. Louis. A parody of its 1920s vibrancy, the once-proud downtown district was still dominated by Gothic revival and Ritz-style three-to-eight-story buildings, faced on their street facades with brick or white-glazed terra cotta, with pilasters between arched, ornamented windows. Devoid of pedestrians, the street was nonetheless congested with a steady stream of cars headed for the interstate ramp at the southern edge of downtown. Roxie stopped her car and he drove alongside. At street level a wig shop elbowed for position with clothing stores, consignment shops and cocktail lounges. She pointed to a humble two-story building chinked in between the taller structures.

"Park in the lot behind that building. The hideout is in the basement of the tall white building next door. Lotsa luck," she said in her dispirited manner. She peeled her tires on the asphalt and roared up the street.

At the crumbling parking lot behind the wig shop, Patrick pulled between a couple of parked cars in the shade of the taller building. A padlocked chain-link fence enclosed a stairwell leading down a dozen steps to a basement door. He scaled the fence, dropped gingerly to the gravel surface on his good leg, descended the stairs and tried the door. It was secured, but an adjacent window yielded to his prying and he climbed over the sill to a mosaic tile floor. He was surrounded by tall columns clad in white terracotta matching the building façade, which rose to white gothic arches forming a-vaulted ceiling. Bronze chandeliers hung on chains from the center of each arched vault.

He puzzled for a moment. What was this unusually lavish space doing in the basement? Then he recalled that throughout this district of East St. Louis, this level had once been the ground floor. As a flood protection measure, the entire downtown area had been filled with earth in the early years of the twentieth century to raise the ground-floor elevation of the buildings to the second story level.

The furnishings of the space made up in technology what they lacked in style. Rows of metal desks occupied the center of the room. A half dozen computer terminals, a few of them turned on, provided alternating views of various outdoor spaces and interior offices. Tipped off by the winking screens that he wasn't alone, he hid behind a fat column clad in clusters of terracotta colonettes. Holding his breath, he carefully scanned the space for signs of life. Detecting none he started rooting for files in metal cabinets stuffed with real estate records, monthly files of paid bills, tax information and property plats, suggesting their real estate transactions were handled here. In a large flat-file along one wall, he discovered drawers full of architectural drawings. With mounting excitement, he searched until he found a set that showed the latest remodeling design for this building. He rolled up the set, tucked the parcel under his arm and headed for his exit by the window.

"Hold it, buster," a gruff voice called from behind his back. He whirled around. A muscular bald man, who looked like Kojak without the lollipop, towered behind him. He held a service pistol pointed toward Patrick's chest. "What're you doin' poking around here?"

Caught red-handed, Patrick improvised. "I'm an architect. Solly sent me. He said I could find plans here for the building so we could remodel this office."

"It is customary to knock before entering someone's office."

This guy had one thing going for him—besides the gun, of

course—a sense of propriety.

"I did, but I didn't hear anybody, and I hated to waste the trip." Patrick had often been told he had more brass than sense. "Solly's really in a hurry to get this project moving."

The thug lowered the gun and scratched his bald head.

As they stood exchanging niceties in the secret hideout, the floor under him shuddered and he staggered to one side. Kojak had the same reaction.

"Get the hell out of here," Patrick suggested, as politely as the situation permitted. "Earthquake. Move it!"

Kojak ran the other way. Maybe another door in that direction led outside. Or maybe he left his lunch in the other room. Patrick didn't stick around to find out. He left the building the same way he'd entered. He was very glad he did, as the violent shuddering continued. He scrambled over the chain-link fence. Another tremor moved the ground as he landed and left him sprawled on the cracked pavement. To shield himself from falling masonry, he dashed into the shelter of his car.

Twenty-Four

Momo came into the cabin for a late lunch.

"Where's Jake?" Erin asked, as she made sandwiches for all of them.

"He's working in the shack. He can hardly walk on his left foot and wants me to bring him some food."

"What did he do to his foot?" Erin already knew, but she wanted to hear Momo's version.

"I guess he twisted it getting out of the car," he mumbled. "You got that food ready yet?" Right now she needed a heart-to-heart talk with Momo and she didn't have much time.

"I'm working on it." She cut the sandwiches and put the food on plates. "Momo. I'm lonesome. Could you just sit here and talk to me?" She brought their lunches over, sat down and pointed to the chair opposite.

"Sure, babe. You know I'd do anything for you—no matter what Jake wants."

"What do *you* want, Momo?"

"I just want to see my daughter again. If I screw up he'll send me back to the pen. I'll never have the chance to go look for her."

She was a prisoner, too. But she almost felt worse for Momo. He didn't seem to be a callous criminal. But Erin had a family and friends. He had nobody but nasty Jake and his greedy boss. She wondered if she could solve both of their problems.

"Momo, I'd like to help you get away from all this and find your daughter. I have a plan to get you out of here. But first I need you to do something for me without a word to Jake. Will you do it?"

She whispered her request in his ear.

"Gee, I dunno, babe. He'll kill me."

"By the time he realizes what you've done, it'll be too late. If you stay around here, he might kill you anyway, or send you up for good. If he doesn't deliver on his contracts with the Mob, the Chicago boys will get to him before he has a chance to hurt you. What have you got to lose?"

"Nothin', I guess."

"Here, take him his lunch and come back."

Ten minutes later Momo came back with Jake's cell phone and a map of Illinois. "Here they are, babe. Now I've gotta get back before he misses me. Good luck."

Good, he was helping. If she were to get out of here safely she had to call someone outside. But whom should she call first?

Her thoughts turned again to Jimmy. After their fight, even if he would take her call, she he wasn't sure he would come right away. He would need convincing. Someone who could talk with him if he balked and make sure he'd do it.

She turned to the one she could rely on in all dire situations, her loyal friend, Kelly. With her stocky build, she wore her black hair in two ponytails—or sometimes braids! She and Erin had been close since childhood. Loyal and motherly, this fleet athlete was her strategic partner, always positioning herself to provide assists and help Erin make winning plays, both on and off the hockey field. She would know how to counter Jimmy's objections, and she wouldn't give up until she had achieved Erin's goal.

Erin punched in a familiar number. She let it ring until finally it was answered

"Erin! Where are you?"

"Kelly, can you talk?"

"Wait, I'm in the library. I'll duck out to the john." A minute later, she was back. "Erin! Okay. I've been panicked about you. What's going on?"

"Do you remember the game against Assumption, when we were in double overtime, down to strokes by the opposing forwards to break the tie? You know how you caught their goalie off balance and drove in the winning stroke?"

"Right. Just luck, I guess."

"And skill and guts, as I recall. Kelly, if I ever needed a winning stroke, it's now."

"Anything, you know that. Where are you?"

"I'm locked in a cabin in the middle of a forest with gangsters. But that's not important right now."

"That's a line from 'Airplane.'"

"This is serious. You've got to do me a favor."

"You know I will. Erin. Are you okay?"

"Yeah, yeah. But I won't be if I stick around here much longer."

"What happened?"

"Look, I don't have much time. The short version is, Dad was right, after all."

"Huh?"

"You know how he warns me about drugs and sex and meth in the Ozarks, and how bad people are out to get young girls?"

"Oh, yeah. My dad, too. It goes right over my head. We don't know anybody like that."

"Well *I* do, and they're about to make me do horrible things."

"Oh, God. Like what?"

"They want me to be a star in a strip show."

"O-oh. You'd be great at it! You've got the looks and the bod for it."

"Plus I'd show Dad a thing or two. Trouble is, it comes with strings attached—puppet strings. I'd be head mistress for the big boss. Yuck, you should see him, the fat greaseball. And then when he got tired of me, it'd be someone else's turn, some younger, prettier thing, with bigger boobs, and I'd be hooked on drugs and sent off to the sex trade."

"Oh, wow, Erin, we've got to get you out of there. What can I do?"

"I'm angry with Jimmy but I've got to talk with him. I want you to tell him I need to see him this afternoon, over here in Illinois."

"You mean you want me to call him? He's probably in class."

"Text him first, then call. I've got to see him."

"But why Jimmy? Wouldn't it be better to call the cops?"

"Too dangerous. Besides, he can save my hopes. My world. Maybe even my life. I've got to get his attention out here in the wilderness and help him fix what's wrong with his head. I want *him* to save me. He *is* my hero, after all. You're the only one who could possibly understand."

"Oh, right. I'm sure he'll just come over and risk getting killed to be lectured by an angry girlfriend, or should I say ex-girlfriend?"

"Oh, shut up. You can tell him it's a matter of life and death, which, after all, it is. Tell him they're about to sell me to a striptease night club and make me dance naked on the stage."

"Oh, God! Do you think they'll really do it?"

"It supposed to happen tonight! But not if I can get out of here."

"What am I going to tell your father?"

"Whatever you do, DO NOT tell my father, and swear Jimmy to secrecy."

"But there's an Amber Alert out for you. You're wanted in six states."

"All the more reason to keep it hushed up. This is between me and Jimmy. And remember, not a peep out of you about my...uh... condition. That's not what we're going to talk about. And anyway, I don't really know what my condition *is*."

"Understood. So what's he supposed to do, come and get you right now?"

"No, silly. He's in class!"

"Hey, that's what I just said. You know you're going to owe me big time for this."

"Big victory dinner?"

"Deal."

"I knew I could count on you, Kelly. Listen carefully. Here's my plan. He's to drive downtown after school, cross the river toward East St. Louis and take Highway 3 south through Waterloo, Illinois. A few miles further south, he needs to turn right on County Road G toward the town of New Design. When he gets there, he should turn right toward Burksville. About a mile past that town, he'll see a gravel road off to the left. It leads to a cabin in the woods, but tell him not to turn in. I'll break out of the cabin and be waiting for him right there at the side of the road. If I'm not there, tell him to come to the cabin, and bring a tire iron. You never know how it might come in handy. By five o'clock—and no later, or we'll both be in big trouble."

"Oh, Erin, be careful. Wish me luck."

She ended the connection and waited for Momo to return.

Minutes later, he entered. "Here, Momo. Slip the phone back in Jake's pocket. You keep the map. If he misses it, too bad. You'll be long gone. I've marked a route on it for you to escape toward St. Louis."

"Jake's gotta take a big shipment to town. He wants me to help him load up."

"Tough break. You've got to leave right now. This is your best chance to make a run for it. When he comes looking for you, we'll both be gone."

"But what about you?"

"Don't worry, it's all arranged. First chance you get, you call this number and tell Bobbi Romano at the FBI everything you know. I mean everything."

"The FBI? Oh, man...I don't know."

"You can trust her. I can't make any promises, but I'm pretty sure that's the only thing that can keep you out of the big house."

"If you say so, Erin. Thanks for trusting me. Good luck."

"Lock the door when you go out. I've gotta make this look real."

He gave her a big hug, grabbed his AWOL bag from the bedroom and disappeared out the door.

She took a last look around the shabby cabin, walked to the kitchen drawer and removed the tools. She thought about her plan to pry open the bedroom window and slide down a post from the porch roof. Nope, she was never going to shimmy down a pole again. She decided to leave in style through the front door, had it open in five minutes and walked out into the dappled sunshine.

But the elation she expected to feel was somehow missing. An eerie silence gripped the forest. She took a deep breath and smelled a burnt odor. Two snakes crossed the trail in a hurry. An army of crickets in formation streamed across the path. She needed to run, but her limbs felt heavy and too weak to move. Unaccustomed dizziness, a pounding heart and perspiration took over her body. Was this a self-induced fear of suddenly being on her own, or was it something else?

She glanced down the path where Jake always disappeared. She didn't have much time before Jake came looking for Momo. She had to get out of here. But her curiosity got the better of her. What exactly did they make back in the woods anyway?

About 500 feet down the path she came upon an old fishing shack next to a stream, the windows dirty and cracked. She peered through a dust-caked window. Jake sat on a stool at a cluttered workbench with his back to her, his left foot propped on a stool. He was deep in concentration amidst a colossal mess. Tables surrounding him were cluttered with vials, jugs, retorts, beakers, tubes, large-sized plastic Coke bottles, cans of drain opener, eye protection goggles, gasoline additives, rubbing alcohol, ether, benzene, paint thinner, Freon cans and half full bottles of substances she couldn't even pronounce. More two-liter pop bottles, blenders, camera batteries, wooden matches, propane cylinders and hot plates occupied every surface and large sections of the floor. Mr. Van Dyne, her chemistry teacher, would have flunked him for his messy workbench alone.

Hunched over the work Jake looked like a mad scientist. Her eyes watered. The combination of smells leaking though chinks in the walls almost overpowered her. Ducking from the window, she noticed a stream of brownish-red sludge dripping from a corner of the cabin toward the creek. What a mess! Was this the source of the curious air pollution? But even as she distanced herself from the building, the airborne smell, like that of a burning match, grew stronger. Sulfur!

Erin ran from the shack past the cabin and headed down the gravel track toward the main road. As she raced along the path, a loud rumble filled the air. The earth shuddered. A whoosh from the treetops, as they swayed in unison, momentarily dimmed the sunlight. She lost her footing, staggered and fell into a ditch alongside the gravel drive. She landed on the side of her foot and twisted an ankle. Pain shot up her right leg, and into her brain, turning her vision blinding white. The ground shuddered again. She didn't dare move or try to get up. She lay with sharp stones digging into her back and waited. After a few minutes, the shaking ceased. She glanced back through the woods at the cabin and glimpsed one cracked window—its wood structure had absorbed the shock.

After thirteen days of captivity she was free, but disabled and hidden in the forest where no one could find her. With night coming on she had to find a way to get back to the main road, so Jimmy could pick her up and take her back to civilization. She tried her legs. It was useless. She collapsed again into the ditch, exhausted, weak and unable to move.

Twenty-Five

Patrick started the engine and headed for the street in front of the white terracotta building. The six-story structure he had just left rocked. Cornices and window glass fell in apparent slow motion ans crashed to the street. The building came to rest at a tilted angle, leaning toward the sad-eyed wig shop next door.

The service level indicator on his cell phone showed three bars—iffy, but possible. Aliesha had escaped and Solly's staff was in open revolt against their boss, but still, Patrick had to find Erin before they dragged her off to the night club. He took out Roxie's hand-drawn map and studied the route. His cell phone rang.

"Oh, Mr. McKenna, This is Kelly. I've heard from Erin. She told me not to call you, but I have to. I just this minute got home from school, and this is my first chance. It was the most bizarre conversation I've ever had."

"Is she okay? Where is she? What did she tell you?"

"Wait, wait, it was kinda weird, almost surreal." She described the call. "She's planning to escape. She had me call Jimmy to help her." She told him what she knew about Erin's situation.

"Thank heaven she's come to her senses. But, Jimmy? I don't get it." Patrick was appalled, but after what he'd heard from Aliesha and Roxie, he could believe it.

"I'm afraid something might happen before Jimmy can get to her."

"Kelly, where is Jimmy going?"

"I talked to him a couple of hours ago. He has probably picked Erin up at the cabin by now. She might even get home tonight. Here's

Jimmy's cell number." Patrick copied it down.

"Oh, please, Mr. MacKenna, hurry, before these killers get on her trail. She needs your help desperately!"

"Don't worry, Kelly. I'm in Illinois, headed for her right now."

"Oh, thank God! Good luck and please tell her—"

The connection failed. Patrick's phone showed "No Service." He couldn't call Jimmy to confirm his location. He was on his own.

With his communications shot, he looked above him at the elevated highway ramps leading to the Mississippi River Bridge. While the highway department's earthquake reinforcement for the structures seemed to be holding up, the high-speed complex had become a parking lot. He switched his hissing radio to the emergency broadcast channel and was soon gratified to learn that the recently reinforced tower had kept the station on the air. The announcer reported that the epicenter of the tremor was centered once again in southeastern Missouri, but bigger this time, measuring 5.7 on the Richter scale. The bridge above had become impassable, with multi-car pileups in both directions. Later he'd have to find an alternate route to get home.

Satisfied Abrams wasn't holding Erin at the secret hideout, he swerved around the backup at the bridge approach and found his way clear to Highway 3. He headed south through the infamous Village of Sauget, population 249, known for its heavy industrial polluters and strippers, another venue where innocent victims were initiated into their tawdry trade.

He didn't have time to waste hunting on his own for the cabin in the woods. He needed help, and the sheriff knew the territory. When he reached the town of Waterloo, he drove up Third Street to the handsome, restored historic house next to the jail, which Judge Burton Scales had described, the temporary office of the Monroe County Sheriff.

Werner Schluetter hung up the phone and greeted Patrick.

"Evenin', MacKenna," he said, shaking his hand and sighing wearily. "We've got a full plate tonight, and your daughter's case is only one of 'em." He pointed at dozens of files littering his wooden desk.

"Move this one to the top of your stack. I've learned these hoodlums are planning to feature her in a new strip act tonight and move her permanently to a new location. Right now, I think I know where she is—or was, until a short while ago." He handed Schluetter Roxie's crude map.

"Don't worry, I'll get on it." He studied the piece of paper in his hand. "Hmm. Haven't thought about the old Hanson place in a while."

"Shouldn't we go out there right now and look for her?"

"Come to think of it," the sheriff said, "old man Hanson died last year. He had a hunting cabin and a fishing shack by the creek. Used to fish out there to his heart's content. I miss the old coot."

Schluetter's unhurried pace was maddening.

"Listen, Sheriff. It's no longer used for that. Some murderers have taken it over and they may be making meth in that shack. My daughter's been held prisoner there for almost two weeks."

Schluetter whistled and shook his head. "Well, I'll be damned." He called his wife and told her not to wait dinner for him. As Patrick fidgeted, Schluetter made a pot of coffee, heated a chicken and cheese burrito in the microwave and gave Patrick half of the huge wrap.

"Saved it from lunch. Maria's Cantina stuffs 'em so full that it's impossible for me to finish one order."

"Thanks, Sheriff. This could be a long night."

Schluetter filled a coffee cup for Patrick and refilled his own, adjusted his foam cushion in a ragged green cover, planted his lanky frame in the curved wooden swivel chair and invited Patrick to roll his chair around next to him. After he finished his half of the burrito, the sheriff leaned forward and dug into the stack of cases. The name of each one was underlined in colored marker, corresponding to a same-colored push-pin in a pockmarked wall map of the county. He had them arranged into piles—red, orange and yellow—and searched the red stack for Erin's file.

He compared Roxie's crude drawing to the map of Monroe County on his wall. "Here's New Design. That's kinda funny—didn't you say on the phone you're an architect?"

"Right. Could we get going here?" He watched, practically jumping out of his skin, as Schluetter took his time placing a red pin in the map.

"In recent weeks," the sheriff continued, "there's been more than your average auto traffic on that road. Last week the proprietor of the local gas and food mart gave me a suspicious packet, dropped by a customer who'd said he was fishing in the vicinity. It turned out to be methamphetamine. They could have been in old Hanson's cabin."

"That's what I thought," Patrick said. "What are we waiting for?"

Twenty-Six

When Erin opened her eyes, the sun had sunk lower beyond the treetops. A dark green Mustang approached the shallow ditch along the gravel track and stopped beside her. She sank back to the ground with relief.

"Jimmy, you found me! I must have dozed off," she said.

'Erin, are you alright?" Jimmy bounded from the car, tire iron in hand.

"Ouch!" she cried in pain as she crawled out of the ditch. "Be careful with that thing." She rose to a kneeling position and reached to meet his embrace.

"You're hurt. Did they do this to you? I'll kill 'em." Dropping the tool, Jimmy lifted her off her feet.

"No, no. I twisted my ankle in the earthquake. Thanks for rescuing me."

He held her to him and squeezed her so hard she forgot her pain.

"Oh, Jimmy, I missed you. I was afraid I'd never see you again."

"Me, too. Here, let me lift you into the car."

"Did you have trouble following my directions?" she said, once she was belted into in the passenger seat.

"No, but then I couldn't find you by the road. I've been cruising this drive for the last fifteen minutes. I've got to get you to the hospital."

"Forget it. The foot will be fine. We've got to talk."

"Hey, I just found out you're still alive. Shouldn't I get you home to your dad, so you can get whatever help you need?

"All in good time. Right now let's go someplace was can sort things out. I've got the perfect place in mind. Just get out on the main road and drive."

He retrieved the tire iron, climbed in and followed the gravel lane to the main road, turning west toward St. Louis. They drove in silence until they came to a fork in the road. Erin pointed toward the narrower pavement. "Turn left here."

"You sure? What's going on?"

"Yes, Trust me. I know what I'm doing."

He turned and followed the road. Erin looked straight ahead and not at Jimmy. "You didn't call me for three weeks," she said, with icy precision.

"I thought we agreed we're too young to be making long term commitments," he said. "I've got college ahead of me, and so do you. Then the Army. Who knows when I'll be back in town and how you'll feel about me then?"

"That's what *you* said. *We* didn't agree on anything. It ended in a huge fight, remember?"

Further along, Jimmy followed a curve in the road to the left into Mill Street, which narrowed to a single lane and crossed an old, arched stone bridge. Ahead unfolded the panorama of an old-fashioned town. In the twilight, they meandered into narrow streets bordered by buildings set among woods and creeks.

It was like stumbling on Brigadoon, an ancient village asleep for the past hundred years. On land rising steeply from the left side of the main drag, high stone walls created platforms for one- and two-story wood and stone houses.

"Where is everybody?" Jimmy said. "I don't see a single lighted window at this hour, when people normally would be home making dinner."

"Stop here," she said. "This town seems deserted. Let's just stay here and have our talk."

He pointed the car into a side lane off the main street and parked beneath the canopy of a rare ancient elm. The rising moon lit his clear eyes as he turned to her.

"Don't look at me," she said.

"Huh? Why not?"

"Because I'm too humiliated to say this, but I have to."

"So talk."

"Just turn away," she said.

He faced the windshield, gnawing his fingernails, and watched the rising moon. She sighed and began. "The past four years have been the hardest time of my life, Jimmy, but having you near me made it all bearable—and more than that—worthwhile."

"Hey, me too," he said to the moon.

"Sure, but you're willing to give me up for your career, your college and the Army."

"No, no. It's been wonderful for me, too. I don't want anyone else but you."

"But you're so different from me. You're willing to go away for years and put me in a drawer called 'girlfriend'. You'll only take me out to look at when you need me. I got a taste of what it would be like these past days when I was cut off from you."

"Hey, that wasn't my fault. Your phone mailbox was full. I called your father every day to see if anyone heard anything."

"Even before I was captured, ever since we had our fight, I couldn't stand to be apart from you like that. I had no one to tell about my problems, no one to talk to, no one who could reassure me that everything would be alright. If you were sent overseas I could wait for you. But not if you don't need me as much as I need you."

"I do need you."

"We've drifted apart, Jimmy. Three weeks ago, you were willing to give me up for good. Then things went from bad to worse, when I fell under the control of these...thugs." She turned to him and put her hand on his chest, to show she still needed him—that he was the only one that could cure the ache in her heart. "Can you imagine what it's been like for me out here, without knowing if I'd ever see you again? You called it off so fast, I didn't know what hit me, or why I felt the way I did."

"Do you still want me?"

"I probably could have escaped on my own, you know. I had a reason to call you instead of the cops and drag you over here. But I was confused about who to go to, where to go."

He leaned over her and stared into her eyes. "Are you now?"

"No." She giggled. "I'm pinned in. I can't even move."

He released the custom bucket seatback and lowered her gently.

"There, is that better?"

"Hmmm. Maybe." She stared into his eyes. In the reflected moonbeam they took on a shade of cobalt, piercing, cool and relentless, into her heart. "Why can't you commit to me, even though you're going to be gone?"

"I'm afraid. Leaving you alone like this." He leaned over her, closer. "You're too beautiful. There will be lots of other guys to distract you and take you away from me. I want you for myself. How can I expect that to work when I'm away at college next year?"

"So you think the others will make me laugh the way you do, talk with me for hours about everything under the sun, and attract me when we do ordinary things like raking leaves, when we kiss, even when we fight?" There were so many ways she loved him, she couldn't begin to list them all.

"Well, when you put it that way, maybe not."

"You can trust me to keep you as my Number One, if I can trust you to be yours."

"That would be okay, if we were willing to forgive each other's occasional lapses. I'm not a saint, you know."

"I can forgive you if you can forgive me."

"The military discontinued their 'don't ask, don't tell' policy."

"We just won't discontinue ours," Erin said.

"Deal."

"How do we seal it—write it down?"

"How about like this?' He pressed his lips to hers and kept them there as his firm chest pressed down. He lifted her polo and slid strong hands along her sides, up her back, across her shoulders and down again. Her breath surged with the released tension as her bra fell off. He explored her breasts. An electric warmth suffused her body and tingled to her very toes.

"Oh Jimmy, don't ever leave me." She thought he felt the same way as she, but even if he didn't, she had said what she needed to say. Now if she perished out here in the wilderness, or if he were killed in a war, he would know how she felt.

He raised his body to look in her eyes. "Ooh," he groaned, abruptly pulling back. "Ouch."

Erin giggled again as he freed his back from beneath the shift lever. "This isn't working. Are you hungry?"

"Starved. I ran off straight from school to get you. Never gave a thought to dinner."

Jimmy opened the door and disentangled his long limbs from the cramped space. She sat up and raised her seat back. "Why don't you drive us around this deserted burg and see if there's any place to eat?"

He walked around to the driver's seat, got in and backed into the main street. He drove toward a light in a building in the next block, a corner tavern. He got out, helped Erin to her good foot and supported her weight while she hobbled toward the inn. He swung open a heavy oak door. Inside, they faced a bar. A woman behind it talked with an old timer sitting on the last stool.

"Where are we?" Erin asked.

"Maeystown. Child, you're hurt. My goodness, what brings you here?" said a plump, rosy-cheeked woman in puffed sleeves and a Bavarian pinafore.

"We got caught in the earthquake. It knocked me off my feet."

"Yep, it was a doozy. This old town's seen worse 'n that, though. These old buildin's ain't moving nowhere," the old-timer said.

"Here, sit." The kindly woman pointed to a round table just inside the door by the near end of the bar. "Tell me what happened."

Erin eased into chair, and Jimmy sat opposite. "Where is everyone who lives in this town?" he asked.

"I'm one o' the few. Most of the folks live in surrounding area. They come here to run the tourist shops and to celebrate the festivals, but not many folks live here."

"How strange," Erin remarked.

"Tell me how you got here."

Jimmy opened his mouth to speak, but Erin shook her head to warn him off. "Oh we were out exploring and got lost. We were wondering if you have anything to eat."

"Nothin' fancy. We got very few customers this time o' night. I just have my pot roast for ourselves and my regulars. That be okay?"

"Great, I'm starved," Jimmy managed to utter without contradiction.

"Mmm." The thought of a hot meal made Erin salivate.

"Comin' up."

The old timer at the bar turned to face their table. "You better watch yerselves around here. We're too close to the damned city, that's what. Them beautiful woods used to be full o' deer and beaver. And now look what we got. The scum from the city uses them as bases for their drug trade, meth labs and raids on the town folks. It's a crime, I tell you."

The woman reappeared, her arms loaded with plates. "You'll have to excuse Toby," the innkeeper broke in. "He does run on and on. This is a historic town. Why, we've even got the old mill built by the city's original settler, and a museum."

The woman set their dinners before them—plates of pot roast and potatoes, dark bread and apple butter—and poured Jimmy a cup of strong coffee. Erin asked for milk. They devoured the meal.

Erin's head cleared. She didn't like the way the woman and the old timer were gossiping at the bar, casting significant looks back at her and Jimmy.

When Jimmy had paid the woman for their supper, Erin asked, "Can you give us directions back to St. Louis?"

"Margaret, I gotta go. My dog'll be wond'rin' what happened to me. Can you wrap this young lady's ankle so she can walk to their car?"

"You don't think I survived in the country this long without knowing how, do you?"

"Oh, that's okay," Erin said, anxious to be free of her well-meaning host. "Jimmy will have me home pretty soon."

"Nonsense. You kids just stay here until this good woman fixes you up," Toby said.

"Thanks, Toby. We'll see you tomorrow."

Toby glanced at them and pushed through the heavy door.

Turning to Erin, Margaret said, "Now looky-here, young lady, you relax and finish your apple pie. You just stick out your leg. While I'll fix your ankle so you can walk on it, you can tell me the whole story."

Erin dreaded the pain of getting up, so she didn't put up much of a fight. She extended her right leg. Margaret went into the kitchen and fetched an Ace bandage. She pulled up a chair, put Erin's foot on her lap and executed numerous figure eights around her ankle and the arch of her foot, taping the loose end to Erin's leg. Despite the woman's urging, she remained silent, feigning discomfort at the bandages when she asked questions. Finally she was finished.

"There. Stand up," she said.

Erin squeezed into her moc and cautiously put weight on her foot. She discovered she could walk almost pain-free. "Wow, thanks!"

"Now you'll be strong enough to make it out to your car. You take it slowly and finish your pie. By the way, what's your name?"

Twenty-Seven

"Let's see, to get there, I might have to get back on Highway 3—"

"What are we waiting for?" Patrick said, fed up with the sheriff's methodical pace.

Schluetter's phone rang. "You never know. Could be this." The second hand swept haltingly across the face of the clock on Schluetter's wall. It showed 7:18 p.m.

Patrick pointed to his ear. The sheriff turned on the phone's speaker.

"Sheriff, this is Toby Plunkett. I just been over to Maeystown, havin' my normal supper with Margaret, ya know? These two kids—"

"Right, right, Toby. Look, I'm kinda busy right now. What is it?" He looked at Patrick, shook his head and whispered, "Town busybody."

"They said they wuz just sightseein' and got lost. Her story sounds kinda fishy, and I was just wonderin'—"

"What does she look like?" For once even Schluetter seemed excited. He pressed the speaker button.

"Oh, medium height, her Levi's all muddy, long hair—"

"Come on," Patrick said, impatient, "distinguishing characteristics—her height, weight, hair color, eyes?"

"Oh, I see what ya mean. Her hair is sorta reddish orange, green eyes, kinda skinny—her boyfriend carried her in here."

"Oh my God. It's Erin, and Jimmy. And she's hurt!" Patrick yelled.

"Thanks Toby. She might be our missing person."

"You better hurry. Margaret's tryna stall 'em with her hot apple pie, but they're itchin' to clear out."

The sheriff thanked Toby again and hung up.

Patrick was familiar with the historic village. He'd visited the restored mid-nineteenth century buildings. But he didn't know what to think about Erin. Wild thoughts crossed his mind. He didn't know whom to believe or trust. Was her kidnapping story made up? Could he believe Kelly's account of the phone call? Why was Jimmy with her? And how long had he been there?

At last Schluetter swung into action. He pushed back from his desk, grabbed a scruffy felt cowboy hat and his gun belt from two pegs on the wall and put them on. "Follow me in your car."

In the falling dusk, Sheriff Schluetter took the road headed west toward Maeystown. Patrick was surprised on this deserted route by the headlights of a powerful car in his rearview that overtook them and sped past on the wrong side of the two-lane road, in excess of any posted speed limit. The sheriff took no time out for traffic patrol tonight. At last he was on a mission.

When Patrick and the sheriff pulled open the oak door, they almost stumbled on Erin's outstretched leg. She and Jimmy sat finishing their pie, listening to the innkeeper prattle on about their route home and its dangers.

"Dad! What are you doing here?" she blurted.

"The more relevant question is, what are *you* doing here? And why is Jimmy with you?" Patrick said.

"Escaping. Jimmy's my hero. He saved me from perishing in the woods," she said with a dramatic flourish.

Patrick rushed toward her and lifted her out of her seat in a teary-eyed embrace. "Oh honey, it's so good to see you."

"Yeah, me too. Ouch." Erin lunged, cringed as she stepped too hard on her bound ankle and clung to him to prevent her collapse.

"Erin, you've hurt your foot. I need to get you to a doctor."

"I'm fine. It's just a twisted ankle from the quake. Margaret taped it."

"I hate to break up this joyful reunion, Mr. MacKenna," the sheriff said, "but I'm not quite through with your daughter. She's the only one who can point out the cabin in the woods and confirm where she was held captive. We've got to get over there fast so we'll have the evidence. Then you can both go home."

"Thanks so much for taking care of my daughter, Mrs. Hoffmann. We'll be back soon to enjoy your town and some more of your good cooking. Here's a deposit on that." Patrick laid some cash on the bar.

"T'aint necessary, you know. The young man paid for their food." Nonetheless she rang "No Sale" and put the money in the drawer.

"My parents will be worried." Jimmy said. "Can I go home?"

"Yeah you can go. Just give me your phone number and address for my report."

"Your father phoned me at seven, frantic that you didn't come home for dinner. You'll have to take the Jefferson Barracks Bridge. The earthquake jammed up the others." Patrick said.

"I guess I'd better. No one was at the stupid cabin anyway."

Erin embraced him, the sheriff jotted down Jimmy's information and he left through the heavy oak door.

"Lead the way," the sheriff said to Patrick as they climbed into their cars at the granite curb.

Patrick drove, and Erin guided them along their route to the rutted lane in the woods. The procession turned right and she led the sheriff down the gravel lane to the hunting cabin.

They found the door ajar, its jamb broken out as she'd left it. It was pitch black inside. Patrick stumbled over a chair as he entered. He brushed against the light chain in the center of the room and yanked it.

The main room was a jumble of upended chairs, dishes smashed on the floor and cabinet doors hanging open.

Erin stepped inside. "The earthquake didn't do all this. Jake's been back, and he's fit to be tied."

"Sure looks like someone made a frantic search." Sheriff Schluetter surveyed the destruction.

Erin pointed to the loft. "They made us sleep up there,"

Patrick climbed the single run of open-riser stairs and passed through the hatch to satisfy his curiosity about Erin's attic cell.

While he was poking around upstairs Erin invaded Jake's bedroom. Ignoring the shambles he'd left, she made beeline for the top dresser drawer. She was in luck. There on top of some tee shirts lay her locket, with the broken chain still attached. She grabbed it, stuffed it in her pocket and rejoined the others.

"If we send out the alarm right now, we might catch them," Patrick said.

"What did they do out here during the day?" the sheriff asked.

"They worked in a shack over there." She pointed into the woods. "When the wind blew from that direction it smelled awful. I looked at it today before I left. It was a big, messy chemical lab. Momo said they made meth."

"What did it smell like?"

"Sort of like cat pee."

"Ammonia—that's meth all right," Schluetter said.

Further down the trail, they spotted a glow beyond the trees.

"You two stay back here. Let me go see if I can save any evidence," Schluetter said.

The glow brightened. The shack was on fire. Despite Schluetter's warning, Patrick followed, snapping pictures of the blaze. Erin limped behind her father. As they approached, the flames flared up, licked out of the windows and poured foul smelling black smoke through the open door.

"Look out. Run!" Schluetter shouted.

Before they could turn to obey, the windows blew straight sideways toward the woods. With a roar, the roof blew off. Sheets of metal, pink clouds and white and orange sparks shot up to the blackening sky, showering surrounding oaks and pines and igniting the their dry upper branches.

"Get a move on, you two. Now!" The sheriff, on his cell phone, ran from the growing conflagration, pushing MacKenna. Erin walked stiffly behind them, coughing up the putrid fumes.

Back at the cabin they stood by their cars and watched the inferno rage.

"They aren't coming back here," Erin said.

"The kidnappers could be inside," Schluetter said.

"Jake might have been in the shack, but I told Momo to make a run for it. There's no way you'll find him within ten miles."

Schluetter called Bobbi Romano and reported his success in retrieving Erin. "How can I help you?"

He relayed Bobbi's instructions. "She wants me to sit tight for now and work with the fire department to save what we can. She'll arrive out here with an evidence team at first light to sift through the debris."

"Lemme talk to Bobbi," Patrick said. Schluetter handed him the phone.

"Hey, Bobbi. The sheriff reunited me with Erin." He described her rescue, the meth lab and their failure to find any of the perpetrators.

"That's great news, Patrick. When we got to the club with the SWAT team it was closed. You guys get home and get some rest. I'll need to debrief Erin Monday. I'll need you both at Adam's office by ten."

"Right." Patrick handed the phone back to the sheriff.

"You'd best be getting out of here," Schluetter said. "We'll need the space for fire equipment, and I don't want to put you in any more danger. I'd sure be obliged if you'd send me those photos by e-mail."

"No problem, Sheriff, and thanks for everything."

"I'll take it from here."

Erin looked back into the woods. "That's not just a crime scene. It's an environmental catastrophe."

But with this crisis over, Erin's thoughts drifted back to her other predicament.

TWENTY-EIGHT

Patrick and Erin drove west and turned toward St. Louis. A pumper raced past them, sirens wailing.

"I hope they can keep the forest fire contained," Patrick said, to fill the awkward hush.

"Dad, for once will you let me talk?"

"Of course, honey. I didn't realize I'd been such a terrible father."

"I'm the one who's been horrible. You've always wanted the best for me. Now that I've seen people who don't have a speck of human decency, I understand."

"I've been pretty bad myself. Besides missing the fact that you turned into a woman before my eyes, I forgot that you have grown-up feelings and like to be respected for them. I'll try to make it up to you."

"That'll be great while it lasts, Dad. If I've got to go talk to the FBI on Monday, you won't like what you hear."

"I'll try to control myself. You've been through a lot. I don't want to make it worse."

Patrick drove slowly, back to Highway 3, through Waterloo to reconnect with the outer belt highway. With the downtown bridge jammed, he had to turn southwest toward the Jefferson Barracks Bridge. It took him a while to find the right words.

"I was so concerned," he said. "It's so good to have you back."

"What did you think after I got through to you on the phone?"

"Frankly, I was afraid I'd lost you. Bobbi told me that even teens from good families who have been subjected to trauma are vulnerable to exploitation by sex traffickers, and she quoted me some FBI statistics that blew me away. Hundreds of thousands of young girls, and even boys, are sold into sexual slavery every year. Talk about trauma, both you and I had our share when we lost your mother."

"No kidding. I still feel the effects, but I didn't react the same way as you. You sort of buried it all and tried to put it out of your mind. You even avoided memories of that night by staying away from rivers. I wasn't afraid. I went right back, like you taught me when I fell off that horse. In fact, until the darned earthquake, I was really enjoying the serenity and beauty, where we had so much fun together on our float trips."

"I may have avoided conscious reminders, but they still come back in my nightmares. Then, to make matters worse, Judge Burton Scales, who works with teenagers all the time, explained how prisoners like you and Aliesha react. He said you might side with your captors, the way Patti Hearst did, and fight off efforts to rescue you. They call it Stockholm syndrome. I looked it up: some hostages in a bank robbery in Sweden became attached to the robbers during their six-day ordeal, resisted efforts by police to rescue them and even defended the criminals afterward."

"It was a close call, believe me. I was sympathetic with Roxie, who's really a good person at heart. When she tried to help me, I began to believe her that maybe stripping wouldn't be so bad."

"I can't understand how you could feel that way."

"But earlier today when she followed Solly to the cabin, she leveled with me about what meth does to your life. It made me face reality, just in time."

Missouri had experienced its share of youth kidnappings, including the long captivity of Shawn Hornbeck, a young teen boy, who was found after he'd been missing for four years. The public had never been told the gruesome details of the abuse he was subjected to, and they had imagined the worst. Compared to him, Erin felt very lucky.

"Other than what you say tomorrow to help out law enforcement, you don't have to tell me anything about the ordeal until you're ready," he said.

"Thanks, Dad. I need some time to think." Much as she appreciated her first adult conversation with her father, there were issues, such as her evolving relationship with Jimmy and her "condition," whatever that might be, which she only partially understood and wasn't ready to discuss.

"You were so smart to escape at your first opportunity, before they could get you under their control. We'll get you some counseling."

"Lucky I got out of there before they really hurt me. This scratch on my face was the big tipoff. Jake felt nothing for me at all."

"Thank goodness for that. Hey, Parnell will be glad to see you."

She imagined the high-strung cockapoo's frantic reaction to their reunion.

"And Jimmy called every day."

"Good." She warmed with the memory of their pact. With this ordeal over, her thoughts returned to her next problem. Now she would have to see a doctor and learn what her condition really was. Despite her father's efforts to keep things bright and cheery with small talk, she didn't say much for the rest of the trip home.

When they got there, Parnell jumped on her and wouldn't stop barking. He wrapped his arms—which is how she thought of his front legs—around her *only* legs, practically knocking her over. For once she was glad to be grubby. The dog added his slobber to the filth on her clothes. When she got him calmed down at last, she retired to her room, took off her polo, jeans and underwear, threw them in the washer and set it on Super Wash.

She plunged into the shower and put on fresh underwear, at long last, and a spring jumper. She longed to see her things, lie on her soft bed and listen to her CDs. Her dad called up that he'd let her know when dinner was ready.

She called Aliesha. "Are you alright?"

"Oh, Erin, I was so worried about *you!*" Aliesha told her gleefully how she had practically crippled Jake and dashed due south between buildings to elude him, found a phone and called her uncle in East St. Louis. Within a half-hour she was reunited with her relatives and returned safely home. She and Erin planned a joyful reunion within the next week.

She stared at her prom picture and Jimmy's eyes for a long time. She dug under the pens, calculator, hair ribbon and markers in the desk drawer and reached into the bottom for the hidden drawing. She took it out and admired her body as Jimmy had drawn it with his confident, firm strokes, recalling the way he had touched and caressed her that night. She wondered if she would ever look that fresh and young again. In a way it didn't matter, since that's how Jimmy had seen her, wanted her, taken her and changed her himself. She fell in love with him all over again.

But the drawer seemed neater, with pencils, pens and markers arranged in rows. She never would have done that. The drawing was at the bottom of the pile where she'd left it, but she realized it had been taken out and replaced. *Double dang.* Her dad knew. What else did he know? She would be meeting with Bobbi Monday morning and would have to tell her whole story. The moment of reckoning was approaching fast. She needed support.

"Dad," she shouted down the stairs, "Do we have enough food for Kelly?"

"Sure invite her over." She was like family. Her father was always happy to add a plate.

Twenty minutes later Kelly came into her room, cried and hugged her. Erin swore her to secrecy and gave her a detailed account of everything she did and said, and all that happened in the past thirteen days.

"So now we've come to this." She pulled out the drawing and showed it to her.

"Oh—my—God. It's beautiful. You're beautiful."

She let her study and appreciate it for a while. "I think Dad saw it. He must have found it in the drawer."

"Oh, man."

"Kelly, I'm meeting with the authorities Monday about the murder and kidnapping case, and a lot of this will come out. I'm a grown woman now. I've got to act like one."

"Like, what does that phrase imply, exactly?"

"Like, level with Dad. With you here to give me moral support, maybe I can face him."

"You want to tell him now?"

"I'd like to, but I don't know if I dare."

"Hmm. Let's see how the land lies."

They found him in the kitchen, flattening veal cutlets, chopping onions and garlic and dropping them in a frying pan to sizzle in olive oil. They each occupied a Windsor chair at the kitchen table, facing him.

"Hey, Dad."

"It's so good to see Erin again," Kelly said.

"Dad, there's something I—"

"You bet. It's good to see you two reunited."

Just as he put the meat into the pan to brown and was opening the wine to mix the sauce, the patio door slid open and Meg entered the kitchen.

"You're just in time. Girls, I invited Meg to join us in our celebration."

Dang, dang, DANG.

"Right. Hi, Meg." Erin said, turning pale. Just the person she needed to complete her family heart-to-heart talk—NOT.

Meg hugged her. "Oh, Erin. I was so worried, and your poor father. Are you okay?"

"Yeah, thanks. Kidnapping-wise, I seem to be fine." She had to say something to shut her up, so she conceded one to her, sort of. "It's nice to be back here where people occasionally express loving sentiments."

"I should hope so." Meg said. "Did they hurt you?"

Meg had an old maid quality about her, with her abstract notions of how others must feel, which drove Erin up the wall every time she opened her mouth.

"In that regard, other than a few scratches, they left me alone."

"Well, thank goodness for that. I'd hope you'll still get the chance to grow up more gradually, in a normal, healthy situation."

Sadly, that ship had sailed. How could she even begin explaining it to Meg? The chill in the room put an end to Confession for the time being. There was no shortage of sins, however; she had plenty of others her father would have to hear in Reiner's office on Monday. Why spoil the best meal she'd had in weeks?

"So what's for dinner, Dad?"

Twenty-Nine

Monday morning Patrick drove Erin, rested and refreshed in a tailored blouse, skirt and flats, to the meeting at the Federal Courthouse. The domed high-rise, designed under the latest codes, had weathered the earthquake well. Surrounding structures, though, had dropped plenty of debris. They found the only street parking space not littered with broken glass and took the elevator to Adam Reiner's office.

"Bobbi's in charge of the debriefing, as she often is with female witnesses. I'll be in my office if you need me." Reiner left the conference room and closed the door.

Patrick wished he could leave, too. He sat at a corner of the table, trying to remain inconspicuous. Bobbi had reluctantly allowed him to sit in, so she wouldn't have to repeat intimate and unsavory details he might soon have to hear.

"Erin you were very brave," Bobbi said. "I hope you understand, anything I ask is not to be critical of your actions or decisions, but to find out what happened and who these guys were that abducted you. Can you describe the events of the night you discovered the body?"

She gave her account of that night, told what happened at the cabin, about Jake and her curious relationship with Momo.

"They all work for Solly."

"Solly Abrams?"

"That's him. He…he propositioned me. He wanted to set me up in a nice place."

"Oh, God," her father said from his corner chair.

"He runs several of the clubs in Brooklyn," Bobbi said. "The last time I saw him he was at his Kitty Kat Klub, the afternoon you, uh—"

"Yeah, I know. I was trying out for the new kitty act."

Patrick groaned quietly and slumped deeper in his chair.

"I guess that was you. In your cat outfit!" Bobbi exclaimed. "Erin reddened.

"What got into you, Erin?" Her father shook his head. "After all your upbringing and good schooling."

"It was a nice costume." She looked at her father, her eyes blurring with tears. "Roxie busted her ass to do it for me."

"Erin, watch your mouth."

"Sorry, Dad. It's hard, after so much time with those...bastards."

"Lighten up, Pops," Bobbi cautioned. "Some of us talk that way when we get agitated."

"Besides, I already knew about it," he continued. "I had a little interview with Roxanne Smiley. Your marquee was impressive. I'm sorry. I didn't mean to be critical."

"You're forgiven—the speech thing, anyway. And it's not just the language. Cooperating with Roxie on the strip club act was my only hope for finding Aliesha, after they took her away, and saving my life. I figured playing ball with them would help me avoid a worse job. Besides, you never admit I'm a grown woman, Dad."

"Almost never, anyway, and I *have* noticed," Patrick said.

"And, by the way, when I discovered what stripper stardom would be like, I realized I *did* value my privacy, after all."

"Erin, I still find it hard to think you even considered it."

"I had no choice. I was just trying to squirm out of that situation any way I could, before they threw me to the wolves, or maybe even killed me."

"Pardon me for intruding in this charming family chat," Bobbi said. "You did good, Erin. You outsmarted them before they could get their hooks into you.

"Getting back to the matter at hand, however," Bobbi continued, "tell us more about what happened in the cabin."

Her story matched Aliesha's closely. The only difference was the addition of her take on the situation.

"Aliesha knew from Day One these thugs were bad news. But, still, they were all I had to work with. I was trying to get along with these guys, so they'd treat us better and maybe even let down their guard. I felt just terrible. My mission was to help these kids. Instead I got Aliesha into terrible trouble."

Bobbi turned a page on a legal pad she was filling with copious notes. "That escape must have taken some doing."

"It was a good collaboration between the two of us. Aliesha knew the score, and I knew from Jimmy's Army training how to behave as a prisoner. Then, when Jake discovered me talking to Dad and crushed my phone, he got nasty."

"Tell me more about Momo," Bobbi said.

"His real name is Mick, for Michael, O'Banion. The boys gave him the nickname—it means grandmother.

"He said my hair was pretty. It reminded him of his daughter's. The last time he saw her she was nine years old.

"He was driving the getaway car a bank robbery. In the shootout the other two guys and a guard died. He was the one they caught. He was sent to Menard."

"But why did you make friends with a murderer?" Patrick asked.

"I had no choice. Even if I could have saved myself, I had to stick around to rescue Aliesha. When they separated us I panicked. I had to ask Momo to do favors Jake wouldn't do."

"Erin, you did a good job of getting Momo's sympathy. He was the key to your escape."

"And Roxie. After my tryout she took me into her confidence. She clued me in to what was in store there if I stuck around—nothing good, for sure. And she tipped me off that Aliesha had escaped. After that there was nothing keeping me there. I carried out my plan to escape."

"Good work, Erin," Bobbi said. "This will help us. I'll check out this paroled prisoner O'Banion. Then what?".

"I know I look like those kids who cooperate with their captors and never escape. But it was all part of my plan. I told Momo you could help him, Bobbi, if he'd just help me. He borrowed Jake's cell phone, I called Kelly, and she called Jimmy. You know the rest."

"Why in hell didn't you call Bobbi, or me?"

"I was afraid I'd be killed in a hostage situation. And the rest is personal, Dad."

"Doesn't matter now, Erin," Bobbi said. "The lab is destroyed and we've got you back."

Patrick had to admit he was pleased with his daughter's quick thinking under stress. But he still couldn't get over how close she came to doing a striptease.

"You outwitted them and saved your neck," Bobbi said. "And you made the right call on Aliesha. Luckily she saved herself before you had to do it."

Turning to Patrick, Bobbi asked, "What else did Roxie have to say?"

Patrick was relieved to get off the subject of Erin and back to the murder case. "I asked if she knew where they might have taken Erin. She said there was a chance I could find her at their hideout in East St. Louis."

"What hideout?"

"It's the basement of an old hotel. Do you know how the basements over in East St. Louis were originally the ground floor? It was once the hotel lobby—very elegant."

"Right, and?"

"No sign of Abrams. But there was a guy there who looks like Kojak in a tee shirt. He pulled a gun on me. I talked fast and convinced him Solly Abrams had sent me for the original plans of the building to use in architectural remodeling."

"Hold it just a minute." Bobbi pressed the intercom at the center of the table. "Adam, can you come in here? You may want to hear this."

Momentarily Reiner reentered and sat down. "What's going on?"

"There's a mob hideout in a basement in East St. Louis." Bobbi said.

"Oh? I'd like to hear more about that."

"But first," Bobbi said, turning to Erin, "will you repeat for Adam what you saw in the woods?"

"Jake and Momo buried the body, all right. We saw them do it, so they wouldn't let us go. They work for Sol Abrams."

"There's a missing link here." Adam Reiner wrinkled his brow. "Can you give us some evidence directly connecting Abrams with the murder of Caleb Mitchom?"

"It's obvious that he ordered him taken out," Bobbi said. "Mitchom was trying to clean up the town and close all his clubs."

"Too obvious," Erin said. "Maybe he didn't do it."

"Now look, here, young lady," Reiner said. "You're a victim and a witness, but leave the detective work to the law officers in charge,"

"He'd be the prime suspect," Erin insisted. "He's not that stupid."

"Bobbi will decide that. She has years of training and experience."

"I'm almost eighteen. What do you call my ordeal, if it's not experience?"

"I beg your pardon." Reiner's face reddened. "Don't waste our time with your theories."

"Now look here, Reiner," Patrick said. "She's your key witness. What's your problem with what she says? She's the one who suffered through it. And Erin, you should cool it a bit, too. These law officers are trying to help you."

"Adam, I agree. You need to dial it down here," Bobbi said. "Erin is very observant, she's had direct contact with these guys for a couple of weeks, and she knows how they think. Besides, she has a good head for these matters."

"Hmmph," he huffed, but stayed silent.

"How did you discover this place?" Bobbi continued her inquiry.

"When I asked Roxie where Abrams might take Erin, she led me to their secret headquarters in the basement of an old bank building on Collinsville Avenue, in downtown East St. Louis. Then she left. She said she had to get out of town. I climbed a fence and got in through a window. They run a big operation there—ran, I should say. The building was badly damaged in the earthquake."

"Patrick, you've got to stop taking chances. Leave the cops and robbers stuff to us."

"I was about and turn it over to you when the tremor hit. Who knows? It may be like Pompeii under there, with all the evidence preserved, but now we'll have to dig for it."

"Could you tell what they did in there?" Reiner asked.

"There were lots of computers and screens, for monitoring surveillance cameras, and file drawers stuffed with real estate records."

"It could be how the boys from Chicago check up on their East St. Louis operations, like Abrams' rackets," Bobbi said. "I need to get over there and inspect those files."

"It may not be safe to enter until Ed Mossbach and his crew inspect it to make sure. If there's an aftershock you'll get hurt, or even killed."

"Worse luck," Reiner said. "Just when we're getting somewhere, we've got a public catastrophe on our hands. Now what happened to your captors—what did you call them?"

"Momo and Jake," Erin said

"One of them is dead. We don't know which one. The environmental investigators found a partially burned body in the ruins of the shack." Bobbi looked at Erin. "I didn't bring it up earlier. I didn't want to upset you. Now that we have one real name, we may at least be able to identify the other guy."

"Momo escaped," Erin said, "the other's probably Jake. If he's the one on the loose, I'm still in trouble."

"Even if both of them are out of circulation," Bobbi said. "You won't be safe until Solly Abrams is put away for good."

Thirty

That night Erin holed up in her room and arranged her schoolbooks. She opened her sociology text to the chapter on Societal Influences on Criminal Behavior. What drivel!

She picked up her new cell phone—a special gift her father bought her on the way home from the interview with Bobbi and Reiner—and called Kelly.

"How'd it go?" Kelly wanted to know.

"I got busted."

"Arrested?"

"No, worse. I don't have many secrets from my father anymore. But I have to say he's been pretty cool about it. He's actually smarter than before. It's amazing how much he learned in a couple of weeks."

"Parents can sometimes surprise you like that."

"This sociology book is a hoot."

"Compared with what you went through, you could probably write a better one."

"It would be more fun to read, anyway. Now I know what they mean by 'deviant behavior.' I could give them a few examples."

"Are you ready to get back into the routine and attend classes?"

"I feel like parts of my brain have shut down. I used to be an ace at these Identities. You know, where you have to match the two sides of the equation by substitutions? Now they're swimming before my eyes."

"I'll help you with that. What about the rest?"

"I gave up when I got to my English lit and the first lines of Chaucer's *Canterbury Tales*—get this: 'Whan that Auerylle with his shoures soote/ The droghte of March / Hath perced to the roote'— I might as well have tried to read Chinese. But biology's okay. I have a new, very real interest in and the workings of my own body."

"No kidding."

"Dad's letting me stay home until next week, for the legal stuff, some counseling, and to catch up. I've got to buckle down, finish the school year and pray that none of the catty girls in our class will guess my condition—if that is my condition. It's already April. If this is really true, I'll be three months along by graduation in May. I figure the baby wouldn't be due until December."

"You might just pull it off. But meanwhile you need an OB. Do you have one?"

"No. Dad never took me—not that I blame him. He doesn't know any."

"I'd ask you to see mine, but then we'd have tell my parents, which means they'd tell your dad. How about asking Meg?"

"Oh, right. She's the last person I'd ask."

"Look Erin, she's practically part of your family. She's dying to do something motherly for you."

"I know. It's her judgmental manner I can't stand. Couldn't she at least be kind about it?"

"Didn't you say your father will be traveling the week after next and that she's staying with you?"

"Unfortunately. I told Dad I don't need a baby-sitter."

"Maybe that would be a good opportunity to ask her. You can pick your moment."

"She'll be here, all right. I may even be glad to get back to school. Compared to what I hear about the 'big house,' I guess I'll have to stop saying saying St. Agnes Academy is like a prison movie."

"You'll do fine. I'll take care of Moira and her twin sister."

"They're the least of my problems. Kelly, what am I gonna do?"

"If you *are* pregnant," she said, "here's what they'd say at that clinic. You have three options. You can get an abortion before it's too late, put the baby up for adoption, or keep it and devote your life to motherhood, abandoning all hope of a good education, a career and a self-sufficient life."

"I won't do the first, and I can't bear to do the second. The baby would be mine and Jimmy's, conceived in love. I'll bet he'd agree with me if he knew—if I dare tell him."

"How can you *not* tell him?" Kelly, the practical one, continued with her cold analysis of the situation.

"I'm so torn. By breaking the news I wouldn't just be making a decision for myself, I would be obligating him."

"He helped create the problem. Why shouldn't he be part of the solution?"

"I don't know if I have the right to ruin his life as well as my own. I really want the third option—to marry Jimmy so we could raise our child together. And maybe Jimmy does, too, if we could find a way."

"Lot of luck with that one," Kelly said. "Besides, I'm not sure that would be such a good idea."

"What do you mean? It's my dream!"

"I-I don't know how to say this, so I'll just blurt it out. This is all over school. And you'll hear it soon enough. I don't think you can trust him."

"Not trust Jimmy? Why?"

"You know how Mrs. Sharpe is always gone on weekends when her husband is out of town on business?"

"'Fraid, I do." She knew about her father's affair with Liza Sharpe.

"The twins had a big party last weekend at their house. I went because Jimmy told me his friend Eddie Peabody would be there. He's so cute, and I think he kinda likes me."

"How did it work out?"

"Oh, great—but that's not the point. Eddie stayed later than I did, because he came with Jimmy. Lots of them were smoking pot, so I went home early. I asked him what time he got home, and he said two a.m., because he had to wait until Jimmy came out of the bedroom with one of the Sharpe twins."

"He went to bed with her?"

"All Jimmy told Eddie was that they were smoking together. Jimmy said he didn't even want to tell him that, because I'd tell you."

"The pot is bad enough. If he made love with Myrna, I really *am* screwed."

THIRTY-ONE

After lunch the next day, Patrick set out to show Gary Archer his new concept for expanding Deerpath City Hall. Although Erin wasn't scheduled to be back in school until the following week, Tuesday was the school's annual Take Your Daughter to Work Day. After being deprived of her for so long and concerned about her safety, he jumped at any excuse to keep her near him. With a stern warning not to rouse the city administrator's quick temper, he brought her along. Maybe her feminine outlook would soften Archer up. Maybe for once he'd worry about something other than his own problems.

On Archer's battered wooden desk sat a teakwood box, pristine by contrast. "What in there?" Patrick asked.

"That's a restored 1911 Colt .45 caliber pistol, a souvenir from Vietnam—stainless steel body and polished a walnut stock. Got it in Saigon."

"Aren't you afraid to have it around?" Patrick said.

"Naw. It has a safety and I have a permit. I'd be afraid to work in this crazy job without it. You should see some of the kooks who come in here and complain."

"I believe it," Patrick said.

"So what's this big solution you couldn't wait to show me?"

Patrick took a drawing out of his portfolio case and propped it on an easel. "See, the new fire bay is located over here, next to the old ones, with the dormitory above it."

"Where's the fire pole?" Erin asked.

"Right here." Patrick pointed on the plan to a circular hole in the dormitory floor with a pole in the center. "Beside the old city offices will be a new office wing for the police department, with the emergency operations center in the basement directly under it. Here's a new stairwell with an elevator and lobby, between the old and the new sections."

He set another display board in front of the first one. "On the new third floor, you arrive here and go down the hall right into your office, with the department heads in offices along this wall. The mayor is at the opposite corner of the building, over here in front with his staff."

"Still too close for my taste," Archer said.

"Don't you get along with the mayor?" Erin asked.

"You listen here, girl. I said you could sit in for the benefit of your education—not so you could sharpshoot me. You got that?"

"Yes, Mr. Archer."

Patrick glared at her.

"I was just thinking that good communication between the two of you would be more efficient for the city," she said.

"I'll decide that," Archer snapped.

"That's not how it works, Erin. Gary works with his staff every day." Patrick jumped in to avoid further friction. "In fact, the offices will be further apart than they are right now."

"Where are we supposed to work while construction is going on?" Archer asked.

"That's the beauty of this design," he said. "You can stay right where you are until the new section is finished."

"Right, if I don't die of a splitting headache. This isn't going to be easy. What about earthquake resistance for the old and the new parts of the building?"

"The new section will be designed to meet today's earthquake resistance standards. The added upper floor straddles the old building with columns that go right down to new foundations. These columns also connect to walls and brace the existing building. Ed Mossbach has worked out an ingenious structural design."

"Where is Ed today?"

"With these latest tremors, I had to send him over to Illinois to look at some pretty critical earthquake damage."

"Hmmph." Arched looked displeased. "What about the cost for

this Taj Mahal?"

"That's the best part. You remember, when we were planning to build a whole new fire station on the other site, how we were running a million higher than your two and half million dollar budget? We can build this whole project now on this site for just under three million."

"Right. And where am I gonna get the extra half-million dollars?" Archer seemed stingy, not just with the city's money, but with his praise, even though her father had just saved the project.

"Gary, we've talked about this before. Now we're down to a small enough overrun that you'll be able to borrow the difference, with much smaller loan payments."

"Who knows if anybody's going to like this harebrained scheme? Let me keep these drawings, and I'll let you know how I do with the mayor and alderman."

"Sure, no problem. I'll even come to your next council meeting and explain it myself. Then I'll be available to answer any questions."

Erin stared at the pistol case and squirmed in her chair.

"Fine, fine. Get outta here and let me think." He reached in his lower right desk drawer and pulled out a bottle of scotch and a short glass and looked up. "On second thought, you want a drink?"

"Hmm. This afternoon's shot, anyway. Sure."

Archer glanced at Erin. "Not you. Why don't you go down the hall and talk to our receptionist, Cora. She'll tell you about her new litter of puppies."

"Look, Mr. Archer," she retorted, "since the kidnapping, I stick with my dad. And don't treat me like a child."

"I'll decide how I treat you."

Erin's face registered disdain and she twirled a strand of hair in her fingers, squirming in her chair.

"Stop fidgeting!" Patrick said aside to his daughter.

She reached for the teakwood case on the desk and lifted the lid to reveal the shiny pistol, the kind with bullets in the handle, sparkling in its blue velour cradle. Shocked, she drew back. The lid clattered backward and hit the desktop with a sharp crack.

"Freeze!" Archer grabbed the gun, stood and pointed it at her.

Erin dropped to the floor beneath the desk.

Patrick leapt and grabbed the muzzle, twisting it toward the wall until Archer let go.

"Gary, what was that?"

A shudder starting at the man's shoulders passed through his torso and down to his legs. He collapsed in his chair.

"Nothing. Just a touch of battle fatigue. I've been jumpy ever since the war."

"Looked like something to me," Erin said, scrambling to a standing position. "Good thing I got jumpy too—had to, with those armed creeps around me all the time."

"Aw, kid, forget it." Here, you want a drink, too?"

"Nope, don't drink."

"Then beat it."

"Wait, Gary," Patrick said. "I feel responsible for Erin. She's the only family I've got left, and I promised to let her shadow me today. She's too young to drink, but she's perfectly capable of joining in adult conversation."

"You're the doctor, Patrick." He let out one of his exasperated sighs, took another glass from the drawer and poured Patrick three fingers.

Patrick sipped, breathed easier and sat back in his chair. Informal chat with his clients often relaxed them and gave him better insight into their personalities. "What was it like over there in 'Nam?" Patrick asked.

Archer took a swallow and leaned back in his creaky swivel chair. "Boring, and tense at the same time. Enough to drive you crazy."

"I'll bet."

"You been in the military?"

"Oh, not much. When I was in reserves, it was a peacetime army, all spit and polish, a lot of saber-rattling going on. My reserve unit never got called up. You guys did the hard stuff."

"Yes, and no. For me, inside the main camp in the rear, lots of boredom. Mostly chicken shit inspections, reports, guard duty—until the company got short-handed and we had to fill in as replacements. We went on maneuvers and convoys to support field units... hard to get sleep, and..." His voice trailed off, and his eyes went glassy. He took another gulp.

"One day on patrol we went into the forward area to hunt for VC in a village."

"V. C.?" Erin asked.

"Viet Cong. Usually we rounded up the villagers in a central area and posted guard over them, so we knew what they were doing while we inspected the hootches. Half of our company secured the perimeter, so nobody could go in or come out. It was our squad's turn to go in and inspect. Behind a family hootch, I found a little girl who was coaxing a dog to come in. I called the dog to get it to come with me to safety while our troops were inside, 'Here, boy.' He didn't respond. She looked at me as if to say, 'Try this,' and called, 'coo coo coo coo coo.' The dog trotted over to her. I tried it, the dog came to me. The little girl and I exchanged a smile. She reminded me of my daughter, Ruthie, back home. She went inside with her mother and an old man.— must've been her grandfather. Just then—" He choked a sob.

"What, Gary?" Patrick leaned forward.

"She knocked over a chair and made a noise. One of our men, who was looking for hidden VC inside, heard it and fired off a round. She…fell…instantly, shot through the heart. Then he killed the old man and her mother…and some children."

"Oh, that's awful!" Erin said.

"Poor dog, too. No mistress," Patrick added.

"Can't erase the look in the little girl's black eyes. She didn't understand. I lie awake nights. Those eyes still haunt me."

"Turns out, when we returned the villagers to their hootches, nobody else came back to the little girl's place. He'd wiped out a family. We all felt terrible. For an instant, I thought better them than me.

"Anyway, it was payback time. We'd been out too long, numbed by all our troop losses, so we got even. That's how we dealt with the loss of our buddies and innocent civilians out there. Best I could do was take the dog and care for it in our area supply room at the rear."

Patrick was glad he stayed to listen. At least he understood Archer better. Years later the man was still paying for those suppressed feelings.

Thirty-Two

Great news! Momo had called Bobbi and wanted to talk.

Late the next morning Patrick drove Erin to the East Side. Bobbi had agreed to meet Momo at an old roadhouse in Centerville, frequented mainly by the locals, where his pursuers were unlikely to find him. If there were any clues to be had about Abrams's whereabouts, Momo was one of the few they could ask. Besides, with the prospect of return to prison hanging over his head, he was motivated.

They found Bobbi at a table in the dimly lit bar.

"Hey, Patrick. Erin, good to see you. Playing hooky today?"

"This is my week off to recover, but they're letting all the seniors off for a day anyway to shadow our dads at work. It's a great chance for me to help you solve the case."

"Makes sense to me."

Patrick noted how easily Bobbi accepted his daughter on the team.

They took seats opposite her at a four-top, facing away from the bar.

"These birds are slippery," Bobbi said. "Abrams has vanished, but I got some ideas from talking to my training classmate Radi in Chicago." She peered over his shoulder.

They looked behind them to follow Bobbi's gaze, which focused between Patrick and Erin to the back of a man seated at the bar.

"Is that Momo?"

Erin recognized a barrel-chested man in a tee shirt and jeans hunched over a draft beer. She ran over and embraced him. "Momo, I'm so glad you made it out alive." She led him back to the table. He sat in the vacant chair and set down his beer.

"Hey, Momo," Bobbi said jauntily. "Or should I say Mick? Glad to see you made it."

"Where's Bobby?" he said to Patrick. "The woman I talked to said we could meet up with him."

"Yeah, I get that all the time." Bobbi displayed her badge.

"That's better. I hate those tough guy cops anyway. But what is this, am I busted?"

"Maybe not for long, Mick," Bobbi said, "if you'll cooperate."

"It's so good to see you, Erin. I was more worried about you than savin' my poor ass. Who's this?"

"Name's MacKenna," Patrick said, "Erin's father. I think I owe her decent treatment to you. Except for a sprained ankle she got in the earthquake, she made it home almost unharmed."

Momo flashed an 'aw, shucks' grin. "Sorry about that scratch from Jake. I had no control over him."

"So, Mick," Bobbi continued, "tell me what happened at the cabin. The day you left."

"I was gone by that time. I didn't work in the lab, except to deliver supplies. My job was as driver, and to guard Erin, so she and Aliesha didn't get away, and so no one else could get to them."

"Why were you holding them prisoner?" she asked.

"Solly and Vince had plans for 'em and besides, they saw us—" Realizing too late where this was heading, Momo interrupted himself in mid-sentence.

"Right, Erin and Aliesha saw you burying Caleb Mitchom's body," Bobbi said. "What were you doing the day she escaped?"

"I had just unpacked some stuff and put it on shelves in there for Vince and headed back to watch Erin."

"What kind of stuff?"

"Boxes of chemicals, powders, test tubes. Jake used all that stuff and making his junk."

"Then what did you do?"

"He told me I was done, so I went back into the cabin. That's when Erin asked me to borrow Jake's phone and a map and said I should escape. I beat it out of there and managed to hitch a ride up here."

"The shack exploded and practically started a forest fire," Bobbi said.

"Oh man, Jake must have been in a hurry and made a huge mistake."

"Several, in fact. We can't identify who got blown up in there, but since it wasn't you, it was probably your buddy. What was his name?"

"Jake Gibbon. With him gone, my problems would be over, but—"

"I know, Mick. I checked with the authorities at Menard prison. You're in violation of your parole."

"Yeah. Now what?"

"Just work with us, Mick. At the very least you're an accessory to Erin's kidnapping and maybe the murder of Caleb Mitchom. I'll talk to the State's Attorney myself and get you the best deal I can."

"I don't know how he was killed. Jake just told me to haul and dig."

"If that turns out to be true, it's good news for you."

"I'll do anything to avoid going back to that crib. What do you need?"

"Solly Abrams has disappeared. Any idea where he went?"

"Boy, Jake would be glad to hear that. Things were getting pretty hot. He was way behind—not producing fast enough, and Solly wasn't providing the shipments he'd promised to the big boys. Even if Solly ran away, he couldn't hide from them for long."

"Where would he go?"

"Don't know. Maybe he'd go up to Chicago to protect his interests with the bosses."

"That figures," Bobbi said. "Where would he go up there?"

"He used to run a club on the west side, in old Cicero."

"That was once Al Capone's territory," Patrick said, "but it's Hispanic these days."

"Billie owns it now. She's an old friend of mine," Momo said. "Maybe she'll know if he's around."

"I'll call our agent up there," Bobbi said. "Radi can ask around."

"Wait. I could call her if I had a phone. I still know the number."

Bobbi looked around the mostly vacant bar and held out her cell phone. "No time like the present."

Momo took it and punched in a number. Before long he was deep in conversation. Bobbi grabbed her cup, got up and beckoned Patrick and Erin to follow her over to the bar. "Let's give him some breathing room."

"Bobbi, I'm in deep trouble," Erin said. "We've got to find Solly."

"Soon we will, Erin. For this guy," she nodded toward Momo, "it's sing or Sing-Sing, if you get my drift."

Momo got up and returned the cell phone to Bobbi. "Solly came into Billie's bar last week. She thinks he delivered a load in person and is meeting with some of the local bosses. It's called Billie's Place, on Cicero Avenue." He wrote down the address of the bar for them on a cocktail napkin.

"Meanwhile, Mick, I'm sorry, I'll have to put you on ice for a while. Best I can say is it's three squares a day and you'll be out of danger from the big-city goons. "

"But you said I'm not in trouble."

"I'll tell them to go extra easy on you. If you'll agree to be a witness in Abrams's trial, maybe I can get you protective custody."

She called for backup.

Thirty-Three

When Erin came down for breakfast Wednesday, her father was poring over a set of tattered blueprints.

"What're you doing?" she asked.

"Looking over these remodeling plans for that old building in East St. Louis. They were made when the ground floor was converted from a bank lobby to an office. These show the retaining walls and entrances they added when they filled all the ground with dirt to raise the downtown area out of the floods."

She looked over his shoulder at the faded blueprint, etched with white lines showing walls, stairways and windows. Even the wrinkles formed a web of white tracery, making the drawing hard to read.

"What does the diagonal shading mean?" she asked. Most of the window and door openings were hatched through with diagonal white lines.

"That's where they filled in the old windows and doors with brick masonry, to keep out the new earth fill. But look what I discovered over here."

He pointed to a corner of the sheet, where two double lines led from a side door to an exit door some distance away.

"This is a hidden passage under Collinsville Avenue. What looks like a closet door really leads from the lower level space out to a remote exit. "It was built when the downtown was filled in, so the tunnel would go under the new elevated street."

"Wow," she said. "A secret escape route!"

"At the time they raised the level of downtown, it was designed as a loading dock to bring supplies into the building. Back in the twenties, when the heat was on, Chicago gangsters needed hidden locations for their operations, where they could chill for a while. They couldn't still need them today, unless..." His words trailed off and he seemed lost in thought.

"What are you thinking, Dad?"

"Erin, can you fix your own meals and catch up on your studies today? I've got to explore a bit."

"Where? Over there? Dad, can I come with you?"

"Absolutely not—it's too dangerous."

"You think I can't handle danger? It's my neck too until we catch those guys."

"Hmm, maybe you'd be safer with me."

"At least I wouldn't be home alone all day by myself, looking over my shoulder for trouble."

"Okay, put on your hiking boots and your Levi's and let's go." He unlocked his bottom desk drawer, took his police-style Glock 9 pistol from its case and stuck it in his pocket.

Erin returned moments later in her freshly laundered jeans, "I wore my Levi jacket just in case. I spent too many chilly days without enough clothes."

Her father handed her a construction hard hat, showed her how to adjust the webbing to fit her head and led the way out the front door toward the driveway. She hopped into his car, proud of her first assignment on the case.

The interstate bridge had been cleared of debris and opened again, and the light mid-morning traffic flowed at reasonable speed over the pavement, now cracked and bumpy after its violent shaking. They parked across Collinsville Avenue from the old bank building. The structure looked beaten up, with a broken cornice, missing face materials and broken windows, like a street kid who'd just been in a fight. Instead of turning to cross, Patrick looked over a railing behind them toward a parking lot a story below, occupying the rear half of the block.

Patrick went down a flight of stairs from the sidewalk's railed overlook to the parking area, strewn with weeds poking through cracked pavement and a few cars. Erin followed until they found a loading dock directly beneath the spot where they had just been standing. Next to the truck docks and up six steps was a rusted man-door, which appeared to be cracked open. Patrick pushed inward and it swung wide. Beside an interior receiving area for the loading dock, a long tunnel led under the street. He pulled a flashlight out of his pocket and probed with the beam. Scurrying sounds indicated they weren't alone.

"Rats!" Erin squealed. She smelled stale urine and rotting garbage.

"That's why you need the Levi's and boots."

He urged her forward into the space illuminated by the beam. She shivered in the chilly underground passage and fastened her jacket, thankful for its protective long sleeves. Stumbling over chunks of crumbled concrete, slipping on wet spots from a stream of water underfoot and bumping into stacks of empty crates, they made their way to the end of the passage, followed its right turn and confronted a battered metal door. Her father aimed the torch at the knob. She saw a single keyhole of the type requiring a skeleton key.

"Ha!" Erin shouted. Her voice echoed down the tunnel and took a couple of seconds to die out. She reached into her jeans pocket for the hated skeleton key, a souvenir of her victorious escape. Since she'd forgotten to empty her pockets before tossing the pants in the washer. Here it was, clean and shiny. Patrick held the light and she tried the key. After a couple of wiggles in the balky lock, the bolt yielded. Her father pulled out his Glock 9 and led them inside.

"What *was* this?" she asked, as they picked a path though shards of broken terra cotta and looked up at steel beams and the concrete slab of the floor above.

"Last week, with the power on, I saw a beautifully preserved bank lobby from the 1920s, with Gothic arches and vaults. Here you can see the remains of one, springing from this corner." He pointed to a steel column still partially clad in white terra cotta colonettes, broken off about two feet above the springing line of an elegant arched rib-vault at the column.

"What a shame," she said, "gone forever." The catacomb had the eerie silence of a tomb. The faint odor of skunk wafted into her nostrils, getting stronger as they progressed through the space. "Hey, I smell something awful. It seems familiar."

"'Fraid so." Patrick said, as he panned his flashlight back and forth, scanning the floor. "Oh, man, there he is." He pointed the beam toward a pile of rubble.

Two huge legs projected from the debris where a vault had collapsed. One arm stuck out from a side of the pile. The smell was overpowering, and she gagged. She now recalled where she had encountered the scent—the burial site in the woods.

"Geez," Erin said. "Not again. Gross."

"You wanted to come along." Patrick sighed, knelt by the body and pushed rubble from the victim's head. He was bald, with a neck as thick as his brawny thigh. "It's Kojak. Still heading for this door. That's where he was going when I scrambled out of there, not a minute too soon." He pointed toward the still open window.

"I almost lost you." She knelt down and hugged her father's shoulders. "This is all too depressing."

Patrick held up his handkerchief. "I'll tie this over your nose and mouth—it'll help with the smell. He secured the mask.

"We'd better stick together from now on," he said. "It'll be safer."

Her eyes watered, maybe from the stink, but maybe not. She looked back at the body. "Who is he?"

"He must have been Abrams' man, because he lowered his gun when I said I was working with him."

Patrick called Bobbi Romano's cell phone, hoping service had been restored. Soon it rang and was answered. "Bobbi we're over in East St. Louis—in the gangster's hideout. We have situation here. A body."

He listened to her questions. "Can't see his face, but it think it's that Kojak guy I met the other day. You need to get over here, Bobbi." Patrick ended the connection.

"She coming?"

"She's on her way."

Twenty minutes later, Bobbi appeared at the basement door. Erin let her in.

"This is how we found it," Patrick said. "Except to remove some rubble from his body, we haven't touched a thing."

"Look at this mess."

"The earthquake did that." He waved at the shambles.

"Bobbi, look over there." Erin pointed toward the doorway. "I'm scared."

"Whew." She whistled as she sniffed. "He's gettin' ripe. When did you last see him?"

"Last week," Patrick said. "He ran in the wrong direction. You know this guy?"

"That's German Herman," Bobbi said.

"You serious?"

"That's what they called him. He worked for Abrams. Solly runs the rackets on the East Side, but he's not the big fish. He reports to Chicago. Those boys are mean. When they're in town they must work from here. So it remains to find Solly and dig out the evidence—literally."

"Now that you're on the case," Patrick said, "I'd feel better if we all got out of here until the structural engineers finish analyzing the damage. I escaped once, and there might be an aftershock. We'd better not push our luck."

"We might have to take our chances on that," Bobbi said. "I'm sure they'd appreciate it if we removed this rotting corpse first. I'll get an evidence team out here right away. We also need to find Sol Abrams."

"Is this hideout you were talking about?" Bobbi asked. "We've been so busy with problems created by this disaster, we haven't have a chance to check out your lead."

"Yeah. Roxie led me here."

"She might want to know about her associate."

"Wait." Erin reached into her right jeans pocket and retrieved a freshly laundered piece of paper with Roxie's number on it. "She said she was leaving town, but I have her cell number."

She whipped out her new Smartphone and tapped in the number. On the fourth ring, she heard, "Hullo?"

"Roxie, where are you?"

"Put it on speaker." Bobbi showed her how.

"Sholly, I'm waitin' for you. Sh'about time you called!"

"No, Roxie, this is Erin."

"Solly, I miss you. When are you coming? I need y—"

"Where are you?"

"At our pad. Oh, please, Solly, come quick. I don't have much ti—"

They heard a clunk on the other end of the line and then silence. "Roxie? Roxie! E-eeeee!" Erin let out a blood-curdling scream and stood, frozen, pointing into the phone.

"She must have passed out," Patrick said.

Bobbi recovered first. "Let's move it, folks."

They ran to their cars and Bobbi led them through the streets to Illinois Route 3 and the warehouse in Brooklyn. Bobbi jumped from her car. She leapt up the three metal steps, burst open the door, dashed through the office and led them to the velour-draped bedroom, Erin and Patrick right behind her.

"Roxie. No. No. NO!" Erin wailed. She took Roxie in her arms and held her tight.

Bobbi knelt by the satin-covered bed and felt Roxie's wrist. "Weak pulse. Crap, now it's stopped." She pried Erin loose, pounded the woman's chest and applied her CPR training. She ran for her car trunk, retrieved an oxygen tank and mask and continued her attempts at resuscitation. After twenty tense minutes of frenzied efforts, she felt her pulse again. "Nothing. Dammit all, too late."

They stood in reverent silence. Bobbi inspected the needle marks on her arm. Patrick shook his head. Erin viewed Roxie's perfect form, her blond hair splayed across a blue satin pillow and her flawless features, finally at peace.

"I'll call this in, too," Bobbi said. "Looks like the forensics crew will be doin' overtime."

"She helped me—drew me a map to the cabin where they held Erin," Patrick said.

"She saved my life," Erin said. "She warned me of the danger I was in. Losing Solly must have been the last straw. She died of a broken heart."

Bobbi inspected the vials on her night table and a used syringe. "Hate to disillusion you, but that's not the whole story. Shame she got mixed up with these creeps."

Thirty-Four

After her week of meeting with authorities, sifting through crime scenes with Patrick and counseling, Erin was eager to get back to school. But on Monday, time to start classes again, she dreaded having to drive with her mending ankle. While she was still in the shower her father knocked on the bathroom door and called her to the phone. "It's Jimmy."

Swaddled and turbaned in terry cloth, she hobbled to the phone.

"I figured you might need some help getting to school today. How are you feeling?"

"Much better, thank you," she lied, her hair dripping with soap and burning her eyes.

"Can I drive you to school?"

"Oh, Jimmy, how thoughtful. I was freaked about driving today. Anyway, there's no way I'm playing field hockey, or even staying late to watch practice."

"Be ready at seven-forty-five. I'll take you and bring you home."

"See you soon."

Maybe their heart-to-heart talk in Maeystown had done some good.

Her father left for the office at seven-thirty. She wolfed down the tiny powdered sugar doughnuts, a favorite treat her father had bought to celebrate her homecoming.

She listened nervously for Jimmy's honk in the driveway, doing a slow burn over what she'd just learned about him and one of the Sharpe twins at their party.

Arriving five minutes early, he appeared at the front door. "Hello, Jimmy," she said, in a restrained, distant tone.

"Why the chilly reception?"

"Oh, no reason. I want to thank you for your consideration in arranging to pick me up."

"You look great this morning—rested, even radiant."

She'd heard the early months of pregnancy described in just those terms.

He helped her into the passenger seat of his '66 Mustang, British racing green. Over the past year he and a friend had installed a rebuilt eight-cylinder 350 cc engine and painstakingly restored it to cream puff condition.

"Tell me what happened. I want to hear every detail."

"First, I believe we need to talk. I just found out about Moira and Myrna's party."

"Oh that. Nothing much to tell. Just a lot of kids making idiots of themselves."

"Including you?"

"Naw. Those girls were just trying to act big, smoking pot and all."

"You know how I feel about drug use. When were you going to tell me you were experimenting with one of the Sharpe sisters in her bedroom?"

"What? Who told you that?"

"Does it matter? Well, were you?"

"Hey, what about our 'Don't ask, don't tell' policy?"

"Sure, when you're thousands of miles away, at college or off to war. Did you really smoke pot with her?"

"Sure, everybody was doing it."

"Do you have any idea what drugs can do?"

"Oh, my brother taught me all about pot. It's no big deal. That's all we did."

"You say pot isn't addictive, but soon it won't be enough, and some girl will get you to try crack and then heroin. As soon as you do that you're hooked for life—a short one at that."

Jimmy said nothing.

"Do you know which one of the twins you slept with?"

"Slept with? Who said anything like that?"

"Kelly. While you were still conscious, you might recall she was at the party."

"I guess, technically, I slept in Moira's bed while she was there. I was too stoned to do anything, and beside I didn't want to. I told you, I won't have anything to do with her."

"You sure weren't acting like it. If it was really Moira, you're off the hook. I'm pretty sure she's gay."

"She wasn't coming on to me. She was just digging for dirt about us. I wouldn't give her the satisfaction. And besides, I fell asleep. When she woke me up she said it was time to go. I know it was Moira, because she has a birthmark on her back."

"You saw her bare back? That's hardly reassuring."

"Honest, it was just the cut of her dress. Erin. I love you. I smoked with her because I was feeling sorry for myself over our breakup, and sad for you."

She laughed. "I guess you're telling the truth. About Moira, anyway."

"I don't blame you for being jealous. We were both under tremendous stress. Now we don't have to be—not as much anyway."

"Jimmy, we'll have to talk about this dope thing. You've got to give it up, cold. I wouldn't want you so stoned you'd rather sleep than make love to me."

"With you back, I can do anything." They came to a stoplight. He looked over at her and smiled. "I'm glad we cleared that up. Now tell me more about your ordeal."

She told him things they hadn't discussed in their hasty meeting in Maeystown, about discovering Caleb Mitchom's body, her capture, Vince, Jake, Momo and Roxie. She blushed when she told him about her audition—relishing every detail, even Solly's proposition, proud of her new sense of womanhood—and her daredevil escape in the nick of time.

"Wow, you really did all that? Who is this Solly Abrams, anyway? I could kill him."

"Why thank you, my noble knight." She explained Solly's role in the East St. Louis rackets. "I'd sic you on him, but he's missing. His girlfriend Roxie died—that's what drugs will do to you. He ditched her. That bastard, I'm ready to kill him myself."

He pulled to the curb in front of her school and regarded her with arched eyebrows. "You've certainly gained a new command of the profane."

"You've noticed!" She smiled and kissed him lightly on the cheek, grabbed her backpack and alighted.

"See you here at four."

"Thank you, James," she said, loud enough to be heard by the Sharpe twins, who happened at that moment to be approaching the gothic archway of the school's main door.

Erin attended classes with a new sense of purpose. During her imprisonment she'd often thought how easy it was to show up in class, do homework and excel on tests, compared with navigating the shark-infested waters of the real world. For once she took pleasure in the class discussions. But when the time came for gym class her anxiety rose.

She was determined to tough it out. Her doctor said the stress-free water exercise would limber up her sprained ankle and hasten its recovery. She dashed through the halls, paid fleeting attention to the greetings of Barb, Kelly and other friends and arrived at the locker room early. She found a seldom-used corner in a dead-end row of lockers, unwound her bandage and changed. Despite the rules, she would shower in her one-piece swimsuit.

Alone in the shower room, she turned her face toward the warm spray, feeling it caress her closed eyelids as the sizzling shower head soothed her ears. She heard a sputtering sound on the opposite wall. When she turned around to rinse, Moira Sharpe, her long-limbs, pert breasts and sculpted hips, like Venus rising from the mist, was staring at her.

"I see your ankle is all black and blue. They sure treated you rough. What else did they do to you?"

"The ankle sprain is from the earthquake. All they did was tie me up, shove me around and lock me in."

"Maybe that's a good thing. Kept you out of trouble with Jimmy. You sure you're not already in it? I don't recall you having that tummy."

"You wish—you just want me out of circulation, to leave the field open for you." Her dad always said an attack was the best defense.

"In fact," Moira continued, "I'm amazed my mother never got pregnant from all that carrying on with your father."

"Frankly, with all the *eligible* women fighting to get his attention these days, I don't know why he ever gave her the time of day." She casually surveyed Moira's naked form as she turned away to rinse. She did have a birthmark between her shoulder blades.

"I can't swim today, but Miss Henderson says I've got to suit up and run on the track above the pool. I've got my period," she said, gloating.

"Whoopee," Erin said, with mock enthusiasm. She wished it were the other way around.

"Why the swimsuit, Erin? You know the rules. Is Jimmy the only one who gets to see you naked these days?"

"They treated me pretty rough. I'm a bit self-conscious about my bruises."

"You're just ashamed of your body."

"Why, are you interested? I heard about you and Julie."

"Well, that does it!" Moira's pale face and neck reddened. She spun on her bare heel and bolted from the room.

Thirty-Five

"Patrick!" boomed Manny Marancik over the phone, "I've got a terrific idea!"

"What is it this time, Manny?" He'd rather shoot himself than hear another of Manny's brilliant schemes. "We still haven't found a place to moor your deep water lake freighter."

"That's why I called. Remember that riverfront town in Illinois, with the odd New York name. What was it, Bronx?"

"Wrong borough—Brooklyn. Forgot the name already? You remembered they didn't approve your casino boat."

"Now there's a new administration in town."

"Whoa, hold on." Now that Marancik's opponent, the mayor, was dead, did he think Brooklyn would just approve his plans? Something smelled rotten.

"The governor likes my plan."

"The governor! What does he have to do with it?" A cold sweat broke out on Patrick's forehead.

"He says it's just the ticket to relieve poverty in Metro East, with jobs and tax revenue."

"But what did the ticket cost you—or your father?" A chill ran down his back

"The situation's changed in the past couple of weeks."

"I doubt it, Manny. The City of Brooklyn wants family entertainment. It won't fit in."

"You remember how the Missouri Gaming Commission wanted a boat that looked old-fashioned? In Illinois they don't care, just so it's profitable. They just follow the money."

"No doubt about that." Gaming revenue wasn't the only money they followed. What did Marancik know about the murder of Caleb Mitchom?

"Patrick, you gotta see my latest plan. Can you take a look at it this afternoon?"

The less he knew about Manny's cockamamie plan, the better. But he wanted to know more about Manny. "Yeah, you can come over here at three-thirty."

Later Marancik appeared in the lobby toting a bulging briefcase and one of the firm's presentation boards, with tissue overlays streaming behind. Patrick led him into the conference room and shut the door. "Now what's so urgent it couldn't wait until next week's meeting?"

"The schedule. Did you know that for any item on Brooklyn's agenda, you have to apply for it two weeks in advance? That gives us until tomorrow night to schedule a presentation at their next council meeting."

"You sure it's Brooklyn? You seem to know a lot about it, considering I just had to remind you about the name of the town. What's up?"

"You said what I wanted to do is impossible on the Missouri site. So I'm reconsidering, that's all."

"I doubt if it's going to be approved over there, either."

"You don't understand. I've got connections."

"I've been meaning to ask about that. So?"

"See, there's this guy Sol Abrams. He has a lot of pull on the City Council. He's practically got them in his pocket."

"You don't say?" Patrick tried to conceal a smile.

"He runs a lot of the clubs over there and pays a fortune in license taxes."

"Why would Abrams help you?"

"Actually, it's...it's kind of personal."

"Oh." Patrick considered Roxie's secret contact with Manny's "boys" and changed the subject. "What's the governor got to do with it?"

"Since Chicago pretty much runs the State of Illinois, my dad's business associates have introduced me to some influential people up there. We know what buttons to push to almost guarantee a casino license for Brooklyn."

"No kidding? Brooklyn is trying to clean things up—and dead set against opening up gambling. They told me they were trying to be family friendly—amusement parks, kiddie rides and all that."

"Right, but the Council has had a change of heart, now that the mayor's gone."

"You sure you didn't have something to do with his convenient removal from the scene?"

"Huh? Aww, no! What do you think I am?"

Patrick had a few ideas but kept them to himself. "I don't really know what you are, Manny. But political deals are made every day, and I just wondered if maybe this one got a little out of hand—I'm not saying it's your fault, of course."

Marancik looked at him wide-eyed. "Hey, wait a minute. I'm just trying to get a legitimate business license. The governor is a good guy. You don't think he would—"

Oh boy, another legitimate business. He'd heard the phrase so often in Brooklyn, it had become a red flag.

"I don't think anything. It's obvious you want to take advantage of the mayor's demise. I'm just curious whether you helped it along."

"Certainly, you don't suspect me?"

"Why not?"

"Are you investigating this?" Marancik's permanent wide-eyed stare got wider.

If this guy was somehow involved in a murder plot, he surely didn't want to mention that his daughter had found Mitchom's body.

"I'm not a cop, Manny. But you can't blame me for wondering who did in the mayor."

"Nonsense." He shook it off. "We merely think with the right people behind this, we can get it approved."

"As for getting help from your buddy, Abrams, you'll have to find him first. There's an all-points bulletin out for him."

"Really? I just saw him last week. Anyway, what do you think of my new plan?"

He examined Marancik's crude sketches, overlaid on the site plan. He was proposing that the entry building and accessory structures look like a shipyard, with cranes, hoists and industrial machinery.

"We'll put elevators inside the accessory building, so people can get to all the decks without climbing stairs. See how impressive the whole complex will look? My lake freighter will fit right in!"

"Gee, wish I'd thought of that! You ought to quit trying to get casinos approved and get an architectural license. Now if you'll excuse me, I've got to get to home and have dinner with my daughter."

Thirty-Six

"We need to talk about how to split up the housework." Meg said as they sat down to the grapefruit, pancakes and link sausage she'd prepared.

"Housework? Give me a break, Meg." Erin laughed. "Dad's a neat freak, and I make my own bed. The maid comes once a week."

"Your father wanted me to keep things proper while he's gone."

"And I didn't ask for a babysitter, especially not you."

"Erin, I'm not trying to pick a fight. I'm not perfect, either. I forgive you for lots of things. But I need a break from the daily chores, too."

"Then just stay home. After all I've been through on my own, I can handle it."

"Your father's right that we can help each other. You should listen to him once in a while. Maybe you'd get in less trouble."

"Maybe you should cut me some slack. I was trying to plan a simple canoe float for my friends. You act like it's my fault I discovered a corpse, was kidnapped and almost got killed."

"Maybe I can share some of my experience."

"Right. You've never been married, never had children and barely know me. And you think you can give me advice."

Meg stared back at her, looking hurt.

Touché! This was too easy—it made Erin feel bad. "Okay, fine. I'll try to help."

"We'll do it together, make it fun."

This all sounded pretty lame. The only way to endure this for a week was to get real.

"Hey, I'll admit I have my flaws, too. I eat too many sweets, spend too much of Dad's money on clothes and, well, there's other stuff. But the last thing I want would be to wreck your relationship with Dad." Ravenous from her days of deprivation, Erin gobbled her pancakes, brushed some red hair out of her eyes and took a sip of milk. "I'm concerned with bigger things."

"At least you're succeeding in school. When I was seventeen like you, I had a lot of trouble with that."

"Dad treats me like a kid. I'm more mature than he thinks."

"At least he doesn't hit you. I could tell you some stories."

"Really! I'd like to hear about that some time. I have plenty of bad experience, too."

"I'm sorry you lost your mother. But you have to move on. Your father wants to marry me soon. But he won't consent until he knows you're okay with it, and neither will I."

"Thanks for that, anyway."

"Your father and I have really had to rely on each other against all his problems. I'd like to think I even help him forget about other women."

"You can't. He'll never forget Mom. Besides, he has a roving eye for beautiful women. How could you ever compete with that?"

Not that Erin admired that trait, but Meg was asking for the impossible. Meg had this wholesome, girl-next-door look about her, far from her mom's raving beauty, with flaming red hair, a perfect figure and glowing emerald eyes. Erin was still wondering what kind of luck it was that she'd inherited her mother's good looks.

"He loves me, I love him and we both want to get married." She studied the large diamond on her left hand he'd given her almost a year ago. We need each other."

Erin sighed. "It would be great if he'd settle down again. We were so happy."

"I think you'll see—he's changing."

"Maybe with things back to normal now, he'll cool off."

On this lazy Sunday morning, they lounged at the kitchen table, still in their pajamas, finishing their pancakes and sausages. As Erin got up to refill her milk, Parnell, sniffing the ambrosial scents of breakfast, wandered into the kitchen to beg for food. She gave him her last savory sausage and shooed him out the sliding glass door into the yard.

"Erin, if I can ever be accepted into your household, I'm hoping to do some of the things for you that your mom would have done."

"Meg, since we're being frank here, can I tell you something?"

"I g-guess so."

"On the plus side, you're good for him. He's been less crabby with me lately and I guess I can thank you for that—at least for boinking him on regular basis."

"Is that all you think I am—his sex toy?"

"Oh, that's just how my girlfriends and I talk. You've only worked with him for a year. I've known him all my life."

"Granted, Erin, but we're coming from different places—you as a daughter. I want to be his mate and, I hope, the love of his life."

"I get it."

"Can we be friends? I can show you some beauty tricks I've learned, and help you shop for clothes. Maybe just be someone to talk to when your father's gone or too busy."

"We can try."

After her ordeal it felt good to have a real person to sympathize with her feelings. "I guess I appreciate all you're trying to do for me. It would be nice to have someone to depend on besides Dad. I should be more...self-sufficient."

"Don't be too hard on yourself. After a taste of that nasty reality, you're probably aware of all the things you have to know and do to be truly independent. It takes time to develop those skills."

"No kidding."

"I've never been a parent, but I'm trying to learn, too. Parents can help you gather all this knowledge gradually. You're only seventeen—there's time."

Erin's eyes filled with tears. "But you don't understand. There isn't time. For me it's already too late."

"Now *I'm* confused. Why on earth do you think that?"

"I've been trying to tell Dad ever since I got back home. First, that night when I had Kelly over for my homecoming dinner—but just then you came in and ruined that moment. Meg, I'm in trouble."

"But...I had no idea. Tell me, what is it? Did those gangsters hurt you?

"No."

"Did you help them commit crimes?"

"No, just in trouble, in the usual sense. Can't you tell?"

"What other kind of trouble could there—?" Meg's eyes widened. She took a long, appraising look at Erin in her thin pajamas.

"I'm-I'm pregnant."

"B-but—I didn't think you had sexual experience."

"Dammit, don't treat me like a textbook case." Erin wailed. "Up until recently, I didn't. I'm human, after all."

"Who did this to you, that skinny—swimmer?" She stared at her in disbelief. "I didn't know he had the balls to imagine it, much less do it."

"That's not funny, Meg," she said. "Jimmy has lovely balls. He didn't do it *to* me. We did it *for* each other, the first time for both of us, and it was beautiful. And I'll have you know, Jimmy is very good in...on the loveseat." She burst into tears.

"Oh, honey. I had no idea... How wonderful! But, was he...did you—? Meg stared at her, open mouthed.

"No, and no!" she said, through uncontrollable sobs.

Meg took Erin in her arms and hugged her tightly.

Her story poured out. The innocent study date that got out of hand. Her confession to Kelly, even the fact that telling Momo had spurred him into action, to defy his bosses, save her and escape. She described her thoughts while in captivity, the appreciation she had reached of Jimmy's superior qualities and his unique virtues.

"Are you considering an abortion?"

"Meg, how could you?" She pulled away and glared at her. "This baby is part Jimmy and part me! Jimmy's a great athlete. He's smart in math and science, and an artist, too. Erin described the long thought process she had worked through to list and analyze her options, doubtful that Meg would follow it and reach the same conclusion. "You have no children, and maybe you never will. What do you know about how I feel?"

Meg cast down her eyes. Tears formed and dripped on her cheek. Erin had hurt her again. She could barely stammer a reply. "I didn't mean...I would never suggest... Oh, dammit, I don't know what I mean. The baby could live here—"

"That's fine for you to say," Erin shot back. "You don't even live here yourself." She ran into the den and flopped down on the sofa, weeping.

For a moment Meg left her alone in her misery. She approached cautiously and sat on the edge of the very loveseat where Jimmy and Erin had discovered each other.

"Erin, you may not believe me, but I can accept that you may be pregnant and why it happened. I've been worried about that a few times myself. It sounds as if you're truly in love with Jimmy. Why don't we address the problems one at a time? First you'll have to see how Jimmy feels about all this."

"I don't know if I dare tell him. Do I have the right to ruin his life? I'm not sure he'll back me on this. How can he tell his parents?"

"I'll go with you when he talks with them if you want. But first you've got to tell him and decide how you both want to handle it."

"The one person I can count on is Jimmy. When he came to rescue me we pledged our love to each other. And we plan to get married someday, after college."

"That's a good start. What about finishing your school year?" Meg said.

Now Meg was asking the right questions. Between sobs, she said, "I'm afraid the girls will catch on. I can't bear the thought of going to gym class for the next month. And this semester it's swimming. We're supposed to shower nude in the big open shower room before going into the pool. Even when I wear my swimsuit, I'm afraid I'll show."

"For starters, you can tell them it the bad food gave you stubborn intestinal virus when you were held prisoner. The suit is to cover your bruises. Beyond that, it's none of their business."

"The biggie is telling Dad when he gets back. I can't wait much longer."

"I'll support you. I didn't realize I interrupted your plan to tell him when I barged in that night."

"You didn't barge in. Dad invited you. I had no right to object."

"I'm really thrilled for you, Erin. If Jimmy accepts your decision, you've found a real man who will stand by you. You know for a fact that you can have a family with him. It's marvelous. I may be getting too old for all that—maybe you're the only child I'll ever have, your child the only baby I'll help care for. I don't want to mess that up."

"Thanks, Meg. I guess I need you more than I knew."

"And Jimmy has no clue?"

"No. Until I see a doctor, I don't know what to tell him. Then again, I don't want to tie him down, unless he agrees with me. What am I gonna do?"

Meg put her arms around her, kissed her forehead and brushed tears off her cheeks. Erin sobbed into her shoulder

"First we'll see my gynecologist. She's a lovely person, and I trust her. I'll call her tomorrow to see when we can get you in. For all we know, maybe you're not pregnant at all."

"I'm afraid there's not much hope of that. I haven't had my period for two months now, and I can feel my body changing. My emotions are going crazy. Crying like this has never been my nature, and the tenderness I feel for Jimmy and what we've created inside me is unbelievable."

"Soon we'll know for sure, and you can see how Jimmy feels about it. Next we'll have to train your father and me. It's been years since you were a baby. He may not remember what to do. The final piece of the puzzle is your father's reaction. We'll get everybody together."

"That will definitely include Kelly, for moral support," Erin said. "We can assure him we've thought of everything. I also want to help Dad solve the case. He's treating me like an adult since I came back from the woods, I don't want to blow it now. And there's still that darned swimming class."

"There's more?"

"I dread what it does to my hair. When I go in the pool it gets messed up. It straggles down my neck in tangled kinks. I can't go back to class like this anymore."

"Maybe we could find an easier style, so you could fix it quickly afterwards. Let's have a beauty salon. Go get me some tools."

"Really? Great!"

Erin disappeared for a few minutes and returned with her mirror tray, stacked with a barber's scissors, her hairbrushes and combs.

"Could I have a Dorothy Hamill wedge?" she asked.

Meg sifted through a handful of her russet locks. "Your hair's too fine and too curly. Maybe there's a better style." Meg sat her on a kitchen stool and wrapped a towel around her shoulders. She began to comb and snip tentatively. She developed an idea of a style, and took bolder strokes. She framed her features in burnt orange curls of different lengths. Meg held up the mirror. An auburn halo set off her creamy skin.

"Voilá, a shag! You'll have no trouble blow-drying and combing this out in a jiffy."

"Oh, thank you, Meg!" They hugged. Erin turned to her "Do you think I'll ever be a pretty as Mom?"

"You'll have to ask your father about that."

"That's her picture at about the same age." Erin pointed to the bookshelf and the first publicity shot of Kitty O'Connor, the pub's Irish singing star. Patrick had taken it of his future wife for his father's newspaper ad.

"I can't believe my eyes," Meg said. She looked first at the picture and then at Erin's image in the mirror, "You look just like Kitty back then."

Something clicked into place for Erin. She was no longer worried about competing with Meg, her dad's new life companion. Her dad had lost his wife but soon would see her again in his own daughter.

Thirty-Seven

Since her dad would be at a meeting Tuesday evening, Erin figured this would be her best chance to tell Jimmy. Using her chemistry homework as an excuse, she called and invited him to come over to help.

She greeted him at the door and kissed him. Although they had made their new ground rules, she took his hand to lead him up the stairs. Her heart was beating fast.

"Are you nervous?" Jimmy said.

"Yeah, aren't you?"

"A little, I guess. Are you sure you don't want me to make love to you again?"

"Jimmy, you know how I feel and what I want. Why even bring it up?"

"Hey, I'm a guy. That's what we do."

"You're more than just a guy. You're Jimmy Steele, and I admire and respect you. I wouldn't want to be disappointed if you broke your promise."

They went into her bedroom and she closed the door. If they were putting themselves to the test, she figured it might as well be a good one.

She sat on the edge of the bed. She had to—her knees had turned to jelly. "In addition, we agreed to obey my father's rules in his own house." This was going to be tougher than she thought.

"Erin, you know that I only want to do what you want—what you think is best. Haven't I always cared about your feelings?" He sat next to her on the bed.

"Of course, Jimmy, but—" His thigh pressed against hers and set her flesh on fire. "I'm not sure I trust myself." Her heart raced and her cheeks burned. She turned toward him, put her arms around his neck and pulled him to her. His lips were soft. She explored the inside of his mouth with her tongue. "Can't we just be like this and enjoy each other?"

Jimmy groaned. "I'm not made like that. I'm afraid I'm not going to be able to resist for as long as we'll have to wait." He reached his arms around her back and stroked strong fingers up and down her spine and down to her hips. The feeling was soothing, and yet it made her want more.

"Oooh." She purred like a satisfied kitten. "Don't stop."

His strokes became firmer and now his palms massaged her back and down to her butt. As he moved them upward again, his fingers slipped under the fabric of her shirt and caressed the bare skin of her back, around to the sides under her bra.

"Ooooh." She felt his hard pecs against her breasts, his heart pounding as hard as hers.

He reached with trembling fingers for the clasp of her bra.

"Wait," she said. "Stop."

"What's wrong?"

"Feeling under clothes—it's sleazy. Our clothes should fall off like they did the first time. It's not the same as before, when we were innocent, like Adam and Eve in the garden. We need a big bed and flowers and beautiful music. Like my mom and dad had in their love nest downstairs. I want to wait until it can be like that."

"Erin, I know what I said and how you feel. I'll do my best, but this won't be easy."

"Now that I know more about the world and myself, there are complications." She got up, walked and pulled the sepia toned drawing from its new hiding place in the closet. "Exhibit A. While I was away, Dad found this in my desk drawer."

"How do you know? Did he mention it to you?"

"No, I know he found it. I'm sure, because he hid it again and neatened up the drawer."

"The drawing's better than I recalled, and you—you're unbelievably beautiful."

"Jimmy, I can't exactly frame it and hang it above my bed like I want to. I know you gave it to me with love, and it rips me up to part with it. But, it's too painful to be constantly reminded of what we can't share. But since you can't have me right now either, I want you to take this home."

"You're letting me? You know how I'll treasure it."

"Maybe you can even put it to good use." To satisfy this big guy. She grinned and patted the rigid bulge beneath his belt. "It'll do you more good than it will me."

Jimmy's ears turned bright red. "But how did you—"

"Believe me, I know. Girls act a little naïve around guys, but we're not stupid. Kelly has a big brother and, well, she walked into his bedroom one time. It wasn't a pretty sight."

"Can you imagine how he felt? That was a sticky situation."

Erin roared. "Shut up! You're making it worse."

Jimmy's whole face reddened.

Her smile faded and she said, "Well, speaking of tight spots, Jimmy, I'm in one now—a really bad one—and I need to share it with you. Seems like I screwed up, in the original sense."

"Does it have anything to do with our night together and the full moon?"

I don't even know if I can say this..."

"Out with it."

She stared at the roses on the scatter rug. "No doubt about it, honeybee. You pollinated my flower."

"You're sure?"

"I'm afraid so, Jimmy. I thought it wouldn't hurt to try it. At school some of the girls think you get a free pass the first time. Guess what? They're wrong."

"I was afraid of that. Your body doesn't know whether you're married or not, or how many times you've done it before. God just wants to make sure the human race continues."

"Maybe He wants *us* to continue."

Jimmy's eyes narrowed. "You sure it's me?"

She looked at him with a shy smile. "No question! You're the only man I've ever—"

"Wow!" Now Jimmy stared at the rug.

"I'm so sorry. I ruined our lives and your future." She threw her arms around him, put her head on his shoulder and broke down in tears. "I've thought about my options, Jimmy. I'm willing to do anything for you. I'll move away and raise the baby by myself. I'll put it up for adoption. I'll give you up forever. Whatever will allow you to reach your potential. I love you so much. I don't want to ruin your life."

"Erin, get a grip. I'm not stupid, either. I realized what could happen. Maybe nothing, and life could go along as before." Jimmy pushed her away and brushed tears from her cheeks with his fingertips. "Have you seen a doctor?"

She kept staring at the flowered rug. "Meg took me to her OB, so Dad wouldn't find out yet. I got the test and it was confirmed. Our baby is due at Christmas." She looked at Jimmy for his unwelcome response.

Instead, Jimmy's eyes lit up. "That's wonderful news! You mean we really did it? We really can have a baby together? Erin, think about it. We can have the family we hoped for. Some couples go on wishing for years and are never so lucky. You remember the title of that O. Henry story, 'The Gift of the Magi'? He'll be ours."

"I can hardly believe it. I hope he's as strong and as smart as you." Then she frowned. "But what if it's a girl? Are you okay with that?"

"I'd be thrilled. She'll be as beautiful as you."

"Maybe both smart *and* good looking, no matter which kind we get." She squeezed Jimmy hard, kissed him and whirled him around the floor. He'd lifted a huge burden from her. She was positively giddy with relief.

"There's only one minor detail, Jimmy. I don't know how to break it to my dad. He'll kill me, and maybe you too."

PART III: RECOVERY
THIRTY-EIGHT

When Patrick returned from work Thursday night, Erin was in tears. "Dad, I quit the field hockey team. While I was gone the coach took me out of the starting line-up for the season. Even when my ankle heals she won't let me start."

"Incredible! You and Kelly led the team that brought home the state championship last year. None of these troubles were your fault. Are you sure she understands?"

"Positive. While I was gone, she put in that new girl from the sophomore team as forward. She's scored goals in every game. They want to give the younger players a chance."

"I've a notion to go over there and change the coach's mind."

"Don't even try, Dad. It's way more important to help you catch these crooks."

"What can you do that Bobbi and the law can't?"

"For one thing, I know how these dudes operate. Besides, they've all seen me, and I'm in trouble until they're caught. Also, Roxie gave me this before I escaped. She removed the flash drive the cord lanyard around her neck, which also held her locket. I think it's full of his business contacts and files.'

"I'll bet that's why Solly Abrams broke up with Roxie".

"I think he abandoned her because she double-crossed him to save me."

"We'd better get that to Bobbi right away."

"But I won't be safe until we find Sol Abrams. Just lock up that zip drive until we have time to study it."

"Tell you what, Erin. Since we know Abrams is in Chicago and you won't be playing hockey this weekend, would you like to take a little run up there with me and look around?"

"Chicago? How cool. Wait until I tell Kelly."

"No. It's not going to be that kind of trip. It will be dangerous enough without you telling anyone about where we're going. Bring mostly jeans and sneakers. You can bring a nice dress, though, and I'll treat you to a fine dinner."

"When do we leave?"

"You've got school and I can't break free from the office until the weekend, so we'll head out early Saturday morning."

When Patrick told Bobbi Romano about his plan, she was none too happy about it. "After we all busted our asses to get Erin free, you're taking her right back into the fire."

He explained Erin's logic that she might recognize some of the lowlifes that had hung around Solly's operations.

"We'll just pay a visit to Billie at her bar in Cicero and see where it leads."

"For cripe's sake, Patrick, go early in the day. I'm not concerned about the liquor laws. Erin can pass for eighteen, or even twenty, but she's too pretty; she'll attract too much attention in a dive like that after dark. If you get in a jam, you make sure to call Radi." She gave him the number of Piotr Radwinski, her counterpart in the Chicago FBI office. "We've discussed Billie's Place in Cicero. He watches it in case old time mobsters show up there. I'll give him a heads-up that you'll be in the area."

At seven a.m. on Saturday, he and Erin set out in his Honda on Interstate 55 for the five-hour trip to Chicago. The fair April skies soon greyed as they slid under a broad cloud deck coming out of the northwest. They coasted out of the Mississippi floodplain onto flat, glaciated Illinois farmland. The only landscape features on the endless prairie were tall hedge rows and moraines, wide, curved ridges left as glacial residue. As they approached Springfield, the gloom depressed Patrick's spirits.

"There's the Capitol dome," Erin said. "I remember when you brought me up here and I sat in the governor's chair. Isn't that where we took the Lincoln trail?"

"You have a good memory, Erin. You were only in fifth grade."

Erin's sparkling green eyes reminded him how Kitty looked that day. In Lincoln's historic New Salem Village, restored and rebuilt as a museum site, she had virtually floated along the path from cabin to cabin through the woods in her peasant blouse and billowing skirt. The displays of old farm implements: buckets, ladles and kitchen tools reminded her of her grandmother's Ireland.

Patrick slowed the car as they approached the Sangamon River "Dad, can we stop up ahead?" Erin asked.

"Why?" Patrick slowed at the bridge approach, afraid to hear her reason.

"This is the spot where we lost Mom."

"If you must." Before the bridge he pulled off the highway on the paved shoulder.

They got out of the car. Patrick stood before a guardrail at the edge of a steep embankment leading down to the river. He kicked the guardrail hard; it responded with a solid ring.

"What, Dad?"

"You know the story. I'd rather not go over it again."

"I'll never forget that sinking feeling when the guardrail failed and the car pitched down the slope."

"Damned crooked contractors! Your mother said she'd be okay and to save you. She never woke up. Why do you want to go over this again?"

"I just wanted to be near her. It would do you good to recall her like this once in a while you're awake, instead of in nightmares."

They stood still and peered into the gully where the river flowed under the bridge, absorbed in their own memories. The stream flowed peacefully now even in spring, compared with the icy torrent that had robbed Kitty of life and breath. He hadn't been here for three years, since the investigations had concluded.

"Your mother believed in her family, Ireland and the ancient Irish legends: how St. Patrick rid the country of snakes, Brian Boru unified the Irish people and the tricks of the Wee Folk—capricious sprites who could grant great favors, or as easily steal babies and brides."

"That's all *her* malarkey, but it's the first time I've heard it since Mom died."

"She also sought their blessings, to help ward off dark forces."

"Whatever." Erin shrugged, but smiled. "Remembering her will help us both,"

They climbed back into the car and drove near the town of Lincoln, Illinois.

Patrick pointed out a two-story building on the right side of the road with a mansard roof bearing its title, "THE MILL."

"We're riding along the trail of the Syndicate," Patrick said. "Here's one of their watering holes." Next to the building stood a statue of a wide-shouldered black steer. "That place opened in 1929 as a Dutch themed restaurant," he said. "It was a regular stop for Al Capone. It used to have a windmill that revolved and was lighted at night. New owners bought it in 1965 and ran it as a dance hall. A few gals even operated out of those motel rooms constructed on the back, as a convenience for passing motorists."

"Yuck," Erin said, "Those parasites show up everywhere, don't they?"

"The local people eventually revolted. It closed in 1996 and reopened as a museum and historic site."

Three hours later, the towers of downtown Chicago loomed on the prairie, and the road widened to eight lanes of heavy traffic. He turned north on Cicero Avenue as jets roared overhead from nearby Midway Airport.

"I'm famished. Can we eat?" Erin said.

"Hang on a few minutes. We'll see what Billie's got to offer at her bar."

They headed north on Cicero, past airport hotels, fast food joints that made Erin drool, big-box stores and industrial plants. Then they entered a commercial stretch lined with two- and three-story buildings, their ground floors occupied by bustling shops with signs in Spanish for *taquerias, carnicerias* and *Viva La Musica*. Tucked into a narrow storefront next to *Taqueria Jiminez* was a bar with the name painted in gold script on the glass, Billie's Place. It was one-thirty when Patrick and Erin pushed through the door. A sixtyish woman with brassy blonde hair was polishing glasses behind the bar. "What'll it be, folks?

"Are you Billie?" Patrick asked.

"Yeah, what about it?"

"I'm Patrick MacKenna. This is Erin."

"Sonofabitch. I shoulda recognized you. So you're the two Momo said wuz comin'! Radi told me, too. He helps keep the mob in line so's I can stay in business."

"We're trying to give you one less thing worry about," Patrick said

"I'd be more'n happy to help you out. My husband died about five years ago, and this place is all I got. I'm too poor to retire and too young to die. That's not so easy to avoid around here."

"So I hear." Patrick glanced at a couple of morose types at the bar and the rest of her rough lunchtime customers.

"What can I get you to drink? On the house."

"I guess a beer would go down nice after our long trip."

"You too, honey?" she said, addressing Erin.

"No thanks, I'm seventeen. A Diet Coke will do."

"Oh, gosh, you look much older, even to an old barmaid like me. Besides, if you're old enough to get kidnapped by those crumb bums, I'll bend the rules and serve you a drink."

"No," Patrick said. "No point in risking your license over us. Got anything to eat?"

She fixed Erin and Patrick up with their lunch special—a giant cheeseburger and fries. As they munched she asked, "So what's this big sting Radi told me about?"

"Erin, you might as well start, since you're the one who stumbled into this mess."

Between huge bites of her burger and gulps of her drink, Erin told the story of discovering Mitchom, her kidnapping, and her adventures in and around Brooklyn.

"Those bastards, abusing young women like they do."

"To cut to the chase, Billie, we think Solly Abrams is up here somewhere, and we wondered if you've seen him."

"I've seen him all right. He sold me this place. He was in here this week with some pretty nasty folks. One guy I never saw before—kinda flighty, sort of fruits and nuts, if you know what I mean."

"What were they saying?"

"I couldn't hear much—they were sittin' at a table in the back. Besides him and Abrams there was Walter Wonkowski—they call him Wally Wonka—a computer geek. Word on the street is, he hacked into City Hall's computers, and now he's workin' on the police department. But the guy doin' most of the talking was Scarface McGurk, after the huge gash up his cheek."

"Who does he think he is, big Al himself?" Patrick grinned.

"Delusions o' grandeur, I suppose. He was braggin' about his knife throwing—says he can trim a cigar in a man's mouth at twenty paces."

"That's enough to make a man give up smoking." Patrick fingered the Glock eight in his pocket, glad he had it. "What else can you tell me about him?"

"Scarface is enforcer for the Bohannon Gang. They say he killed three women, but nobody's been able to lay a finger on him. I don't envy you lookin' around here for him. You'll be in a world o' hurt 'fore you know it."

"You catch the other one's name—this gay guy?"

"Couldn't hear much. They sat way in the back, called him Danny, or maybe Manny?"

"Manny Marancik?"

"Could be. He was braggin' about some boat he bought with his father's money."

"That's Manny, all right. He and Solly have had dealings down in Metro East."

"Sounds like a real goofball."

"You got any idea where Solly's hanging out?"

"He's got a secret girlfriend in a house somewhere in town."

"A girlfriend?" Erin said.

"He's moving up in the world," Patrick said. "He normally keeps his girlfriends in an abandoned warehouse."

"Abandoned whorehouse is more like it. It's somewhere up on the Northwest Side. The city oughta tear it down."

"You know the address?"

"Sorry."

"Hey, thanks, Billie, we're much obliged. And thanks for the lunch." Patrick plopped a twenty-dollar bill on the bar and got up to leave.

"'Twarn't nothin'," she said, "and keep your money. You might need it. It's worth it to me if you can take Solly and some of his friends out of circulation."

"We'll give it a shot." Patrick left the money on the bar and continued toward the door.

"You watch out, MacKenna," Billie said. "Don't ever surprise Scarface from behind, or you'll get yourself stabbed to death."

Thirty-Nine

Patrick headed east on the Eisenhower toward downtown, grateful that the heaviest traffic was in the opposite direction.

"Hey, Erin, watch this."

They barreled toward a block-long structure dead ahead, which appeared to obstruct the multi-lane freeway. As they topped the next rise, a wide viaduct appeared beneath it.

"Wow, We're going underneath."

They glided through a wide tunnel under the main post office building. Stopped at the light on Michigan Avenue, Patrick decided to continue east across Grant Park to the Outer Drive. "Let's have a look at the lake." He found a turnoff where they could park. Boats lay at anchor in the harbor, their sails stowed in tarps, cowering beneath the dull clouds.

"Those boats look like ghost ships," Erin said.

"The whole city's that way—beautiful, but mysterious."

They walked along atop a seawall of mammoth dressed stones.

"They're taller than a man," Erin said. "How did these get here?"

"During the depression the Works Progress Administration built the wall to hold the man-made shoreline and create jobs."

"Man-made?"

"Most of the open space you see between here and Michigan Avenue is filled land. They say Chi-ca-go was the Potawatomi name for a swamp smelling of wild onions."

They turned to face the park. The distinctive skyline of the Loop was silhouetted against a yellow sunset. Patrick pointed out the Gage building fronting on Michigan Avenue, remodeled by Louis Sullivan, part of a midget hedge bordering a forest of towers.

"In the 1850s, when the city had no paved streets, cracks in the wooden sidewalks oozed with the soupy muck, making it impossible to keep carriage wheels, and especially ladies' fine dresses and boots, free of the muddy mix. The city's ingenious founders decided to jack all the buildings, which were built of light wood, ten feet into the air and pave the raised surfaces with stone. For about ten years, the city existed on stilts. The space created below was known as the "underworld," a maze of tunnels, enclosed spaces and underground streets."

"No kidding?"

"Oh, yeah. The nation's largest collection of hoodlums—pickpockets, highwaymen, jack-rollers and killers-for-hire roamed down there. But worst of all were those who preyed on women. In this underground dungeon, girls as young as fourteen and fifteen were gang-raped, terrorized and forced into "the life" as prostitutes, kept pliant with opium, and sold to the whorehouses for $200 plus a percentage of their earnings. The girls, in turn, paid 60 to 90 percent of the ten dollar fee for "tricks" to their owners. This huge industry was taken over by Al Capone's Syndicate, and its successor, the Outfit. Remnants of it still exist today."

"Not much has changed in all those years, has it?"

"It comes and goes. The good guys won for a while, but it's getting out of control again, in places like you discovered."

He drove them around Grant Park, passing the band shell, Shedd Aquarium, the Field Museum and the reborn Soldier Field, updated as a modern sports stadium. New grandstands emerged like giant petals blooming from its classical shell. He doubled back on Roosevelt Road over the Illinois Central tracks and past the railroad's main Victorian terminal building, where he headed north again on Michigan.

"What say we treat ourselves to a decent hotel tonight?"

"After the cabin, I won't know how to act."

"I'll chance it."

From a suite in the Hilton Towers overlooking the harbor, they watched the last flecks of light on the water's choppy surface dissolve into an endless expanse of inky blackness. They changed into their good clothes and set out.

They walked north along Michigan Avenue, past Sullivan's Auditorium Building, turned left on Monroe and continued north on Wabash toward the family pub. Elevated trains thundered, squealed and spewed sparks overhead. They pressed north amid the din of rush hour car horns and suffocating diesel bus exhaust to the family's popular watering hole.

Patrick pushed through the door of MacKenna's Irish Pub. Dermot, the loyal, mustachioed bartender, waved in greeting. A few tables were occupied by early diners. The happy hour crowd was well-established, six-deep at the bar, and diners were beginning to filter in. He'd warned the family of their arrival and his timing seemed about right.

Nonetheless Lily MacKenna practically dropped a tray of glasses, hastily set them down, and embraced Erin in a body hug.

"Sure, and you're a sight for sore eyes, me little darlin'," she said, her eyes brimming. "What with yer abduction and all, I feared I'd never see you again."

"Hi Grandma, it's good to see you, too." As she extricated herself from her grandmother, she cast down her eyes, hoping she would interpret it as shyness, but ashamed of what she would have to tell her someday soon.

Patrick bent and kissed his mother on the cheek.

Seamus MacKenna swung the kitchen doors wide, draped his apron on a barstool and hugged Erin. "Them blackguards turned ye loose, I see." With twinkling eyes, he addressed Patrick. "To what, might I ask, do we owe the honor of this visit—and why so brief?"

"Serious business, Father," he said. "I'm hoping you can help me answer some questions.

A frown darkened his father's brow. "Of course, son. The Saturday night crowd won't arrive for a while. Let's sit a bit and chat." He led them to the family booth, a round table in the far back corner of the restaurant surrounded by a curved banquette and three chairs. Here his father and mother met with salesman, food wholesalers, liquor distributors and friends, and here they'd held many a family parlay.

"Where might ye be stayin', since 'tis not with us?" his mother wanted to know.

"This is just a quick trip, Ma. Erin has to be back Monday for school. So after all these troubles, I decided to treat us to the Hilton Hotel and Towers."

"Puttin' on the dog," Lily said, "and rightly so. Just don't be forgettin' your family."

"Here we are, Ma, just now comin' to visit."

"Now what is it, son?" the senior MacKenna asked.

"Have you ever heard of Scarface McGurk?"

"Ah, haven't I, now? He's the stuff o' legend and story—rascal, scoundrel, and, sorry to say, gang underboss."

"That much. I know, but what rackets is he mixed up in?"

"Haven't you heard of the time when he rounded up all the customers at the downtown Third National Bank, had them lie on the floor and made off with five million dollars? Didn't he stage a daring raid in broad daylight on the Riverside casino? In that one he absconded with three of their prettiest hostesses, not that I could blame him."

"Seamus!" Lily cried.

"Ah, that leads to my real objection, but I hate to talk about it before the child."

"Grandpa, after my ordeal," Erin said, "I'm not an innocent child anymore."

"Oh, heavens! They violated ye?" Mrs. MacKenna said, visibly shaken.

"No, no, I managed to escape that. But they had big plans for me as an exotic dancer, and I got out just in the nick of time." She was glad she could at least tell her grandparents this much.

"You poor dear." Lily wiped tears of sorrow mixed with joy from her eyes.

"That's just it," said the elder MacKenna. "He's lurin' these women into a life of sin, sex and seduction with habit-formin' drugs. I might forgive my countryman for some of his transgressions. So might the Holy Mother Church, God knows, this bein' Chicago and all, but the rest of it I cannot abide. What of it, son?"

"This McGurk has been seen here with a client of mine and a man who runs the rackets in East St. Louis, one Solly Abrams. He's the man whose henchmen kidnapped Erin. He's suspected of murder. Erin and another girl discovered the body. He's been missing for a week now. I'm pretty sure he's in Chicago, and I'm wondering if you have any clues to where these birds hang out."

"Hmmm. Those desperate men don't frequent our place any more, praise the Lord, and I'm not current on their whereabouts."

"Seamus, what about that hoodlum that tried to shake ye down fer protection last year? Didn't he mention McGurk?"

"Sure an' he did. He said to deliver the money to a grand old house somewheres. They use it as a halfway house. I called Captain O'Donnell at the police, an' didn't he find 'em there? But somehow they had a heart-to-heart an' that was the end o' that. I may still have the address." He got up and returned with an old ledger, from which he copied the information on a slip of paper. "Here it is. Now Patrick, don't ye be gallivantin' about these perilous precincts with me only granddaughter. Let her stay here with us."

"Grandpa," Erin said, "I can take care of myself with these thugs, and besides, I have a few questions of my own to ask Solly."

"Erin and I will be together, and besides, father, I'm armed. He patted the weapon in his front pocket.

"Be careful with that thing," his mother warned. "Ye can carry it around, but don't be puttin' any bullets in it. You might injure someone."

"Grandma!" Erin exploded in guffaws. "That's the whole point!"

◊

They returned to the hotel, where they enjoyed the fine dinner Patrick had promised Erin and turned in early.

Awakened Sunday morning by a spectacular purple, red and gold sunrise over the lake, they dressed quickly and set out in hopes of finding Sol Abrams.

"I doubt if he'll be at church," Patrick said.

"Nor at temple, either. The only thing he worships is money."

His father's directions took them to an industrial neighborhood along the north branch of the Chicago River on the Northwest side. Nestled among coal depots, rusting manufacturing plants and an auto junkyard, they found a single residential street lined with once elegant homes. Some were in ruins and others had windows boarded up and bore For Sale signs. Tall windows, an occasional conical roof turret at one corner, spindle-railed porches and cutout curlicue decorations at the gable peaks graced the handsome Victorian structures. Patrick figured they dated from the 1880s or '90s. A half-dozen houses appeared to be occupied, with trimmed lawns and window curtains. Since few bore street numbers, he puzzled where to begin.

They'd proceeded almost to the end of the block when Erin said. "Look, there's Solly's car." She pointed to a black late-model Mercedes parked at the curb in front of one of the occupied homes.

"You're right—looks like the one I saw at his warehouse apartment."

Patrick checked the address and knocked on the front door.

"Suzie?" boomed a voice from a cavernous interior.

Patrick motioned for Erin to respond.

"Solly—it's Erin—Fifi, that is," she yelled though the door.

After the sounds of shuffling and the rattle of locks, the huge deep-carved door swung wide and Solly Abrams appeared in the opening, his sleeves rolled, in wrinkled dark slacks. "What a pleasant surprise." Then, when he saw Patrick, "Oh, and you."

"May we come in?" Patrick said.

"In regard to what?"

"Your goons kidnapped my daughter and another girl."

"Where's Vince Scullin?" Erin asked.

"How the hell would I know? He's supposed to be working at my club."

"It's closed," Patrick said, "and we needed to ask him some questions."

"Then go find him. I had to come up here on business." He kept looking at Erin, torn about what to do.

If he didn't even know where Vince was, Patrick figured, it was unlikely he would know about the explosion at the cabin, Jake's demise and Momo's survival.

"Too bad you forgot to tell Roxie," Erin said.

"Roxie? She never likes it when I travel. So what?"

"We'll fill you in, if we can just sit and talk," Patrick gestured toward the foyer.

"All right you two." He couldn't take his eyes off Erin. "Come in."

He stepped back and admitted them to a hallway with a cobwebbed chandelier and guided them to a dusty parlor. Erin and Patrick sat on the edge of a worn burgundy plush sofa of flamboyant Victorian design. Solly brushed off the needlepoint upholstery on the seat and back of a carved side chair and sat.

Abrams looked Erin up and down and shook his head. "Cat-Girl," he said, "you're still beautiful. You should have come to the club that night as we planned. When you didn't show up, all hell broke loose."

"Darned good thing I didn't, Solly," she shot back at him. "I lived to tell about it. Maybe I even did you a favor by not letting you get caught red-handed with my underage goods."

"And you, MacKenna, how's your sexy little friend, the FBI agent?"

"She's still layin' for you, Abrams, and not the way you want."

"Such language, in front of your own daughter."

"That didn't seem to bother you when you were ready to put me to work in a gin mill, peddling watered-down drinks, bad drugs and easy sex," Erin said.

Patrick stared at her, open-mouthed, shocked at her gutsy speech.

"Hey, I wanted to give you top billing. As I told you, MacKenna, I operate a legitimate adult business, providing entertainment services for affluent clientele."

"Spare me, Abrams, I already saw the ads," Patrick said. "You were spotted up here the other day meeting with Scarface McGurk, that playboy Manny Marancik and Walter Wonkowski. What's your hookup with Marancik, anyway?"

"Aw, come on. You know as well as I do. Marancik is as queer as a three-dollar bill. I sent him to Vince to find some pretty boys for his amusement."

"You sure you didn't blackmail him to kill Mitchom?"

"Hell, no! Trying to please a customer, that's all."

"What about McGurk?" Patrick said.

Abrams sighed and spread his hands, palms up. "He's the enforcer for the boss. They're tryna move in on my operations down there. It got really hot. I had to come up here to protect my interests. "

"Are you sure that's your only connection with him?" Patrick asked, annoyed.

"MacKenna I have better things to do than answer questions for you and that stupid FBI broad. She'd make more money in one of my acts."

"She's a lot smarter than you." Erin held up a thumb and forefinger. "And she's this close to bringing you down."

"If I knew who killed Mitchom, don't you think I'd tell you?"

"Who mentioned Mitchom?" Erin said. "Is his murder starting to bother you?"

Patrick stared at her, amazed, and put a hand on her arm. "Cool it, Erin. I think we'd better go. Thanks for nothing, Abrams." He beckoned Erin toward the door.

She wasn't through.

"I'm sure Roxie would love hearing about Suzie—if she could. Is she blonde? Does she have big tits?"

"What do you mean, if she could? Don't you dare tell her!"

"Too late for that. Thought you knew—you caused it. She-she's dead." Erin could barely speak.

"Roxie, dead? Oh—God... NO-O-O!" Abrams let out a howl that could have been heard downtown and slumped in his chair,

"Hmmph. Pretty good act, Abrams." Patrick said. "All of a sudden, you care."

"Where? When?" the man said, his eyes misty.

"In that warehouse pad of yours in Brooklyn, where you abandoned her," Erin said. "Last week we found her dying. She was asking for you."

"I can't believe it." He pressed his palms to his eyes. Such a great showman. She ran my acts, chose the girls and produced the shows. Her eye for talent was flawless. And she'd cheer me up whenever—"

"I'll miss her too, Solly. All the more reason not to mistreat her," Erin said.

"But I've only been here since last Friday. Who could have killed her without any... ." He seemed lost in thought.

"You did, Solly. She died of a drug overdose, waiting for you to come back. You're the supplier." Erin enjoyed watching Solly squirm, for a change.

"The last she heard out of me were angry words about your escape."

"So much for the love story," Patrick said. "Now, think. Who killed Mitchom?"

"Maybe Marancik. He wanted a favor from Mitchom and didn't get it. He expected Mitchom to welcome his gambling venue with open arms. When old Caleb said, 'Too bad, we don't want a casino in Brooklyn,' he was— how shall I put it delicately?— annoyed."

"Such a pussycat. I can't imagine him lifting a limp wrist against anyone. Maybe I should've put him in one of my shows—ha ha."

Solly had spent so long with Roxie he'd begun to sound like her.

"McGurk, on the other hand, likes to victimize women," Abrams continued. "He enjoyed his visits to our town. We made sure he got plenty of his rough stimulation—and left happy."

"That may help us solve this, Abrams," Patrick said.

"Oh boy, now I'm as good as dead. You don't cross Scarface. He's deadly with a knife."

"Hey, thanks, Solly. Maybe this wasn't a wasted trip after all," Patrick said.

"See. I'm not such a bad guy. Not like McGurk. You stick your nose into his business and he'll cut it off."

Patrick shuddered. What if Solly had forced Erin to entertain McGurk? She'd escaped not a day too soon.

Forty

Patrick took the driver's seat, pulled away from the curb and checked the mirrors to see if anyone was following them.

Back on the Dan Ryan Expressway, Erin said, "Look at all this traffic, filling a dozen lanes of pavement, early on a Sunday afternoon."

"Big city. A nice town to be *from*," Patrick said. "You took some chances in there. He could have pulled a gun on us. I came close to calling Radi for backup."

"I think we got some more clues out of him just now."

"You handled it well, but I can't put my finger on a pattern here."

"We must be able to use some of Solly's information," Erin said. "What do you make of Gary Archer and Caleb Mitchom being in the same unit in Vietnam?"

"It doesn't mean much. This First Air Cavalry Division was huge—with helicopter squadrons, engineers, infantry and medic units all attached to it. Maybe it's not important."

"Seems like most of your recent clients were in the Army."

"Let's see, there was Mitchom, the murder victim, Archer, and then a contractor, Mercer Tomkins, who's been giving Archer all those high bids. I believe he said they were even in the same company over there. I still don't see how that could relate to Mitchom's murder."

"They'd be pretty tight, after going through the war together."

"But what about this McGurk?" Patrick said.

"Could he have been getting revenge on Mitchom for resisting the Chicago mob's move on Brooklyn operations?"

"Everyone says if you mess with McGurk, you're really asking to get yourself hurt."

"But he wasn't killed with a knife. What about Archer? And this Tomkins— I'd never heard of him until just now."

"Now Erin, Tomkins is just a chiseling contractor, and Archer is what we used to call shell-shocked, from the Vietnam War. He's a troubled neurotic, and he drinks too much. But how that could connect either one of them with a murder over in Illinois, I don't have a clue."

"How about your other client, Marancik, the gambling casino guy? Abrams said he was upset with Mitchom for not helping him get his riverboat casino approved."

"Erin, I don't see why you're trying to involve all my clients in this. Before you're through, I'll be out of business."

"You're so eager to keep their business, you don't even suspect them."

"Come on. That won't influence my judgment."

"The way Gary Archer explained it the other day, someone in his company went ballistic and killed that Vietnamese family."

"Maybe Mitchom could shed some light on it, and he's dead. Sounds fishy, huh?"

Patrick was pleased to have an adult conversation with his daughter, but her theories were wildly speculative. How could they help solve the case? He tuned the radio to Chicago's classical music station. The Mozart symphony must have had had a calming effect. Erin fell asleep.

When they arrived at McLean, the halfway point between Chicago and St. Louis. Erin awoke. Patrick pulled into the parking lot of the Dixie Truckers Home. In the restaurant on this sleepy Sunday the section marked with a big "Truckers Only" sign was nearly vacant. At Patrick's urging the waitress allowed them to sit in one of these booths, larger and equipped with amenities for the drivers.

"This is how you live on the road," he said. "They even have showers and wi-fi."

"Pretty sweet deal."

"The food's good, too."

They ordered the lunch special—a hearty beef stew.

"Dad, there's something we need to talk about." Erin said.

A trucker sat across the aisle browsing the Internet on the restaurant's wi-fi connection.

The waitress arrived almost immediately with their order.

Hungry, Patrick dug into his lunch special. "With our and no food in the house, this will be our big meal for the day."

The trucker with the computer turned toward them and asked, "You folks headed south?"

"In fact, we are. To St. Louis."

"You'd better watch it. Says here there's been another earthquake down there."

"We're not done yet?" Patrick rose from his seat and stood behind the trucker. He stared at his screen in disbelief.

They hastily finished their meal. Patrick paid the check, led them back into the car and steered back on the ramp to the highway.

"Dad, it's been really great to be back home with my friends and going to school again. But there's one thing—"

"Believe me, it's a relief to have you back, to resume life just the way it was before all this stuff happened." He fiddled with the radio buttons. They were in a dead zone between FM public radio stations, where he could get detailed news.

"The thing is, Dad, now that I'm back home, we need to talk."

"Sure, sure, honey. Why won't this thing work? To hell with it." He poked the button that changed to the AM band and then hit the button for KMOX, a high-powered network station in St. Louis.

"We bring you a message from the emergency broadcast network..." The transmission came through loud and clear.

"That's the station with the tower we reinforced. It survived and passed another test."

"Dad, I need to talk you!"

"Shh, Erin. Listen."

"...with this emergency broadcast. An earthquake of 6.8 magnitude has struck, its epicenter in Potosi, Missouri. Buildings and structures have been demolished across a wide area in St. Louis, Southwestern Illinois and Southeastern Missouri. The Governor of Missouri has declared a state of emergency. All bridges to the City of St. Louis... Repeat, all bridges leading to the City of St. Louis have been closed due to structural damage, obstruction by disabled vehicles or damage to the roadway..."

"My God, we can't even get home. St. Louis has been reduced to an island city."

"Didn't you tell me that there's one route in and out of St. Louis without crossing a bridge?" Erin asked.

"Right, Manchester Road."

"I'll see if there's a way to get from here to that highway. Erin fished in the glove compartment for a map and unfolded it.

"Highway 100, west of town, becomes Manchester Road," she continued, "but there's a catch: that's on the other side of the Mississippi and the Missouri River from us."

"Hmm. How about the Brussels Ferry across the Illinois River and the Golden Eagle Ferry?"

She pored over the map. "Nope, that takes you across the Illinois River to that skinny Calhoun County, Illinois, and you can cross the Mississippi on the Golden Eagle Ferry. But you still have to cross the Missouri River bridge to get from St. Charles County to St. Louis."

"But here, we could head west on Interstate 72 out of Springfield and cross the Mississippi at Hannibal. Then we'd take Highway 47 south to Washington and cross the Missouri further west at the Highway 47 bridge. I wonder if that's still open"

She fiddled with her new mobile phone. "Remember, this phone with internet service that I had to have?"

"What about it?" The replacement for her ruined cell phone had been expensive, but he was so relieved to have Erin back, he gave in.

"I can use it to check the Missouri Department of Transportation website." She worked the screen with her thumbs. "It says that the new Highway 47 Bridge in Washington, Missouri, is open."

"That works. We can catch Highway 100 out of Washington and head east back to St. Louis. Here, I'll make sure." He pulled out his cell phone and called Joe Sparks, City Manager of Washington, at home.

"Joe, how're you doin' down there? I'm trying to get back to town from Chicago. I thought maybe we could cross your Highway 47 Bridge." He chatted back and forth for a few minutes and learned that damage in Washington was minimal and it would be clear sailing, at least across the bridge. He ended the call. "He couldn't promise we can avoid traffic. Once the word gets out that Manchester Road is the only way to get to St. Louis, he anticipates heavy congestion."

Following their plan, they turned west at Springfield, crossed the unharmed Mississippi River bridge at Hannibal and headed toward Washington, Missouri.

At 7:30 that night, weary but triumphant after nine hours on the road, Patrick pulled into their driveway. Normally they only used the overhead door to get in through the kitchen. He parked in the driveway space next to Erin's car. The garage door failed to open when Patrick pushed the button in his car—the first sign they had no power.

They walked around and entered by the front door. After stowing their bags, he checked the outside of the house in the waning spring twilight and found the cracks beside the windows, which he had recently caulked, had widened. A branch from an old maple had fallen against the garage roof. Some trees fell across the creek behind the backyard, but the house had no major damage. As he predicted, his neighbors hadn't fared as well. Across the street the leaning chimney had collapsed, crushed the roof and broken several windows.

He called Meg and learned she and her mother were secure and safe, although in the dark, and got the same reassurance from Uncle Mike and Aunt Marie. He walked across the street, knocked on Mrs. Jameson's front door. Her bedroom wing and kitchen were undisturbed, and she and her son were managing fairly well. Back inside, they lit candles and made a dinner of cheese, salami and the rest of the melting ice cream from the freezer.

In the morning the battle would resume—between Patrick and the thugs, the Law and the Outfit, Nature and Mankind. Exhausted at the mere thought of it, Patrick collapsed in his bed.

FORTY-ONE

While Monday's sky was clear, the earth below seemed less trustworthy. Patrick accepted the scientific explanation for the recent shaking—shifting tectonic plates far beneath the surface. But his foul mood evoked visions of darker forces beneath for movement in the earth, and maybe for the dismal state of the people on it. Although some were blaming hydraulic fracturing—injection of wastewater into the earth to loosen shale oil deposits—for the current rash of earthquakes, he knew this wasn't happening around here. Feeling sorry for himself, he knew many people in his beleaguered city had suffered damage, but still felt unduly burdened with misfortune.

Since the calamity, broadcast news had arrived on a small digital radio Patrick kept for emergencies. Overhead power and phone lines to outlying districts were cut by falling trees, collapsed power poles and destroyed buildings. Miraculously, due to its underground service in the central part of the city, his one-story office building still had power. While he had to rely on his cell phone to make all his calls, at least he had a place to recharge it.

The only available news reports came from broadcasts on the emergency channel and, of all things, the St. Louis Post Dispatch, the printed daily newspaper, whose underground power supply and original presses, in the sub-sub-basement of their fortress downtown, had been spared. The city's sole surviving newspaper, financially weaker every year, for once had a monopoly. With the only operating presses in town, they were happy to contract for printing services with all takers— neighborhood journals and the St. Louis Enquirer, the local scandal sheet. In a weak moment, the strapped publisher even agreed to distribute this rag using its own delivery network.

When Patrick picked up his morning paper off the driveway, he found a free copy of The Enquirer as well. He almost pitched it in the trash can as he passed, until he glanced at the front page. When he read the headline he stopped walking. Under the kicker, *Fatal Designs: Riverdale's Troubled Project*, the headline screamed, BUILDING FOUNDATIONS COLLAPSE IN QUICKSAND. Patrick's face scowled from an inset photo next to the story. Next to his was the boyish face of Doug Marsh, looking innocent, alert and startled, as if he had just read the adjacent story.

"Miss Gotcha got me again," Patrick said at the breakfast table, He read the story to Erin.

By Mona Springer

In Sunday's earthquake, a building structure in Riverdale Business Park has sunk into the ground, suffering foundation damage and the collapse of new brickwork built just last Friday. Marsh Development's controversial project, in the flood plan of the Missouri River, was approved by the County Council, despite loud objections by residents of adjacent communities, environmentalists and concerned citizens.

During the heated rezoning battle, opponents hurled accusations at developer Douglas Marsh and the project's architect and planner, Patrick MacKenna. In an article from a previous issue of The Enquirer, Steven Mueller, a member of the environmental group, World Advocates for Resources (WAR), said: "The creators of this misplaced monstrosity have concocted the perfect recipe for disaster—they will have blood on their hands." Mueller was unavailable for comment.

Elmer Niederbrucker, Building Inspector for St. Louis County, reached late Sunday night, said, "I told them so. There's places in that floodplain unfit to build on. I said those soils could liquefy when the ground shakes and swallow up buildings, just like quicksand.

"Heck, Dad, you warned those builders a hundred times. Who is that reporter, anyway?"

"Mona Springer and I have tangled before. I fixed her clock the last time she made trouble. She's getting even for what happened in my last case. I can do it again. First of all she's both lazy and just plain lying. She knows the mischief makers have all gone to jail. She neglected to mention they falsified the location of their soil borings, which was proven in court. She doesn't even ask why the County granted a building permit. After all, it was issued after Niederbrucker approved the plans."

"Are you going to sit still for that?"

"I'll get out there later today and get the straight dope on it. Mona always forgets that when we cross swords, she's the one who gets stabbed."

For now he had more important work to do. Confined to the St. Louis "island," Patrick couldn't just run over to Illinois and check on the latest antics of drug pushers, pimps, prostitutes and the "adult" entertainment industry. With Abrams chilling in Chicago and the earthquake here, perhaps those activities would be on hold for a while. Even Bobbi Romano, Adam Reiner and the rest of law enforcement—busy trying to maintain order—were leaving him alone, so he was able to concentrate on his real job.

He focused on dealing with building damage and ensuring occupant safety. He drove to his office, where he found Ed Mossbach and a few of the younger computer technicians and architects on the exterior of the building, installing plywood sheets over shattered plate glass windows and sweeping up debris. The structure had survived, but Mossbach pointed to X-shaped cracks in masonry panels along the exterior walls, which showed how the building's brick walls had been racked back and forth by the tremor's horizontal ground movement. He also warned that aftershocks could be expected in the next couple of days. At least the total disruption of the city's customary activities would also allow him to fashion his own schedule and give him a chance to sort out his many problems.

"Dammit! Will anything in the cursed city stay nailed down?" Patrick kicked a loose brick lying on the parking lot. "Ouch!" He stubbed his toe.

"Got time for lunch, Patrick?" Ed Mossbach rolled down his sleeves and nodded toward his car.

"Why not?" He followed the engineer's lead and climbed in.

Ed drove to the Cheshire Inn, where they sat at a tiny table crowded in among lounge chairs and sofas of the old Fox and Hounds tavern, decorated like a German hunting lodge. A few stalwart lunch patrons had shown up here, one of the few eateries which still had electrical service. Ed picked their famous roast beef. Patrick ordered a corned beef on rye and a round of draft beers. Brooding, he studied a buck's head on the wall.

"What are you going to do about the news story?"

"I'll go out there this afternoon and see for myself what happened. I'll also remind Mona's editor that even his lawyers frown on such sloppy reporting— lawsuits are bad, even for his paper's pathetic reputation. I might also have to remind Mona how much I know about her affairs with married men."

"You're suppressing a lot of anger. I'm concerned about you."

"It's that noticeable?" He counted ceramic beer steins hung above the bar.

"On a personal level, yes. But Gary Archer has confided to me he's worried about the quality of our work. I'm afraid he'll go off and hire some other firm to take over our projects. They still owe us a lot of money. If they go away mad, we'll never get paid."

"He 'confided', eh? Well, I wish he'd 'confide' to me what the hell is eating him. He's turned into a petty, complaining tyrant. Something went wrong in Vietnam, and he can't let it go. Do you know anything about it?"

"Not really. I was assigned to Headquarters in Saigon. I heard somebody shot up a village and killed some innocent villagers. Fog of war I guess." He sighed. "Meanwhile, he seems to be driving you crazy."

"Two of our suspects deal in a side business. Abrams provides Manny Marancik, this gay casino client of ours, with his pretty boys.

"So, what else is new?"

"Seriously, Ed. As if that weren't enough, I suspect Archer's buddy Mercer Tomkins of collusion to be low bidder on our city hall project. Everyone I know is somehow a suspect. But I still don't know who killed Caleb Mitchom. The most likely murder suspects are Abrams and his goons, Erin's kidnappers. The FBI and the U.S. Attorney's office are hampered by the aftermath of the earthquake. On top of all that, Meg's pressuring me to get married. Erin is hiding something about her relationship with her boyfriend from me and the police. Other than that I'm perfectly fine."

"You need to let law enforcement do its job, or you'll have a nervous breakdown."

"Among you, Erin and Meg, I wish everyone would stop worrying about my mental health and focus on their own. I'm beginning to think I'm the only sane one left. Erin says every client I have is either involved with the East Side gangsters or plotted together in Vietnam, and I'm supposed to be the crazy one? I'm beginning to wonder about you. What about your close buddy, Gary Archer. He's been though more trauma than any of us."

"Lay off him, will you?" Ed said. "He's still dealing with battle fatigue. He needs a break."

"I'd like to break his neck."

"Now who's violent?"

"Maybe it's your friend, Archer."

Forty-Two

Patrick was determined to learn more about mysterious city administrator, and he needed to know how the city building had fared in the latest tremor. Besides, he wanted more information about his wartime buddies. He called Gary Archer, who agreed to meet him at his office.

While Erin's historic school campus had survived with minor damage—cracked masonry, broken windows and a lot of ruined plaster—school would be closed for the next couple of days until the power was restored and the mess could be cleaned up. Patrick invited Erin to come along, Erin jumped at the chance, and they set out for Deerpath.

The city hall was still standing, but in unusable condition and strewn with rubble. The staff had been sent home for a least a week. Patrick planned to inspect the damage and then to adjourn to lunch elsewhere. Arriving at eleven, they picked their way through debris to Archer's office, where they found him hunched over his desk, squinting at a sheaf of building plans in the room's gray north light. An empty glass stood at his right hand.

"Hey, Gary."

"I see you made it." He brightened at the sight of Patrick's face and glowered at Erin. "Oh, you again."

"She's off school today and wanted to see how the building fared in the earthquake. How bad is it?"

Archer grimaced. "You can look around, I guess, but don't get hurt. More liability is all I need."

"You won't believe how we got back here. We were in Chicago

when it hit."

"Tell me over lunch." He sighed. "We're in trouble, as usual. See this column?" He pointed to a corner on the floor plan. "It's no longer holding up the roof. It's over the mayor's office, of all places. Damn lucky he wasn't there at the time."

"Let's go take a look."

They walked outside to inspect wall damage. One corner of the building was crushed; the roof drooped as if melted in a surrealist painting. Bricks lay scattered on the ground below. Next they climbed stairs to the mayor's office directly above, where the carpet was strewn with broken glass. Puffs of pink fiberglass insulation cluttered the ornate cherry desk. The mayor's high-backed swivel chair lay on its side. Broken picture frames, a whirlwind of papers and a bust of Washington—its stand toppled and George's neck broken—cluttered the carpet.

"Looks like it was hit by mortar shell." Archer spread his hands. "Where do I start?"

"Stay calm and stick to the basics. It looks as if we may have rain tonight. First, get a crew out here and secure the roof and the broken side of the wall with tarps. Make sure they're properly anchored so they'll stay put in the wind. Next, just in case, move the mayor's furniture and what's left of his fine things to the center of the ground floor, in the conference room."

"Do you think we're miracle workers?"

"No, just workers," Patrick replied. "At least then the mayor can keep functioning and call his council in for meetings when he needs to. We'll bring out a team from the office to evaluate the damage and begin making recommendations for repairs. You did better than I thought in this earthquake. Still, it makes this retrofit project even more urgent."

They returned to Archer's office, where he made phone calls to his field inspectors and his public works director to secure the building against bad weather. "Let's get outta here," he said. "I could use some refreshment."

As they walked to their cars, a chartreuse F250 pickup truck pulled into the lot. A man rushed out of his truck, charged to Archer's side and shook his hand.

"It's about time, Mercer," Archer said. "I'm sure you remember Patrick MacKenna, the architect." He turned to the contractor. "We were trying to assess the damage."

"Hey, MacKenna," Tomkins eyed him warily. "Who's this, your new girlfriend?"

"I beg your pardon. This is my daughter, Erin. She wants to see how this repair work is done. We need to show her the *right* way to do it, so she doesn't learn any cheap shortcuts."

"Looks bad to me. Frankly, you might as well tear it down and start over."

"No way. We're going to have our engineers inspect it first thing in the morning," Patrick said. "It may not be as bad as you think."

"No need. Here's our cost estimate for earthquake repairs."

"Don't you think it might make sense to hear what the scope of the work is before you estimate the cost?"

"Sure, sure. I just wanted you to know that I won't hold you up on this. We want to be your contractor."

"Hold me up? That's what I was afraid of."

"Aw, MacKenna, I'm trying to cooperate here."

"Then let me show you what Ed Mossbach and I had in mind for the retrofit and the plans for the addition. We intend to house the Police Department and a new emergency operations center right here on this site."

"Right, Gary told me. I already allowed for that in my figures. "

"Let me show you anyway, in case our design has a few ideas you hadn't considered,"

Erin tagged along as Archer and her father toured Tomkins around the building, and then showed where the new wing, a new stairwell and elevators would be constructed. They returned to the parking lot.

"You like my new truck?" Tomkins asked.

"Kinda bright, isn't it?" Patrick said, donning his sunglasses.

"I wanted the color of those new fire trucks. We're known for our speed."

"At our firm, we're known for our accuracy. I don't know if we'll be compatible. "

"No problem, MacKenna. We're ready."

"No, you're not."

"But I wish you'd take a look at these figures, I think we'll be able to provide the best deal in town."

"If you want to be considered for this job, you'll wait till I can get you some plans and outline specifications on Friday and then give Gary a price on that."

"But I already put everything aside to get this done for Gary here." He shoved a stack of papers into Patrick's hand. "Now I'm up to my ears in alligators on this earthquake repair work."

"If you're too busy to work on this job, you let me know any time. There are plenty of other contractors out there."

"Don't get the wrong idea. Why do you think I rushed over here?"

"Maybe so you could lean on your old buddy Archer to grant you a no-bid contract. If it makes you happy I'll look them over—if only to see how you do your estimates." He stuck the sheaf of papers in his bag.

"Good. You guys goin' to lunch?"

Patrick grumbled. "I thought you were so busy. Why don't you start work right now?"

"A man's gotta eat."

"Mercer, you instruct your men first and then join us." Archer said. "We're going to our favorite little tavern up the road."

"I'll call them from my truck and meet you there."

They waited until Tomkins climbed into his pickup and roared out of the parking lot. Archer sat in front next to Patrick. Erin got in the back seat.

"Why in creation did you invite him to lunch?" Patrick said. "He's not doing you any favors. If he's your only bidder the city will pay double for these repairs."

"Relax, Patrick. I've known this man for years. We can trust him."

"We'll get his prices, but if I'm involved we'll need to get other bids. And it's the law."

"Maybe that's my problem, Patrick—you're involved."

Patrick stepped on the accelerator, barreled up Manchester Road, into a strip shopping center and parked next to Jill's, Archer's customary haunt. He'd hoped he could still question Gary about his

Vietnam experience before Mercer Tomkins joined them. But the chartreuse truck was already parked at the end of the aisle.

Inside, the waitress ushered them to Archer's usual booth, Tomkins was already seated there, instructing someone over his cell phone. "Go over that building with a fine tooth comb. I want a *detailed* estimate. You hear?" He looked up, surprised. "Gotta go, Charlie. Just do it."

Archer slid into the booth beside Tomkins. Erin slipped into the opposite side. Patrick sat next to her and studied the menu, waiting to see where this conversation would lead.

"You see, MacKenna, I've got a lot of experience in disaster recovery. After those floods last year we restored dozens of businesses."

"Didn't we all?" Patrick said. "I learned more than I ever wanted to know about flood recovery." Tomkins's manner grated on him. "Anyone ever tell you it's rude to address someone using only last name?"

"See, it's not just floods, MacKenna," Tomkins lumbered on. "This year we've been busy all over town fixing earthquake damage."

The waitress came and took orders, starting with drinks. While the other two ordered double bourbons, Patrick and Erin requested iced tea.

Aside from Tomkins's rudeness, Patrick resented his intrusion into his private lunch with Gary Archer. He took the offensive. "I hear you've got all kinds of experience, Mr. Tomkins. Talk to me about some of those patrols you and Gary used to go on in Vietnam."

"I'd rather not."

"It's too depressing," Archer explained for him. "We didn't know who to trust in those villages. If somebody made a false move, sometimes you'd take out innocent people just in case they were hiding Viet Cong."

"Most of the time it was them or us," Tompkins echoed.

"I heard Caleb Mitchom was in your platoon. You know, from Brooklyn, Illinois?"

Archer shook his head and stared at the table. "Poor guy never got a break. Survived his tour in 'Nam, just to get killed in his own home town."

"Dead?" Tompkins stared across his shoulder toward his army

buddy. "I just saw him last month. How did it happen?"

"When you were in Memphis on that industrial job," Archer said. "It was in all the papers. I guess you missed it."

Erin remained silent, taking it all in.

"Man, that's tough." Tomkins rested his forehead on one hand. "First he gets court-martialed and the next thing you know he's dead."

"I hadn't heard about a court-martial. What was that about?" Patrick's eyes bored into Archer, who looked away.

The waitress brought their Swiss steak specials. "Another round for you folks?"

. Tomkins nodded and downed the rest of his drink. Archer handed her his glass.

As they dug into their food, Archer toyed with his.

"You wanna tell it, Gary?" Tomkins said.

The waitress returned with their drinks. Archer took a swig from his glass and began.

"Towns suspected of supporting the enemy were called VC villages. On this particular day, Bravo Company was sent out to search one. As usual, two squads surrounded the village with our half-tracks. Our riflemen stood guard. Our squad, with Mitchom, Tomkins and me, was in the other half, chosen to enter the hootches and conduct the search. First we rounded up civilians and herded them to an open space near the center of the village, where a group from another squad guarded them. Then we systematically searched the hootches for weapons, tunnel entrances and any stragglers who might be Viet Cong."

"Most of these farmers wanted to be left alone to grow rice, make their products and take care of their families," Tompkins added. "But the Viet Cong wouldn't let them alone. In the evenings they sent instructors into the villages to hold 'educational' sessions. They'd hype the 'benefits' of their liberation movement. Because these VC shared their language and culture, the villagers tended to trust and sympathize with them. They didn't really care who ran the government.

"Anyway, in this one hootch," Archer continued, "there's this teenage girl with an old man who's half blind and scared. Then hiding behind a screen we find a terrified mother and three young children. Mitchom, our squad leader, who knew a few words of Vietnamese, started badgering the old man with questions. He asked why he didn't go to the center with the others. It seemed like she was saying he was too old and sick. Then he asked him if he was Viet Cong."

"The old guy kept muttering '*Toi khong biet*'— 'I don't know,'" Tomkins added. "This was their standard answer for anyone who addressed a native villager in English, sort of like, 'I don't understand you.'"

Archer took a big gulp of his bourbon. "Poor old guy—miserable, squatting there, in his ragged shift and bare feet. Kept saying, '*Khong biet, khong biet...*'"

"Then Mitchom said, 'See? He even admits they're Cong-Viet. Now get the hell out. Keep watch.' So we did."

"Next thing I know, automatic fire is coming from the hootch— three bursts. We rush back in and there's Mitchom, the barrel of his rifle smoking. Five bleeding mangled bodies are sprawled across the dirt floor."

"That's horrid," Erin exclaimed.

Archer looked at her, his eyes wild.

"I can't believe he would do something that cold hearted." Patrick gulped his iced tea. "He wasn't like that."

"You don't know what you're like until you're in that situation. It's kill or be killed. But— an old man, a woman and three children— we couldn't believe it either. Archer drained his second double bourbon on the rocks. He hadn't touched his food. "I still see the old man lying on his back, his eyes wide open, a terrified expression on his face. Haunts me to this day."

"The Army didn't conduct a full investigation," Tomkins said. "Something wasn't right." He reached for the green and white slip of paper the waitress had left. "Here, I'll get this check."

"No thanks, Tompkins." Patrick grabbed it first. "Save your money and sharpen your pencil. We need your best number on this job. And don't finish your estimate until I send you those drawings and outline specifications— you'll have them by Friday noon. *My office will decide which items actually need to be rebuilt.*"

"If you say so, MacKenna," Tomkins said

He paid the waitress at the bar and they walked out the door into the daylight glare.

After dropping the city administrator back at City Hall, Erin said, "Archer and Tomkins seem a little too cozy."

"I have an idea of why, but we need some help with research. Let's go see Bobbi Romano."

He drove to the FBI office on Market downtown. They found her wrapping up the day's work at her desk.

"I've put Erin back on the case." Patrick chuckled. "I hope you approve, especially since she's a top-notch interviewer."

"She was never off it," Bobbi said. "What have you got?"

"Our little jaunt to Chicago turned up a few stray facts," he offered.

"Did you talk to Radi, our agent up there?" Bobbi asked.

"Briefly, on the phone. I was tempted to call him in, but I didn't need to. Erin loosened our man up just fine."

"You found Abrams?" Bobbi said.

"With some help from Billie the innkeeper and a tip from my father, we found him holed up in a grand Victorian ruin on the Northwest side. Apparently, he's got a new girlfriend."

"He didn't know Roxie was dead," Erin said. "He was pretty broken up about it."

"At least he put on a good show of grief," Patrick added.

"No, Dad. I know him," Erin said. "He really loved her."

"Good job, Erin," Bobbi said. "What else did he say?"

"He claims innocence," Patrick said. "'I'm a respectable businessman...' and all that bull."

"The devil he is," Bobbi said. "We can get him on enough drug charges alone to put him away for good, not to mention exploitation of minors, prostitution and kidnapping."

"He stonewalled us and offered no clues to Mitchom's killer."

"Hold on here," Bobbi said, "who did Abrams meet with at Billie's place?"

"Billie said he came in last week with Manny Marancik, Wally Wonka, the Outfit's computer geek, and the gangster Scarface McGurk."

"Tell me those aren't really their names."

"Hey, it's Chicago," Patrick said. "We've got plenty of suspects, but no proof."

"Like who?"

"I'd put them in three groups— the Vietnam vets, the casino operators and the mob."

"Turns out Mitchom was in the Army in Vietnam with Deerpath City Administrator Gary Archer and this contractor buddy of his, Mercer Tomkins. All three were in Bravo Company. Something about a massacre of civilians— both Archer and Tomkins blame it on Mitchom, and there was a court-martial.

"Then He made application for a casino in Brooklyn. Mitchom made sure they turned it down flat.

"Finally there's the mob. Scarface McGurk is a Mafia don from Chicago, underboss and enforcer of the North Side Bohannon gang. He's moving into Metro East, working his way into Abrams' operations. He felt entitled to Mitchom's protection for his Brooklyn operations and more support for Abrams's cash cows—his clubs, whores and drug dealers in Brooklyn. He was really upset when he didn't get either one."

"So who do you think murdered the Mayor of Brooklyn?" Bobbi asked

"Don't know. Mitchom had lots of enemies."

"He shoulda taken a Dale Carnegie course," Bobbi said. "It seems the only remaining mystery is what happened in Vietnam. Sounds like I'm due for a visit to the Military Personnel Records Center. Some hippie war protesters tried to burn the place down in the seventies, but maybe I'll get lucky and find that their files weren't destroyed."

FORTY-THREE

Friday night Meg was helping her mother with her weekly chores and Erin went to a movie with Kelly. Patrick used the time alone to study Mercer Tomkins's new cost estimate for the Deerpath City Hall.

Weary of staring at figures, he took his papers into the kitchen to get a beer and let out the dog when Erin entered the kitchen.

"Hey, Dad."

"How was the movie?"

"Good. A chick flick. You'd hate it. What are you doing?"

"I'm trying to make sense of Tomkins's estimate. The cost of each work item seems reasonable, and each trade subcontract is in line with normal costs in the region. But the total doesn't make sense—the cost per square foot appears way too high for this size and type of project.

"It's too perfect," he said, as he sipped from his can. "There's too much money in it for the construction manager—he's only supposed to coordinate the work of the subcontracted trades. Sometimes he does the carpentry as well."

"How much money?"

"He's got almost a million dollars in here for his firm's portion of the work. Who does he think is going to believe his prices?"

"He's probably charging you double," she said.

Patrick grabbed his stack of papers and looked again. "That's it!"

Parnell, just reentering the sliding door, looked up, curious.

"That construction management figure has lots of money in it for—" Patrick fanned through Tomkins' estimate sheets— "carpentry!" But he's already got enough money in his carpentry contractor's bid to do the entire job. Why, he's got duplications of carpentry labor throughout his estimate, No wonder it's so high. He's almost half a million dollars over."

"There you go," Erin said.

"See, I knew Tomkins was trying to cheat the city."

"Maybe they both are," Erin said. "Like they're in it together, or something."

"Now Erin, this is where you get off. I've busted my butt to win this account and I won't have you questioning Gary's motives. He's the client after all. He has a right to be a bit eccentric." However, Erin's suggestion preyed on his mind.

He took his cell phone from his belt and punched in a number. "Bobbi, sorry to disturb you at home."

"No problem, Patrick, what's up?"

"Archer gave me a premature cost estimate, and I've been going over it. I've found a half-million-dollar overstatement in Tomkins's figures. Archer might know about it. What do you make of that?"

"Maybe they're in cahoots."

"How could that be? I've worked with this man for over a year. He's a pretty good public servant, and I have no reason to suspect him. Why would they collude?"

"I found Mitchom's and Tomkins's files at the records center," Bobbi said. "Archer's is missing. It doesn't prove much— lots of records in this archive have been lost. In 1973 Vietnam war protestors set the St. Louis Military Personnel Records Center on fire. It burned for days and smoldered for weeks."

"Do you think Archer's file was were destroyed in that fire?"

"Doubtful. They told me most of the records destroyed by the fire and water damage were from World Wars I and II. Anyway, a court-martial was brought against Mitchom over a 1968 massacre during the Tet offensive in a small village outside Hue, but the charges were dismissed."

"What did Mitchom say in his own defense?"

"He said he sent Archer and Tomkins into the hootch and he went on to supervise other members of his squad."

"That's odd," Patrick said. "Tomkins claims Mitchom went in

while he and Archer stood guard outside."

"The case was dismissed for lack of evidence against Mitchom."

"Somebody's lying."

"And Archer's personnel records have disappeared. It always helps to blame the dead guy," Bobbi said. "At least he can't contradict you."

"I think Gary's clear of anything like this. Tomkins may be crooked, but it happens a lot with the fierce competition of contractors trying to get a job. Tomkins handed these figures directly to me— Gary hasn't even had a chance to review them. He'll disqualify Tomkins once I show him this."

"If they're colluding, that's nothing new in the construction industry." Bobbi paused. "But it doesn't tell us who killed Mitchom."

"I'm working on that. Maybe Gary can fill in the blanks. I'm meeting with first thing tomorrow."

He ended the call.

"She thinks Tomkins and Archer are colluding. I just can't believe it."

"You might give it some thought, Dad. Archer's pretty unstable. His trauma in the war was a lot worse than ours."

"I'll ask Archer what he thinks of these figures when I see him in the morning."

"I probably ought to get to bed, Dad. I'm going upstairs."

"I'm ready to turn in, too, Erin. We'll figure it out tomorrow." He retired to the master bedroom and she went upstairs to her room.

◊

Erin lay in bed, restless. She wasn't ready for sleep.

She recalled what her father had told her about trauma, and how it can affect people's behavior for years to come. She'd been reading about it since that day, in hopes of overcoming the ill effects of the traumatic experiences in her life. Her dad had tried to repress them, and it had made him short-tempered and mean, subject to unpredictable outbursts. Her means of coping was to do the opposite: she had returned to the river to evoke fond memories of her mother, actively trying to overcome the affliction. She learned that people who repress it often do it though drugs and alcohol. She remembered she'd seen the city manager take a drink in his office. She'd learned that people who have been exposed to violence often recreate the violence in their lives.

Archer wasn't stupid. She didn't believe Tomkins could fool the city administrator with a padded bid. What would drive Archer to tamper with the bidding on a public project and violate the citizens' trust? Maybe he was covering something up. Maybe he would be capable of killing a man. Maybe he had even murdered innocent people before, and was capable of doing it again.

Oh. My. God. She sat up, trembling, her eyes wide. It added up. So many things pointed to the argumentative city manager.

She needed to know more about Archer, but she couldn't approach him directly during the day without her father present. With him there, her dad would be too respectful to his client. Something told her this matter couldn't wait until morning.

She called Jimmy. "I'm worried about the city manager of Deerpath," she said. "He's hiding something. It has to do with his Vietnam experience." She told him all she could remember about her luncheon discussion with Archer and Tomkins, her suspicions about their cozy relationship, and Tomkins's phony cost estimate with inflated figures. "Archer's not acting like a city official trying to get a good deal on construction. Even with their war stories, they cover for each other and finish each other's sentences, as if they had rehearsed it."

"That figures. My dad still sees his buddies from Vietnam. As far as he's concerned they can do no wrong. My brother, too. He was—"

"Just as I thought, Jimmy." Erin interrupted him before he could get too deep into sad reminiscences of his late brother. "I think something really rotten is going on at that city hall, and I'd like to investigate. Dad is trying to keep Archer as a client and considers him above suspicion. It's nighttime now and we could sneak in there and look at his files. Maybe we can find a clue to what he's doing."

"I'm game. Can you get out of the house undetected?"

"Dad just turned in for the night. He'll be dead to the world in no time."

Minutes later Jimmy killed his headlights and pulled in front of their house. Erin came out of the shadows of the tall shrubs and slipped silently into the Mustang's passenger seat.

"The building will be locked," Jimmy said. "How are we going to get in?"

"It's no longer secure after all this damage. Trust me, I'm pretty sure we can."

But she hadn't figured that door to the building would be ajar. In addition, when they crept into the parking lot at Deerpath City Hall with the headlights off, a white van was parked behind the construction dumpster.

"Look, Erin. This is too dangerous. We don't know who's in there. Let me go in, and you can keep watch and call the cops if you need to."

"Not a good idea. You don't know what to look for. What if you're attacked? I'm going in there with you."

They eased silently through the doorway and into the main corridor. A rhythmic clanking came from the big council chamber in the near front corner of the building.

She trembled and her legs went weak. The last time she had snuck up on a suspicious sound, she'd been captured and had endured a long ordeal. At least she had Jimmy with her this time. She took a deep breath and motioned for him to follow. She opened a door in the corridor, opened another on her left, climbed five steps and entered a darkened projection booth. Jimmy closed the door behind them, isolating them from the sounds in the council chamber.

Her father had allowed her to view his presentations unobserved from here. It was a perfect vantage point to see what went on without being seen. Tripping on a slide projector, which had slipped off its stand in the earthquake, she muttered under her breath and took a seat on the projectionist's metal chair. Jimmy took another next to her. In the dim available light the entire audience area and a conference table spread out before them in front of the raised stage and dais. Toppled chairs, a coffee stand and a jumble of wires and microphones cluttered the floor. Plate glass corner windows had broken, and plaster had fallen from the walls, revealing bare steel studs and columns.

As her eyes adjusted she realized the only light came from an electric lantern. A man in a dark hoodie sweatshirt was chipping away at the column base in the weakened corner of the building. After he cut a chunk from one side of the column flange, he kicked the column. They heard a faint clang through the glass, and the building groaned. He uncoiled a roll of wire, which he connected to a black box and set it at the base of the column.

"Fuse wire!" Jimmy said. "What if it's connected to explosive charges?"

"He's trying to collapse the structure!" Erin whispered.

Packing his tools in his bag, the hooded man surveyed the floor for any he had missed and restored the scattered rubble to the corner by the column. He whirled around. A man stood facing him in the gloom with a knife leveled at his throat.

"Omigod, we've gotta get out of here." Erin's heart pounded in chest.

"Bad timing," Jimmy said. "Our exits are, so to speak, cut off."

In a movie, that line would have made her laugh. This wasn't funny.

"Stinks," she said. "We can't hear anything. Do something,"

By the dim light spilled from room into the booth, Jimmy surveyed an array of dials and knobs on the control panel. He flipped a switch on the left side of the console and the amplifier sprang to life. Its gold dials and red and green lights glowed. He twisted the largest knob. Immediately they heard shuffling and grunts from the room. She and Jimmy bumped fists in triumph.

"Not you!" the hooded man croaked. He'd been caught flat-footed, surprised in the darkness. His voice trembled. "Wh-what d-do you want?"

"I came to even the score."

Squinting in the dim light, Erin made out a thin form hunched forward like a cat poised to spring. A gash disfigured his left cheek.

Erin blanched. "Jimmy— it's Scarface McGurk!"

"Some folks find your presence, shall we say, inconvenient?" The man's nondescript, scarred face twisted into a sardonic grin.

"Who are they? And what the hell did I do?"

She recognized the timbre of the other man's voice. With his face turned away from her, she had difficulty placing it.

"You know what you did. And you can probably guess who's unhappy about it."

"What do they want?" The man wobbled and leaned on a desk to steady himself.

"First they need their fifty back, plus the sugar. Totals one hundred grand."

"But, I paid it back. Ask Abrams. And then you made me—"

McGurk pointed the knife at his throat, silencing him.

The revelations were shocking enough— these were some pretty high stakes. Then it dawned on her. The voice of the saboteur was that of Gary Archer. Despite the isolation of the soundproof enclosure, she whispered her discoveries into Jimmy's ear as he riveted his eyes on the drama.

"Blood is good enough for Solly, but the Big Boss still wants his cash. If you were removed from the picture, he wouldn't miss you one bit." He stepped closer and grabbed the lobe of Archer's ear. Get it by next Friday. Or else."

"Huh?" Archer gasped and squirmed.

"Just so you won't forget." With a lighting move, he flicked off Archer's earlobe.

"O-o-ww-w," Archer screamed. His assailant disappeared in the bat of an eye through the hall doorway. Archer scrambled toward a demolished plate glass window behind the dais and leapt feet first though the opening, leaving a trail of blood behind him.

They cowered motionless in the dim light for what seemed like an eternity.

"What if they see my car?" Jimmy asked.

"I wouldn't worry about Archer," Erin said. "You're parked on the other side of the big dumpster from him. He has too many problems of his own to find it. The slasher probably parked on the other side, by the main entrance."

To make sure they were alone, they waited fifteen minutes in the projection booth.

"You've got to call that detective. What's her name— Bobbi?"

"Bobbi Romano. I can't. Dad bugged Bobbi once already tonight. He'll kill me if he finds out I snuck out on him. Get me home so I can pretend I've been safe in my bed all this time."

"I don't like it, Erin. This is a crime scene. We should report it."

"It's too late to catch McGurk. I'll tell her in the morning. I've got to get back home and sleep."

FORTY-FOUR

Despite her hopes for forgetful sleep, Erin awoke unrested after a fitful night. She washed her puffed, groggy eyes and rushed downstairs, overflowing with guilt. She needed to confess to her father what she had gotten herself and Jimmy into last night. His bed was made and the kitchen cleaned up from breakfast.

He was gone.

The clock on the stove said 9:14 a.m.

Dang, overslept.

School was supposed to resume today, too. Right. As if that even mattered.

On the table sat a box of doughnuts. Her father had left half a pot of coffee, and it was still warm. Despite her concerns for the baby, she needed to clear her head. She poured herself a cup and let out Parnell. She sat down, munched on a glazed French doughnut and ruminated on last night's events.

She figured the most urgent thing was to report to Bobbi and get her going on investigating Archer. She picked up the kitchen phone and punched in her cell phone number, which she now knew by heart.

"Hey, Bobbi."

"Hey, Erin. What's goin' down?"

She told her what she and Jimmy had witnessed at the city hall.

"Erin, what the hell got into you? I can't be minding you twenty-four-seven."

"You need to get out there right away. There's some evidence to be collected— all sorts of wire and fuses, and some tools— in the council chamber. Also, lots of blood for DNA evidence. Oh, and probably a missing ear. Scarface McGurk came to collect a big juice loan Archer owes to the mob. "

"By now Archer's long gone. The trail may be cold. I'll assemble a team and get out there as quick as I can, probably this afternoon. Just go to school, for chrissake."

"And Bobbi, I took Jimmy with me this time. If he hadn't known how to turn on the sound system, we wouldn't have heard a thing. I think we've cracked the case wide open."

"Dammit, Erin. You almost got yourself killed. Let us cops chase the crooks."

Chastened, she snatched another glazed doughnut, refilled her coffee and resolved to take Bobbi's advice. Then she remembered what her father had said before he went to bed. He was meeting with Gary Archer at nine this morning. At Deerpath City Hall.

"Oh no!" she cried. Archer had weakened the supporting columns of the building. She recalled the floor strewn with wires. Connected to a black box. What if he had set timed fuses for charges to go off? Or was a suicide bomber bent on blowing himself up along with her dad?

She grabbed the phone again and tried to connect with her father's cell. She immediately got his recording.

He must have turned it off for the meeting.

She gorged on her last bite of doughnut, washed it down with the tepid coffee and raced out the patio door. She found Parnell sniffing at a rabbit hole, picked him up and carried the squealing animal inside.

"Damn," she cursed. Her guilty desire to conceal her discoveries from Patrick had led him right into a trap!

She dropped the baffled dog, grabbed her jacket and cell phone and dashed out the front door to the car. She had to warn him before it was too late. On the highway she veered around a balky truck, triggering a honk and annoyed gestures from the driver she had cut off.

What if she drove up to another exploding building, too late to prevent disaster? *My father's in there— he's all I have left of my family.* Heartsick, she realized she would be alone in the world— an orphan, pregnant and without education, a job or the support of loving parents.

What did she do to deserve all this?

◊

As usual, Patrick was late for his meeting with Gary Archer. He pulled into the city hall parking lot and entered the building to do a quick survey of existing conditions before the meeting. As he walked past the corner council room he noticed a wire snaked toward the corner of the room, connected to a box and a packet of some kind. Drywall sheathing had been stripped from the base of the corner column, and the wide steel flanges had been cut away at critical points. He kicked the column; the weakened structure creaked in complaint.

"Sabotage!" he cried aloud. He grabbed the cordite fuse wire and yanked it free of its attachment. He kicked the explosive packet away from the column base. But there could be others. He had perhaps minutes to warn Archer and make his escape.

He headed down the corridor toward Gary Archer's office. Halfway there, he glanced into the finance office. Behind the usually neat row of desks, chairs were overturned, a computer lay on the floor and papers were scattered everywhere.

He stepped into the office and saw no one.

"Hold it right there, MacKenna."

Patrick whirled. Emerging from the vault, Gary Archer, with a two-day beard, disheveled shirt, wrinkled pants and a large bandage covering his left ear, stood with a gun pointed at him, a black leather satchel in his left hand.

"What the hell happened to you?"

"I had a little accident, MacKenna, and now I plan to get well."

"Hey. Put that gun away. I just discovered someone tried to boo-by trap this structure. I'm trying to help you solve this building's problems."

"You're my biggest problem, MacKenna. You've stuck your nose in my business once too often."

A stray sunbeam from the window glinted off the shiny barrel of Archer's souvenir .45 caliber pistol. In the flash of light he saw the whole picture.

"It all makes sense," Patrick continued. "Bobbi Romano did a little digging at the Records Center yesterday. Mitchom was innocent, wasn't he? You've got the story of your army buddies backwards. You were responsible for the massacre in the Vietnam village. Doesn't that sound about right, Trooper?""

"Why, you—" Archer leveled the gun at his head. "That's what the men called me, all right. They looked up to me, the soul of the team."

"And that explains why you're so beholden to your contractor buddy, Tomkins. You keep him well paid, so he won't rat on you."

"Everything would be fine, if you hadn't started nosing around. This project would've gotten built. Everyone would be paid and I would be headed for a comfortable retirement. You force me to create a scene and make a big mess on this nice floor."

"But why kill me? Why not your buddy, Mercer Tomkins? He's the last living witness to your crime."

"There's more to it than that. I was into that bastard Solly Abrams for fifty grand, plus interest, which doubled the damages."

"Whew, that's some serious dough. How did you manage that?"

"Oh, broads, gambling, drugs— Abrams had 'em all, plus easy credit— until now. Man, it's rough, after living through a war like that. Right after the war, I applied for disability based on Post Traumatic Stress Disorder. The bastards denied it,."

"Yeah. Maybe they couldn't find your files. How come your folder's missing? But I can see why you didn't want anyone else to know what you did."

"It's none of your damn business, MacKenna. That's why I have to kill you."

"How did you hurt your ear?" Patrick was sweating like a foundry worker. His stomach was tied in knots. Despite his cool demeanor, he was frantic. He had to prolong this conversation. It was the only thing keeping him alive.

"I had a little accident— ran into Scarface McGurk's knife. And that brings me to you. You know entirely too much now, and he'll be back for his money soon. I have to go. I paid Solly once, but he didn't turn over the cash to the gang. I had another idea, to take a hundred grand from the city to pay McGurk off out of our cash on hand, collections from property tax payments, parking meter revenues and traffic fines—we had a big month. But now I've got an even better one. The treasury here gives me enough cash money and bearer bonds to take early retirement."

"You'll never get away with it. There are too many people on your trail now." Even as he said it, Patrick thought it sounded lame.

Archer patted what looked like a TV remote sticking out of his shirt pocket. "I'm going make your death look like an accident. No one will ever know. First, I have to make sure you don't run away."

Images of Kitty, Erin and Meg raced before Patrick's eyes.

◊

Erin swerved toward the off-ramp for Deerpath to a chorus of honks from alarmed drivers. She was terrified for her father. *Get a grip*, she told herself. She recalled Sol Abrams's leer. Her anger at her unjust captors returned. That was all it took.

She pulled up to the Deerpath building. All looked serene from the outside. She brought her mother's old Chevy to a screeching halt in the parking lot. Relieved to see the building still standing, she hopped out onto the pavement. As she rushed inside looking for Patrick, she heard groans and creaks from the weakened structure. She proceeded down the hall toward Gary Archer's office. Passing a door on the left side of the hall, she heard a raised voice, speaking in angry tones.

She peered through an entry hall into the room. Archer had the drop on her father!

"You'd better shut up now, MacKenna. I need to get outta here before our cops do their rounds."

"Okay, so you owed the mob big bucks. But why murder Caleb Mitchom?"

Her father was stalling for time, until he could think of a way to survive. So she could be sure not to miss a word, Erin crept inside the door jamb, still hidden from view by the passage into the room beside the massive vault.

Erin's heart pounded; her palms grew sweaty.

"Why didn't they honor Abrams's bargain with you?" Patrick asked.

"Scarface never knew about it. I paid Abrams what he wanted, but McGurk never got his money. Solly's drug profits were running behind, and he didn't have the cash. Abrams welshed on his part of the deal. He told them I was a deadbeat and wouldn't pay up."

"And to think Abrams claimed he was a respectable businessman!"

"So McGurk came down to collect. By that time I was flat broke' He gave me a way out—bump Mitchom off and cancel my debt. I didn't want to kill a buddy. They handed me an AK-47. McGurk held me at knifepoint and started digging in. Before I knew it he was dead—in the basement of his club during a show. The band and the crowd were so loud nobody could hear. Seems like everybody at least oughta have the right to a public execution."

So that was it. The Outfit's tentacles reached everywhere. Erin trembled to think how close her escape from them had been. If she hadn't fled when she did, she might never have gotten out alive. She drew in her breath and focused on Archer's words.

"You need to come clean. I'll bet you could get a good plea bargain if you turned state's evidence against Abrams. You know enough to convict him."

"See, you're trying to run my affairs again. You and that piss-ant daughter of yours. You two always get in my way."

Erin resented Archer's choice of words. She inhaled sharply and snorted.

"What was that?"

Darn it. Will I ever learn? She flattened herself against the wall of the narrow passage, trying to become invisible. She was sweating. Her heart hammered like a pile driver against the wall of her chest. She'd given herself away before, and look what had happened.

"Your guilty conscience, Archer. You're hearing things."

"I don't think so, MacKenna. With lightning speed he darted into the passage, grabbed Erin around her neck and held her as a shield, with his gruesome gun pointed at her head Archer held her so tightly around the neck she could barely breathe.

"One false move and she's dead. You count to one hundred and don't move. Too bad I can't stick around to see the building collapse on you."

"Look out! Patrick pointed up. Archer looked where he pointed. Patrick lunged toward Archer and knocked the gun upward with the edge of his hand. He kneed him hard in the solar plexus. Archer crumpled, his grip relaxed and Erin squirmed free. He fell backward toward the wide-open steel vault.

Patrick reached down and recovered the gun. "Now raise your hands where I can see them," he commanded.

"No you don't." He reached for the remote in his packet.

"No, not that!" Erin screamed in terror.

"Erin, run. Now! Go out the side door where you came in. I disconnected fuses wires down there. And wait for me."

"Hurry, Dad." Erin dashed out of the room toward the exit.

◊

All Patrick had to do was shoot, but something held him back.

"Looks like a draw, Gary. Either way, you lose. Maybe we should talk."

"What about?" Archer lowered his hand from his shirt pocket and struggled to stand up.

"I want to know what's happened to you. Until a few months ago, we were getting along just fine. Then I watched you unravel."

Archer regained his feet, shook his head and looked at Patrick. "You ever had nightmares, hallucinations, stuff like that?"

"Yeah." Patrick cast down his eyes.

"I have plenty. They're so real I can't tell them from a dream. When an old man comes into my office and begs for tax relief. In a crowded elevator, when a little black-haired girl holding her mother's hand turns around and looks at me, her dark, innocent eyes wide, I panic. I'm trapped."

"That bad?"

"I can't get that old man out of my head. He reached out to me, pleading. He was her grandpa. I think about him, cradling her in his arms during our shelling of the town, so she could go to sleep. His eyes said it all—sheer terror. When he fell, the little girl was in my line of fire. The automatic kept spouting fire. The picture of innocence. She thought all people were her friends, until we came along. Her pretty little face, ruined. Her beautiful black hair, spread on the floor, her own blood oozing through it. Her mother's eerie scream—not even human. I couldn't take it. I shut her up.

"When I'm in a group of people, I can't join in. I see their mouths moving, hear their voices, their laughter and their relaxed good humor. I see though life. I know all it would take would be a few bullets to make the world silent for me again. I could be in peace, at least for a while, until the old horrors rise up again. And the cycle starts all over.

"At first I was able to forget about it all with a new woman, drinks and a good party, like most everybody does to forget. It worked for a while, but the dead still came after me. Then I had to keep them in check with pot. When that wouldn't work anymore, I started using crack. Abrams had it all, and I needed it. That's how I ran up such a big bill with the Outfit."

"It's that bad." Patrick felt cold, icy water rise around him. He lifted his head for air, fumbled with frozen fingers for a seat belt. Kitty's imploring eyes. Her last request, "I'm okay— get Erin."

He shuddered and remembered where he was.

"Yes, Patrick, it's that bad. There's no escape. I'm in the prison of my own mind."

"If I follow Erin out that door, what happens?"

Archer patted the remote in his shirt pocket. "I'll take my chances— a living hell, or going straight there. Who knows which is worse?"

"And this building, which we've tried so hard to save?"

"Like Tomkins said, you'd be better off to tear it down and start over. By the way—he's clean. That was his second submission you saw. I gave him a number for what I said was an additional building on the radio tower site, by a separate carpentry contractor, and told him to include it in his estimate. He thought it was for the expansion to City Hall."

"I knew something was wrong," Patrick said.

"With all this new earthquake damage, those old estimates were out the window anyway. A new building would serve the city better in the long run."

"Maybe I did I try too hard to save what's beyond repair." Patrick shook his head.

"Okay, you said your piece. Now get out."

"You'll be blamed for the destruction. Any regrets?"

"None. The people have been out of it for days. The place is a wreck."

"I have none either. But you've got to promise me you won't tell a living soul."

"Not too much chance of that, now, is there?"

"Guess not." Patrick heaved a sigh. He felt a lump form in his throat.

"You have my word." He looked Patrick in the eye. "You'd better go now."

Archer pressed a button on the remote. Fuses hissed.

Patrick ran down the hall and cleared the side door.

He rejoined Erin and hustled her off to the far side of the parking lot. A loud detonation shattered the calm, followed by the crumbling of plaster and groans from of the mortally wounded structure. Then another, larger blast. The roof pancaked down to the second floor slab, which collapsed on the ground slab. A mushroom cloud of debris and dust rose into the sky. The dying monster emitted a gruesome roar of protest,

Patrick grabbed his cellphone and placed a call.

"Mr. Tomkins, this is Patrick MacKenna."

"What's up, MacKenna?"

"An explosion has destroyed the Deerpath City Hall building. Your friend Archer's trapped inside. His air supply is limited and we desperately need to dig him out.

"Oh, my God! I'll get a dozer-front loader and a bucket crane over there right away. By the way, this one's on me."

A city police officer approached him. "Here let me put Officer, uh, Riley, on the line to describe the scene," Patrick said, as he read his nametag. He explained Tomkins was on the way with heavy machinery. "He'll explain how the situation looks from out here."

"What happened?" the cop's partner asked.

Patrick related relevant parts of the story—the building sabotage and how he and his daughter had barely escaped. The rest could wait until they could piece together the whole picture with Bobbi Romano and Adam Reiner.

Forty-Five

On Friday, with Patrick recovered from their showdown with Archer, they met with Bobbi Romano and Adam Reiner at his office in the federal courthouse downtown.

Miss Fritz rose from her desk. "Patrick, it's good to see you and Erin all in one piece after everything that's happened."

Patrick greeted Eleanor warmly, glad to see her familiar face. As she stepped toward the conference room door, opened it, and ushered them in. He regarded her birdlike frame, clad in a long brown dress. Once he had looked down on her as an old maid, hopelessly in love with her boss. But now he regarded survival of human kindness in any form with wonder.

Adam Reiner looked up from an intense conversation with Bobbi. "You're just in time, Patrick. We're closing in on the Brooklyn operators."

"That's great. Bobbi told me about it on the phone."

"Take your time and fill us in on the details," the attorney said.

For Reiner's benefit Patrick recounted a play-by-play of the last few days' events and Gary Archer's ambush. Erin described his hostage-taking, the building sabotage and the building explosion.

"With the construction equipment Mercer Tomkins brought in," Bobbi said, "we managed to excavate the collapsed ground floor. There was no trace of Gary Archer."

"Well, I'll be damned." Patrick said, "What about the leather satchel full of cash?"

"We searched for the bag you described—nowhere to be found."

"Did you search the vault?"

"Of course, but there's a time lock. We had to wait until the next day before city could open it. It had been cleaned out. Nothing left but files and petty cash."

"He was in front of the vault when he ignited the fuses to set off the blast. I barely got out in time." Patrick compressed his lips. Erin nodded in confirmation of her father's statement.

When the new vault door was installed, Patrick had studied the security system and discussed the time lock with his client. Archer knew the code to override it.

A puzzled look flashed across Bobbi's face. "There's no way he can escape. We have an all-points bulletin out for him. We've even alerted the border patrol. Based on yours and Erin's testimony, he's wanted for the murder of Caleb Mitchom."

Patrick looked down at the table. "He was a good client and, I thought, a decent enough guy. It all began years before, with a war he didn't start and couldn't finish. I can't help but think it could've turned out some other way."

Reiner riveted him with a serious look. "Don't beat yourself up about that, Patrick. There's a little good in everybody. It's all about the bad choices they make. There's not much you can do to prevent that."

"I suppose you're right..."

"I've asked Radi to pick up Abrams in Chicago," Bobbi resumed. "We'll get him on kidnapping, drug dealing, child endangerment, human trafficking and racketeering charges. I doubt if he'll ever see the outside of a prison cell again."

"Big whoop," Erin said. "Somebody should have done this a long time ago."

"Until your bad luck we couldn't get enough proof make the charges stick," Reiner said. "He could get life plus enough years for all of his crimes to keep him in prison for good."

"Hey, speaking of proof," Erin said. "Here's the flash drive Roxie gave me from Sol Abrams office. We've tried to read it but it's gibberish."

"Gimme a look at that," Bobbi said.

She handed it to Bobbi, who inserted it into her laptop on the table. "Hmm. It's encrypted. I think I can crack it." She fiddled with the files. "Ah, here it comes. Adam can we hook this up to your projector?"

Moments later, what looked like a contact database flashed upon the screen behind Reiner.

"Holy crap!" Bobbi exclaimed. "There's McGurk's cell phone number, and a whole bunch of contacts with Chicago and Detroit area codes— man! By the time we get this sorted out, we'll have names, phone numbers and locations for Abrams's bosses and the whole organization. They can't escape us now."

"I wouldn't get too carried away," Reiner said. "We've already got plenty on the boys in Brooklyn. It's mainly a mop up job from here on."

Patrick wondered if the Assistant U. S. Attorney mistrusted the evidence just because his teenage daughter had found it. Or because a female Special Agent had cracked the code.

"No, Adam," Bobbi countered. "What Erin has given us here will keep us busy for months. We may be able to bust the Midwestern mob wide open."

Bobbi took Reiner aside and they spoke earnestly for a few moments. He sighed and turned toward Erin. "Young lady, I thought I'd never say this, but I'll have to admit you did help us—a lot. Bobbi's going to put in your name, right beside your father's, for the FBI Director's Community Leadership Award."

"I can't wait to write the citation," Bobbi said, grinning at Patrick and Erin.

"And I'll endorse it," Reiner said with a tight smile.

"Why, me?" Erin said, looking bewildered. "Kelly and Jimmy helped a lot, and it's my dad who did it. All I did was save my neck. Bobbi and Mr. Reiner should get credit, too."

"Don't worry about us. It's our job, and this solved case will look good on our records. But this is a pretty big deal," Bobbi said. "You'll be our only nominees from St. Louis. The citation is presented in Washington by the Director of the FBI."

"And of course, I could never have done it without Roxie's—" Erin looked away and burst into tears.

"Hey, you were brave and smart when you had to be." Patrick put a comforting arm around his daughter. "We've got you back in one piece. That's all that matters." He hugged her.

On the way home, Patrick said, "Erin, I'm proud of you. You kept your head in the most trying situations."

"Thanks, Dad." She took his hand and squeezed it. "Some of that advice you tried to give me was good. Now I get what you meant by 'experience.'"

Then she fell silent as her personal storm cloud returned. She would never tell him how close she came to blowing it all— being tempted by Roxie's offer, making her stage debut as Fifi, the Marmalade Cat Girl, and how close she came to her personal ruin. Moreover, she still hadn't told him about her pregnancy.

As Patrick drove around the block and west on Market Street, Erin's view of the Gateway Arch was replaced by the Egyptian-Greek Revival Civil Courts tower, the Renaissance revival City Hall and the art deco Soldiers Memorial. Opposite the elegant stones of the Romanesque Union Station lay a block-long spray fountain. Bronze nude female and male figures representing the Missouri and the Mississippi rivers faced each other from opposite ends of a long reflecting pool, doused by spouting dolphins in a display of gushing fertility. The composition was officially renamed, "The Meeting of the Waters," a prudish euphemism for the original title. Carl Millis, sculptor of the signature water feature, had named it, "The Wedding of the Rivers." Her hope for a future wedding was her biggest challenge.

Her ramblings had somehow come full circle to her original problem, the miracle of creation. She had yet to break the news to her father. She and Meg, however, had planned for that to happen tomorrow evening, at a dinner Meg had arranged, ostensibly as a family celebration of the end of the case. Anticipating what should be a happy occasion for her, her family and their and her closest friends, Erin trembled with dread.

Forty-Six

Meg began the celebration with a present for Erin, a 24-karat gold neck chain with hand-forged links. "It was my mother's, and I want you to have it."

Erin removed her mother's locket from the red cord lanyard and looped it on the old-fashioned chain. Meg placed the heirloom around Erin's neck and kissed her on the cheek. "Now your mother's memento is a gift from my mother, too," she said. "They'd both be very proud of you."

After dinner, with Kelly and Jimmy present, the moment arrived. "Dad, there's something really important I've got to tell you—"

"Uh-oh," Patrick said, looking alarmed. "Did they hurt you when they held you prisoner?"

"No, and I'm almost recovered from the bruises."

"Do you owe somebody a lot of money?" her father asked.

"No, nothing like that. I'm not asking for money. But just don't hit me, okay?"

"What did you do, honey— did you kill someone? Do you need a lawyer?"

"Better just spill it," Kelly said. "Compared with what he's imagining, maybe this won't sound so bad."

"Dad, I'm pregnant."

"Oh, God." His eyes darted to from side to side as she spoke, as if his thoughts were racing like a crawling banner inside his forehead.

"I was thinking a lot while I was trapped in that cabin. There's one clear course of action for me. And I'm determined to take it."

"You're pregnant?" Patrick stood and paced. "I knew it. As soon as I saw that drawing. You did that, didn't you?" He looked accusingly at Jimmy.

"Yes, sir." Jimmy stood up and began speaking. "Oh, you mean the drawing. I did that too. I took art courses to prepare for some kind of a design career."

"Hmpph. I was actually admiring it until I realized who it was. Dammit!" He punched one hand hard with his other fist and paced some more.

"Erin and I have been close for the past four years, ever since her mother died. Then last year, when I lost my brother, Erin helped me deal with the grief, and we've grown to love each other very much. One night last March, while you were gone, our love was just too much, and it happened. It was the only time, and now Erin is going to have our child— "

"You don't have any idea what this means."

"I suppose not, sir, But Erin and I thought— "

"You thought—ha! If you'd have thought first, none of this would have happened."

"Patrick!" Meg said. "You don't want to go there."

Erin watched like a spectator at a tennis match, cringing at each blow.

"Sir, I love Erin very much, and— "

"Well I hope you're ready for the consequences. This is going to cost you and your family—"

"Wait, sir. I'm not finished. I know what a hardship this will be for both of us. But we see it as a joyous event.

"Erin, what were you thinking?"

"I wasn't, Dad. I know I've let you down. But if it makes you feel any better, I have heartburn carving a hole in my stomach, and I haven't moved my bowels in days."

"What Erin is trying to say," Kelly said, stifling a chuckle, "is that she wants to keep their baby and raise it herself."

"Oh, sure." Patrick said. "You're too young to get married. So is Jimmy. He needs to develop those talents of his."

"I know, sir," Jimmy continued. "I plan to attend Washington University here in town. I'm eligible for a full ROTC scholarship. I'll study engineering and get a good job. I want to support your daughter and our child. I want to marry her as soon as we can get on our own two feet."

"But-but, Erin, you can't do it all," Patrick sputtered, "what about the college education I've slaved to save for, so you could get a good start in life?"

"We've thought about that, too," Erin said. "Plenty of women work and raise a family. I could go to college in town, and raise my baby, too. And Jimmy could come over any time he likes, so the baby could know his father. "

"Meg, what do you know about this?" He riveted his eyes on her.

"She told me the whole story the week you were gone. Frankly, I'm thrilled they're in love and know they can have a baby. And after what each of them has been through, I think they know their own minds and are ready for this."

"You should have told me."

"I've only known it myself for a couple of weeks. When would I have had the chance to tell you?" Meg's eyes welled. "I don't know why you're angry with me. At least Jimmy is willing to face facts and settle down." She broke down in tears. "Unlike some people I know."

Patrick slumped into his chair and buried his head in his hands. "It's my fault. The way I've lived, treating women the way I have. First I lost Kitty, though my own negligence. I've raised my daughter irresponsibly."

"Patrick, you're wrong. That's not it." Meg got up, walked behind his chair and put her arms around his shoulders, trying to console him.

Patrick stood up, embraced Meg and dabbed her eyes with his handkerchief. "Erin," he said, "Meg and I have wanted to ask you something for a long time. Tonight is as good a time as any. We all might as well spill our guts at once and see what's left of us.

"As you know, we've been engaged for over a year and we're very much in love. What would you think if I married Meg and she moved into our house?"

Erin remained silent for a minute. She took her time, shaping the words to answer, comparing her father's predicament to her own. Or maybe she was just enjoying the delicious suspense. At least she had the power to fix this one.

"Well, Dad, you've got your education, a house and can afford to support a wife. And I guess you're old enough to get married."

"I have your permission, then?"

"You don't have to ask mine. But I have two questions for Meg."

"What?" Meg asked, hanging on her words.

"Could you love me like a daughter? And will you move in—starting tonight—and help me raise my child?"

"Oh, Erin. Yes, and yes." She took Erin in her arms and held her for a long time.

"Thanks, Meg. I do love you, after all. The pit in my stomach I've felt since I lost Mom four years ago seems filled for the first time."

Patrick walked over and shook Jimmy's hand. "Jimmy, I'm sorry you had to see all this. But I guess it's okay. You're family now. Tonight, you taught me something about how to handle a woman. Congratulations on your plans and your new baby."

"Wow! Thank you, sir. I'll live up to your trust, you'll see."

"Now that I've seen you in action, tiger, I know you will." Grinning broadly, he gave Jimmy a friendly punch on the arm.

Parnell, sensing something was up, sprang up on his hind legs, trying to lick Erin's face, and then ran circles around the standing group as fast as he could.

"Well, I'd better go home.," Jimmy said. "My parents are anxious to know what you said."

"I'll see you out." Erin took his hand, walked him to the front door and gave him a long and passionate goodnight kiss.

"I guess I'm done here," Kelly said to Patrick and Meg. "It's interesting, Mr. MacKenna. You set out to rescue Erin, and she ended up rescuing you. Congratulations, you two—on everything." She walked to the front door and hugged Erin.

After Kelly left, Erin glanced back into the kitchen, winked at Meg, and called out, "Goodnight, all!"

Parnell sniffed around Patrick, who was otherwise occupied, entwined in Meg's arms. The dog rejoined Erin in the foyer and trotted behind her as she disappeared up the stairs.

Patrick led Meg to his big marriage bed to share joyous new secrets.

Erin sat on her bed, petting Parnell and beaming with pleasure.

She had never before been so proud of Patrick MacKenna, her caring father, architect and crime fighter. For her part, she was thrilled that their lonely house once again burgeoned with new life.

Acknowledgments

Many talented individuals helped this project along its winding road to publication. The late Linda Houle and editor Lisa Smith, its intended original publishers, believed in it and employed Cindy Davis to edit early drafts, but their press closed after Linda's untimely death in 2013. Jennifer Stolzer, author and Illustrator, reviewed a draft and clarified my vision of Erin's teenage outlook. Jaden Terrell read early and later versions of the manuscript and made many useful suggestions for strengthening plot and characters. Bruce DeSilva, mystery author, seasoned journalist and writing coach, took time to identify and suggest many enhancements. Special thanks to Sarah Fine, clinical psychologist and author of *Sanctum*, who applied her work with teen trauma victims to fiction writing in a Missouri Writers Guild master class, and to Anne Redelfs, Ph.D. whose understanding of trauma's effects on all our lives enriched this work. Medical mystery author Braxton DeGarmo also offered many suggestions to improve the final draft. Architects Stephen G. Knarr and Mark O'Bryan read portions and early versions and confirmed architects' concepts and character traits presented in the story. Thanks also to Steve Besemer for an inside look a the Missouri Emergency Management Agency.

Published works which influenced my conception and creation of this novel include:

On Point, by Roger Hayes, St Martin's Paperback, 2000
Ozark Meth, by Laura L. Valenti and Dick Dixon, 3Cross, 2005
The Mob, by Gus Russo, Bloomsbury, 2001
Juno, Academy-Award-winning screenplay by Diablo Cody, 2007. Mandate Pictures, Jason Bateman, Dir., Starring Ellen Page.

For all those in St. Louis Writers Guild, Sisters in Crime and St. Louis Publishers Association who supported, encouraged and assisted with this work, I offer my thanks. And to all who helped, your assistance is well appreciated, but I must claim any errors as my own.

About Author Peter Green

Peter H. Green

The son of two journalists, architect and city planner Peter Green found his father's 400 World War II letters, his humorous war stories, his mother's writings and their family's often hilarious doings too good a tale to keep to himself, so he launched a second career as a writer. His first book, recounting the humorous antics and serious achievements of his dad's World War II adventure, Ben's War with the U.S. Marines, and his first novel, Crimes of Design, a Patrick MacKenna mystery, an intrigue of murder and sabotage set in St. Louis during the highest flood of record, were republished by Greenskills Press in 2014, He lives in St. Louis with his wife Connie, and has two married daughters and three very young grandchildren. You can read more about Peter and his works, as well an illustrated short story based on the last dog they owned, "The Night We Ruined the Dog," on his website: www.peterhgreen.com.

Join Peter's Readers

Website: www.peterhgreen.com
Facebook page:
www.facebook.com/AuthorPeterGreen
Twitter handle: @writerpeter
LinkedIn ID: Peter H. Green
www.linkedin.com/profile/view?id=38211772

Before You Go

If you enjoyed this book, please
leave a review comment at this book's page,
accessible from:
GoodReads page: https://www.goodreads.com/author/show/5864519.Peter_H_Green
or
Peter's Amazon Author Page :
http://www.amazon.com/-/e/B008749FPC

Also by Peter H. Green

Nonfiction
Dad's War with the United States Marines
Ben's War with the U. S. Marines

Patrick MacKenna Mysteries
Crimes of Design
Fatal Designs

CPSIA information can be obtained
at www.ICGtesting.com
Printed in the USA
FFOW01n2134290615
14684FF